INFESTATION

INFESTATION

A NOVEL

MARY ROMASANTA

Sagga Publishing House LLC

Sagga Publishing House LLC, October 2024

LIBRARY OF CONGRESS CONTROL NUMBER: 2024912070

Premium Mass-Market Hardback ISBN: 979-8-9886746-5-8

Premium Mass-Market Paperback ISBN: 979-8-9886746-8-9

eBook ISBN: 979-8-9886746-9-6

Published in the United States by Sagga Publishing House LLC, Texas.

Artwork by Robert Romasanta

Cover design by Damonza.com

Visit the author's website at:
www.maryromasanta.com

Printed in the United States of America

This book is dedicated with heartfelt gratitude to my mother and father.

Thank you for the lessons.

Love you always.

Preface

I was four years old when I saw a ghost for the first time. Not exactly your typical first memory, right? My teenage sister and I were home alone when I spotted a man inside the house. The fear in my eyes must have been unmistakable because she didn't hesitate—she grabbed my hand, rushed us outside, and we waited in the yard until our parents returned. Just a short time before, I attended my first funeral. My father, a pastor, had been asked to speak at the service of a man who had died under tragic circumstances—he was killed in a satanic ritual. The details of his death were so gruesome that the casket remained closed during the viewing.

When my parents got home that night, my sister explained what had happened. My father, ever the investigator, immediately checked the house from top to bottom. Finding no one, he started asking questions. *What did the man look like? What was he wearing? Was he thin or heavy?* I answered as best as I could, and my responses left him stunned. He retrieved a newspaper article—something I had never seen before—and showed me a photograph. "Is this the man you saw?" he asked. I nodded. It was the same man who had been laid to rest in that closed casket.

You might be thinking, surely I must have seen the obituary or perhaps photos at the funeral. But according to my sister and parents, there were none, and at four years old, I certainly wasn't poring over the newspaper. Regardless of how it happened, this is my story to tell—just as the one I'm about to share is.

That sighting wasn't my only brush with the other side. *Infestation* is inspired by the personal accounts of events that occurred that began shortly after my parents purchased a house across the street from San Fernando Cemetery #2, the largest cemetery in San Antonio, Texas. They converted that house into a family business—a flower shop. Not long after, the woman living in the house directly behind the flower shop—also across from the cemetery—passed away, and my parents bought that property too. I was maybe eight at the time, and my adolescent brother and I were thrilled. No more long days waiting around the flower shop after school until we could go home. Now we were just a backyard away while our parents finished up work.

But our excitement didn't last long. It quickly became clear we weren't alone in that house. Despite the convenience of having our home just out back, we often found ourselves lingering at the flower shop with our parents, too scared to be alone in the house. Even something as simple as running home to grab a carton of milk became an impossible task. My brother and I would challenge each other to games of Rock/Paper/Scissors to avoid the dreaded trip. The loser would have to brave the house alone—poor sucker.

Of course, the book isn't entirely true. It's a work of fiction, not a memoir. But my experiences were the spark that ignited the story, and in many ways, they've shaped who I am today. Looking back, I wouldn't change a thing.

Happy reading,

Mary Romasanta

INSPIRED BY TRUE EVENTS.

Prologue

THE LAST TWO YEARS WERE SUPPOSED to be different. They had won the war, defeated the enemy, and eliminated the evil that plagued the world. He tried to convince himself that his tears and his brothers' blood had earned him peaceful, quiet nights with his wife and daughter. He told himself that his Chicago home was thousands of miles away from the Western Front. *There are no Panzer tanks lurking behind the trees in the park.* The curtain fluttering in the neighbor's window isn't concealing a sniper. The shouts in the street are from children playing, not his comrades screaming as they're mowed down by machine-gun fire. But no matter how hard he tried, the war had left its indelible mark, keeping him perpetually on edge. He tried to lower his guard, to be *normal*, but the smallest things always managed to set him off.

What the fuck is that? he thought, squinting at his porch from the street. The car rolled to a stop as he kept his eyes fixed on the suspicious feral cat sitting there. It was watching him, like it was expecting them. Waiting for them. Scheming. The cat was comfortable, licking its paw as though it had made itself right at home.

His wife and daughter knew better than to speak when he was locked in like this. They knew where his mind must be, or perhaps where it *wasn't*. They remained still, careful not to make any sudden moves or ask questions that might set him off. So they sat quietly, waiting as he assessed the situation.

"You ever seen that cat around here before?" he asked, his voice low.

"No," his wife replied.

"You, Maddy?"

"No, Daddy."

The cat stopped licking itself and stared at him, unrelenting, as if it knew it was the subject of their conversation.

"It's just a cat," his wife said, her voice tinged with disbelief.

"Not just a cat—a black fucking cat," he replied, his eyes still locked on the feline.

"So?" she asked, a touch of exasperation creeping into her voice.

"So, everyone knows black cats are bad luck. And it's watching us."

The cat leaped from the porch and landed silently on the ground before striding toward the car. Its movements were deliberate, purposeful, as it pounced onto the hood. It drew closer, turning its face to reveal that the left side was mangled—its ear hanging by a flap of skin, exposing a crusted skull beneath dried blood. A single fly crawled out of its hollow eye socket and flew into the night.

He closed his eyes, telling himself it was just another hallucination, a trick of his war-torn mind. But the dull red glow pierced his clenched eyelids. When he opened them, the source of the glow was the cat's single intact eye, shining with an unnatural brightness. The creature continued its approach, placing its front paws on the windshield, meowing and purring as if it were still an ordinary animal. The family winced in unison as the cat revealed its underbelly, where its pale pink intestines hung loosely like grotesque sausage links.

That explains it, he thought. "It wants me to put it out of its misery." He turned to his wife. "Wait here."

He opened the car door, grimacing as the pungent stench of sulfur—like rotten eggs—assaulted his nostrils. Resisting the urge to gag, he bit his lip and leaned over the hood, lifting the cat by the scruff of its neck. The cat maintained its gaze, unblinking, on his family inside the car.

"What the fuck are you staring at?" he muttered.

In the war, he had witnessed the most gruesome injuries imaginable—men with their legs blown off, faces torn apart by shrapnel. But it didn't seem right that this cat, with its insides hanging out and its body riddled with sores, could still be alive. Holding it as far from his body as possible, he searched the yard for a rock, something heavy to quickly put the creature out of its misery. His eyes settled on a cement paver. He glanced back at his wife and daughter. *Maddy shouldn't see this,* he thought as he stepped to the side of the house, out of their view.

"Fuck!" he exclaimed, losing his grip on the cat. He frantically scanned the ground but saw nothing. The smell still lingered, so strong it was as if the cat were right under his nose. *It couldn't have run away—not in that condition.*

Then, he spotted a red orb glowing faintly on the ground. He crouched closer. *A rat.* A big, black fucking rat. It probably came from the cemetery across the street, reeking of death. Nearly as large as the cat, it lay motionless. He leaned in for a closer look and blinked in disbelief. *What the fuck?* Its intestines were hanging outside of its body too.

No time for questions, he thought as he stomped his boot down on the rat. It let out an otherworldly shriek as its body twitched under his weight. As he raised his foot for another stomp, the creature seemed to expand, filling the space beneath his boot. No longer a rat, it morphed into a pulsating mass of black hair and skin, its form shifting and swelling in unnatural, grotesque ways.

He stumbled back, fear rooting him in place as the creature's red glowing eye opened again, fixing its gaze on him. He fell to the ground, scrambling backward on his hands and feet, his mind unable to process the horror in front of him. The beast's jaw, now lined with razor-sharp teeth, extended unnaturally wide. Its deep wheezing breaths were punctuated by the sound of bones snapping and resetting, as its body transformed into the grotesque shape of a massive black dog.

Intestines still dangled from a gaping wound in its belly as the beast padded toward him with ghostly fluidity. The sulfurous stench overwhelmed him, snapping him out of his daze. He tried to run, but the creature pounced, pinning him down with its enormous weight. He gasped for air, his lungs collapsing under the pressure as the beast's claws tore into his chest. Its rancid saliva dripped into his mouth and nostrils—maggots wriggling their way inside.

He wheezed, desperate for air, as pain and disgust consumed him. *What did I do to deserve this?* he wondered. *I'm a good man—a good father. I fought for my country. For the good guys.* His thoughts raced as he fought against the crushing weight of the beast. He turned his head toward the car, where his wife and daughter watched in horror, his face covered in maggot-filled drool. He tried to speak, to utter a final word, but it was no use.

In a swift motion, the beast's jaws clamped around his head, crushing it in a single, violent bite. As his spirit looked down at his lifeless body, he had just one final thought: *What the fuck did they do?*

Chapter 1

"I'VE NEVER SEEN ANYTHING LIKE IT," Emmanuel remarked, staring at the sprawling two-hundred-acre graveyard across the narrow street. Tombstones stretched endlessly over the manicured grass, winding through the rolling hills like an intricate maze. Cemeteries had always made him uneasy; he had avoided them whenever possible. Something about knowing that countless human bodies lay decaying just beneath the earth unnerved him. Or maybe it was the stark reminder of his own mortality—the thought that one day he would take his final breath, his soul departing from the only vessel he had ever known. But that was in the past. Now, there was something almost peaceful, even mesmerizing, about it.

"And it's only twenty minutes from here to the city," his wife, Josephine, said, carrying their six-year-old daughter, Emma, on her back. Emma clung to her mother's shoulders, wide-eyed as she took in the surrounding landscape.

Emmanuel's gaze shifted to an unexpected sight—a mangy black dog wandering freely through the cemetery. Even from a distance, the dog looked emaciated, its ribs visible from a hundred yards away, its tongue lolling as it panted heavily, desperate for water. Normally, Emmanuel, a self-proclaimed animal lover, would have felt compelled to help. But there was something unsettling about this dog, an aura that made him instinctively keep his distance. "Do we need to worry about wild dogs out here?" he asked, turning to his sister-in-law, Janie.

"No, I see that dog a lot out there. It must belong to a groundskeeper," she replied.

He furrowed his brow. *Hideous-looking pet,* he thought. *It looks like it should be put down.* "At least we don't have to worry about noisy neighbors."

"That's not entirely true, is it, Janie?" Josephine said, turning to her sister, who bore an uncanny resemblance to herself and Emma.

"Most days, it's pretty quiet, but occasionally, you might hear trumpets from a mariachi band playing for a burial service," Janie replied, stepping toward the entrance of the quaint, unkempt one-story home.

"Mariachis? You're letting us stay here for free, and we get free live music? How did we get so lucky?" Emmanuel joked with a smile.

Josephine sighed audibly. "I wish he were joking—he loves mariachi music."

"You can take a man out of Mexico, but you can't take Mexico out of a man," Emmanuel quipped.

"I said occasionally—most people buried there are of Italian ancestry, many wealthy families, some famous."

"Like Al Capone?" Emmanuel said, half-joking.

"Yes," Janie replied, inserting the key into the door lock. "That's Mount Carmel Catholic Cemetery—he's buried right through there."

"Are you serious?" he asked, incredulously.

She nodded. "You can visit the grave yourself."

"Very cool," Emmanuel said, genuinely impressed.

Janie scoffed. "Let's see if you still feel that way once you've seen the inside of the house."

Emmanuel turned his attention to their temporary new home. Its once vibrant paint was now faded and chipped, revealing the weathered wood beneath. Rusty steel burglar bars clung to the windows like a prison. He noticed that none of the other houses they passed had bars. His eyes landed on a black vulture perched on the roof, now snow white from layers of bird droppings. He opened his mouth to speak but quickly shut it, not wanting to seem high-maintenance or ungrateful.

He was quite comfortable in their current, more modern, and spacious home, and would never have considered moving on his own. However, as the pastor of a small bilingual Pentecostal church on Chicago's south side, struggling to keep its doors open, he and Josephine had made the difficult decision to sell their house and use their personal funds to keep the church afloat. This place, no matter how much work it needed, was a roof over their heads—they would make it work.

Janie jiggled the key in the lock, struggling to turn it. "Manny, I'm going to need your help," she said.

"No problem," he called out, racing up the weathered steps to the porch. The old wood creaked beneath his feet, but he paid no mind, too focused on reaching the door. As his foot connected with the first step, it unexpectedly gave way, sending him stumbling forward. He barely had time to register the fall before his face slammed into the unforgiving concrete of the porch. The impact was jarring, pain exploding through his skull.

"Are you okay?" Josephine's voice was filled with panic as she rushed to his side, Janie following close behind. They both knelt beside him, their hands hovering over him, unsure where to touch, afraid of causing more pain.

Blood trickled from his nose, his vision swimming as he tried to push himself up. "I'm fine," he mumbled, though the throbbing in his face told a different story. The world spun slightly as he struggled to get his bearings, the taste of blood metallic on his tongue.

"You don't look fine," Josephine said, worry etched on her face. "What happened?"

Janie rummaged through her purse. "Here—I have tissues."

"Thank you," Emmanuel said, dabbing the brim of his nose. "I don't know what happened. I was looking right at where I was stepping—it was like my foot slipped before I was ready. I must have missed a step." He glared at the steps, as if they were the culprits.

Janie turned away, shaking her hands. "I can't stand the sight of blood. Are you sure you're OK? We can do this another time."

"I'm fine," Emmanuel insisted, rising to his feet. He examined the door, noticing that the frame was misaligned, likely warped from water damage. He gripped the doorknob with one hand and pulled up as he turned the key with the other. The lock finally gave way, and the door creaked open. "There you go," he said, casting one last resentful glance at the steps.

"The house was built in the 1940s," Janie said as she stepped inside, the floorboards groaning under her weight. "What year is it, 1996? So that would make it around... fifty years old, give or take."

Emmanuel waved off the musty odor that assaulted his nostrils as he stepped in. The air was thick, filled with floating dust particles. His eyes adjusted to the dimly lit room, which seemed frozen in time, like a forgotten relic. The living room furniture—a couch, coffee table, and end table—sat abandoned, covered in a thick layer of dust.

"Momma, it's spooky in here," Emma said, tugging on her mother's dress.

"A woman lived here with her daughter. They both passed away of old age, I think, and they didn't have any next of kin—which worked out great for me," Janie explained.

"And why is that?" Emmanuel asked, curious.

"I bought it from the city for practically nothing."

"Why?" Emma asked, her eyebrows shooting up in surprise.

"Why what, baby girl?" Janie asked, crouching down to the six-year-old's eye level.

"Why did you buy it?"

"Well, sweetheart, Auntie is going to convert the house on the other side of the fence into a floral shop," she said, pointing toward the back of the house. "I thought maybe I could use this space for storage, or maybe even spend the night here after a long day of work."

"Why would you want to sleep here?" Emma wrinkled her nose. "Why would anyone want to sleep here?"

"Angel, that's enough questions," Josephine said, her face flushing with embarrassment. She turned to Janie. "Sorry, Janie—you know how kids are."

Janie scoffed. "Thank goodness, I don't," she replied dryly.

The circumstances were far from ideal. Emma had just adjusted to her first school and now had to move, something that broke her little heart. The commute to the church would also be longer. But Emmanuel saw Janie's offer to live here, rent-free, in exchange for handyman services, as a sign from God that they were doing the right thing, even if it meant making sacrifices. He and Josephine had agreed to sell their house, pay off the mortgage, and use the extra money to get the church back on its feet while saving up for a new home.

"Do the appliances work?" Emmanuel asked as he stepped into the kitchen.

"I think so," Janie replied. "There's no separate dining room," she said, circling the small kitchen table. She moved to the sink and turned the faucet, only to have the knob come loose in her hand. "Oops."

Emmanuel's eyes landed on a cracked window that offered a view of the backyard. The yard was fenced in with chain link, overgrown with green clovers, and appeared almost picturesque compared to the house. "Did you recently have the yard mowed?" he asked.

"No, not much seems to grow back there for some reason."

He leaned closer to the windowsill and was met with the pungent scent of decay, the wood rotting before his eyes. "Does the place have termites?" he asked, his concern growing.

"Not that I'm aware of," Janie said, stepping out of the kitchen. "Down the hall, we have two and a half bedrooms and a bathroom."

"You mean a half bathroom," Josephine corrected.

"No, a half-bedroom. Follow me—I'll show you."

They followed her through the small kitchen to a short hallway with two doors on the left, one door at the end, and one door on the right.

"On the right, there are two bedrooms—I've mostly cleared them out. The bathroom is on the left."

Emmanuel placed his hand on a doorknob embellished with an intricate brass floral design—concentric wreaths encrusted with deep purple gemstones.

He crouched down to inspect it more closely. "Seems a little fancy for a place like this," he said.

"I thought so too," Janie replied. "They're on every door in the house. I thought they might be worth something, so I had someone come in and take a look."

"What did they say?" Josephine asked.

"Apparently they were custom-made. The gemstones are amethyst—not worth a whole lot, but nice to look at."

"Hmm... Just like your ex-husband," Josephine scoffed.

"Ha! Exactly," Janie replied.

"Interesting," Emmanuel said as he stood up. He turned the doorknob, but the door wouldn't budge. He tried again, this time pushing with the weight of his body, and finally stepped inside.

"Small, isn't it?" Janie said from the hallway.

Josephine peeked into the room. "It's got a sink, a toilet, and a shower—that's all we need."

"Interesting that it doesn't have a tub," Emmanuel noted, examining the mismatched tiles on the floor that suggested a tub had once been there. Nothing else indicated any recent work had been done on the house.

"Maybe the previous owner needed more space," Josephine suggested. "Or maybe she couldn't step into a tub anymore."

Emmanuel's eyes locked onto a ceramic wall heater next to the shower—a vintage relic from another era that blended seamlessly with the mosaic tile. "Wow, I haven't seen one of these since I was a kid," he said, running his hand over its cold metal surface.

"That reminds me—you'll need to install a dryer connection," Janie said.

"No dryer connection?" Josephine asked, unable to hide her disappointment.

"I'm afraid not. But you can use the old clothesline at the far end of the backyard."

"Oh... OK... That'll do," she replied, though her voice lacked conviction.

"Don't worry, honey. I'll install a dryer connection—it's at the top of my list," Emmanuel assured her.

She let out a sigh of relief. "Thank God."

They stepped out of the bathroom. "I assume this is the half-bedroom you mentioned?" Emmanuel said, pointing to the door at the end of the hall.

"It's not much of a bedroom," Janie replied, pushing the door halfway open. "More like a storage room, maybe? But I suppose you could use it as an extra bedroom if you really needed to."

The smell of decaying wood and old paper wafted through the half-open door, seeping into the hallway. Emmanuel stepped closer, peering into the cluttered room that seemed to shrink under the weight of its contents. Cardboard boxes were stacked high, teetering precariously like Jenga blocks that could topple at any moment.

"Help, Daddy. Help!" Emma cried out, her voice filled with distress.

Emmanuel crouched down and scooped her up. "What's wrong? What happened? Are you hurt?"

"I saw something scary," she whispered, her tiny heartbeat pounding against his chest.

"What did you see?" he asked gently.

"I don't know, but I think it lives here." She pointed to something scuttling across the floor—a tiny speck, no larger than a watermelon seed.

"It's just a roach—it's harmless," Emmanuel reassured her.

"Fair warning—those things are everywhere," Janie said with a look of disgust. "I had to have all the window frames replaced. Those little suckers damaged everything in a matter of days."

"Days?" Emmanuel echoed, astonished.

"Yes—days. So, make plans to fumigate."

Fumigating's an expense I'd rather avoid if possible, he thought. *Roach foggers should do the trick.* "I'll take care of it," he replied. As they walked back through the house to the front door, his eyes roved from one area of disrepair to another. Broken window, rotted window frame, broken faucet—and that was just the kitchen. The rest of the house seemed no better.

"I know it needs a lot of work," Janie admitted.

"Nothing I can't handle," Emmanuel said, doing his best to hide his growing concern. "Besides, we appreciate you letting us stay here while we get the church's financial situation in order."

"Yes, and it's only temporary," Josephine added, trying to sound optimistic.

"And who knows? Maybe you'll end up loving the place and make me an offer to take it off my hands," Janie said with a smile.

"Yeah... Who knows?" Emmanuel's eyes drifted to a dark patch on the ceiling where water dripped steadily onto the tattered linoleum floor. He muttered under his breath, "But it's highly unlikely."

Chapter 2

EMMA CLUTCHED HER LOYAL, floppy-eared, white-furred stuffed animal—a puppy dog named Blue—tight as she narrowed her gaze on the colorful snake slithering across the page of the book her father was reading to her. The snake moved with a friendly, approachable grace, but its wide, innocent-looking eyes held a glint of wickedness, hinting at its true nature. Emma hung on every word as her father recounted the tale of how Satan had once been the most beautiful angel. But he didn't want to be just an angel—he wanted to be God. Filled with resentment, evil, and hatred, Satan was cast out of heaven. In the Garden of Eden, God gave Adam and Eve just one rule: don't eat the fruit of the Tree of Knowledge. But Satan, determined to disrupt God's plan, disguised himself as a snake and waited in the garden to trick Adam and Eve into eating the forbidden fruit.

"How did he do that?" Emma asked, her brow furrowing.

"Do what?" her father replied.

"How did he disguise himself as a snake? They didn't have costumes back then."

He smiled gently. "It was an evil magic trick."

She pondered this for a moment, then asked, "If he wanted to trick them, why did he choose a snake? Why not something less scary, like a bunny?"

Her father chuckled. "It wouldn't have mattered. They wouldn't have been afraid anyway. They didn't even know what fear was."

Emma's mind raced with questions. Why were Adam and Eve naked in the first place? How did the snake talk to them? Did he move his mouth? There were so many trees in the garden and so much to eat—why did they choose the one tree they weren't supposed to touch? And if that tree was so bad, why did God create it? She glanced out the window at the darkness outside, knowing there wasn't enough time for all her questions. She settled on one.

"Why didn't God just not make that tree in the first place?"

Her father nodded thoughtfully. "You know what poison ivy is, right?"

Emma nodded vigorously, recalling her class field trip to the Chicago Botanic Garden when her teacher warned them not to touch it. One of her classmates, Aiden, thought it would be funny to touch it with as many parts of his body as possible. "That's why an ambulance took Aiden to the hospital."

"Exactly," her father said. "But do you know what would happen if there was no poison ivy?"

"Aiden wouldn't have gone to the hospital," she replied confidently.

Her father laughed softly. "Maybe, but also, birds like robins, which feed on its berries, would have nothing to eat. Dirt would run off slopes and fill riverbanks, leaving many animals without water to drink, and we wouldn't have some of the medicines we have today."

Emma's eyes moved rapidly as she processed the information. "I think I understand now, Daddy."

Her father leaned over and kissed her forehead. "Sweet dreams, mija," he said as he stood up to leave.

Emma whispered a prayer as her father stepped out of the room. "Now I lay me down to sleep, I pray the Lord my soul to keep; Keep me safe through the night and wake me with the morning light. If I should die before I wake, I pray the Lord my soul to take. Amen." She closed her eyes, ready to drift off to dreamland.

But her eyelids fluttered open as the room suddenly filled with a cacophony of mechanical whirs and electronic melodies. The darkness was pierced by colorful lights flashing from her toys. "Oh no," Emma whispered, climbing out of bed. "You'll wake Momma and Daddy." Her heart raced as she ran to quiet the toys, one by one.

As she turned toward an unfamiliar sound—a haunting, eerie laughter—her gaze settled on her father's prized toy, Tickle Me Elmo. He had gotten it for her as a housewarming present. She didn't care much for it, thinking herself too old for such a baby toy. But her father had spent hours waiting in line at the toy store and took pride in bringing it home. So, she had accepted it with a smile and placed it on her shelf, never to be played with.

Cautiously, Emma approached the doll. *Maybe it needs new batteries,* she thought, picking up the red plush figure. She placed the doll face down on her lap and carefully peeled back the Velcro from its back. With a gentle click, she deactivated the battery pack. "There," she whispered, returning the doll to its seated position on the shelf.

But as she climbed back into bed, an eerie, distant giggle filled the room. Emma's eyes widened in terror as she slowly turned her gaze back to the doll. It was standing now, its large, round eyes glowing like two bright orbs. The doll cackled, its twisted laughter a dark parody of the innocent giggle it was meant to have.

Emma stared at the toy, her heart pounding in her chest. She swallowed hard as the reality of what was happening began to sink in.

It's not supposed to stand like that.

Its eyes aren't supposed to glow like that.

The toy extended its fuzzy, vibrant red arm toward her. Its mouth moved in puppet fashion as it said, "Wanna be my frrrriend?"

She gasped as another realization settled in.

Its mouth isn't supposed to move like that.

It cackled again, its body trembling—the one thing it was designed to do. The trembling stopped abruptly. The puppet opened its mouth wide. "Pllllleeeease." With a grotesque burst, a torrent of roaches erupted from the darkness of its mouth, their wings beating frantically, as though they had been multiplying in the depths of its belly, waiting to break free. She opened her mouth to scream, but fear gripped her, and no sound escaped.

Emmanuel still had the box the toy came in, and he would have much preferred to return it and get his money back. Maybe even store it for a while to see if he could make a little money off it. God knows they could use the extra cash. His gaze lingered on the doll—its fuzzy red fur and endearing grin radiating a childlike innocence—and he thought, *Come Christmas, I bet you'll be worth a thousand bucks.*

He exhaled deeply. He had never seen Emma so upset. It wasn't unusual for her to have vivid dreams—she called them "movie dreams," a term she used to describe how clear and vivid they were, like watching a movie while sleeping. They had never bothered her before. In his mind, Emma's innocent imagination was filled with cotton candy and amusement parks, unicorns and rainbows. She had never complained about a single nightmare—until now. He had known this day would come, but he never imagined that PBS's biggest star would play a leading role in Emma's nightmares.

He promised her the doll would never see the light of day again. *What a waste,* he thought, as he stuffed the plush toy deep into the black Hefty garbage bag. The doll's cheerful giggle now felt like a sinister mockery of the innocence it was supposed to represent.

Stepping out of Emma's room, Emmanuel's face was a mask of disappointment as he dragged the garbage bag down the hall, the sound echoing like a body bag being pulled across the floor, carrying the lifeless corpse of the doll.

The bag started trembling violently, sending a jolt of fear through Emmanuel. He flinched, his muscles tensing instinctively. For a moment, he stood frozen, staring at the trembling bag. Then, with a reluctant sigh, he dropped his head and exhumed the doll from the garbage. *No sense in throwing away good batteries,* he thought, trying to rationalize the bizarre situation as he tore open the Velcro and opened the doll's battery pack.

His eyes fixed on the hard, hollow plastic innards of the toy, and his brow furrowed in confusion. *That's interesting...* he thought as a chill ran down his spine.

No batteries.

Chapter 3

A PUTRID, MUSTY ODOR SPILLED into the small room like a genie unleashed from a centuries-old bottle, assaulting Josephine's senses. She wrinkled her nose, hesitating for a moment before cautiously lifting the creaking lid of the dusty pine-wood chest that had been abandoned in what Janie referred to as the half-bedroom. Surely a forgotten treasure, she thought, her heart quickening with anticipation, like a child on a treasure hunt.

As the lid fully opened, Josephine's excitement mingled with a growing unease. Inside, a burlap pouch sat atop a jumbled collection of handwritten letters, brittle, yellowing newspaper clippings, and scattered clothing, all thrown together in careless disarray. She reached for the pouch first, her brow furrowing as she examined the powdery black substance within. *Charcoal?* she wondered, bringing it cautiously to her nose for a quick sniff. The scent was faint but unmistakable—burnt, earthy, and oddly unsettling.

That's strange... she mused, setting the pouch aside. Her curiosity now piqued, she picked up an old newspaper clipping, the front page of the *Chicago Tribune* dated 1947. The faded ink and yellowed paper hinted at the passage of time, and as her eyes scanned the headline, a shiver ran down her spine.

GRAVESITES DISTURBED AT MOUNT CARMEL CEMETERY

A cold chill crept over her as she processed the headline. *That's just across the street.* Having no interest in the story, she moved the clipping aside and sifted through the chest's contents—mostly a pile of musty-smelling clothing. Her eyes landed on a leather-bound book. Its cover was smooth and supple, marred with slight imperfections. Etched on the cover was an "M," probably using a stylus or a knife—deep enough to leave an impression, not too deep as to ruin the fine leather. A diary. Surely long forgotten, it called out to her, begging to be unearthed, to see the light of day. She brought it to her nose and breathed in the faint smell of leather. The temptation to uncover the stories and secrets of a bygone era proved irresistible. With great anticipation, she opened it, welcomed by the subtle smell of aged paper that evoked a sense of nostalgia. She began to read:

> *September 19, 1946*
> *I love my new home and school, at least so far. Momma was*
> *worried I would miss my friends back in New Orleans and said*
> *she would do anything it took to make me feel like I belong here.*
> *She had this look in her eye that made me believe she was dead*
> *serious. I told her not to worry, but you know mothers... They*
> *worry, and mine is no different.*

> *September 22, 1946*
> *High school is everything I imagined it would be and more! I*
> *have a BEST friend! Her name is Julianne. JULIANNE—the*
> *name just sounds so proper and sophisticated, if you ask me. I*
> *never imagined it would happen so quickly, but Momma allowed*
> *her to come over, and we talked and talked until time completely*
> *escaped us. I told her I have a crush on Michael D (he is so cute!)*
> *Madeline & Michael have a nice ring to it, does it not? XOXO*

Immersed in the pages of the diary, Josephine's quiet room was suddenly interrupted by a faint, mournful cry. She placed the diary on her lap, searching for the source of the sound. Hearing nothing, she dismissed it as a trick of her imagination and continued reading.

September 23, 1946

Julianne thinks it's unusual that Papa had our home built across the street from the cemetery, but that doesn't keep her from coming over. She said her family wouldn't dare do such a thing. I told her it's no big deal—nothing to be afraid of. My family is no stranger to cemeteries. I think it's funny she finds it unusual. The kids back home wouldn't give it a second thought. I just may have to take her across the street and show her myself.

September 25, 1946

Michael D. gave Julianne a love letter between classes today. I was standing right beside her when he did it. You will never believe what she did with it... She walked the letter straight to the nearest garbage can and tossed it away! She didn't even open it! What a terrific best friend she is turning out to be.

September 29, 1946

I don't feel like writing today, so I will keep this brief. Julianne and I have accepted a new friend into our group. She seems fine—a little risqué for our age, if you ask me, but Julianne likes her, so she can't be that bad. I said no promises, but I will give her a shot. Time will tell.

Josephine looked up. There it was again. A faint, persistent wailing. *Where on earth is that coming from?* Her body jolted as a loud, ominous thud rang out, reverberating through the room.

THUD.

She flinched.

THUD. THUD.

What was that? She glanced up at the ceiling, searching for the source of the sound.

THUD. THUD. THUD.

She gasped, her hand flying to her racing heart as the noise continued in rapid-fire succession. *Something is on the roof,* she thought, her eyes wide with fear as the relentless assault persisted.

"Momma! Momma!" Emma cried out.

Josephine rushed to Emma's room. Emmanuel had beaten her to it. "Everything is OK, mija," he said, embracing their daughter. "It's probably just a hailstorm. It will pass."

Josephine peeked through the window blind as the pounding on the roof continued. The sky was clear, the sun shining brightly—no sign of hail or rain. She turned to Emmanuel and shook her head. "Afraid not," she said.

It grew quiet.

Their eyes darted around the room, searching for any sign of movement or sound.

Complete silence.

"What else could it have been?" Josephine asked.

"Only one way to find out," Emmanuel replied. He stepped out of the room, carrying Emma as Josephine followed.

"Daddy, I'm scared," Emma said.

"Don't be, mija. I got you."

They stepped into the yard and looked up at the roof. The penetrating gaze of a legion of black vultures crowding the rooftop met theirs—featherless heads hung low over their legs, beady eyes fixated on them, gleaming with haunting intelligence. Their hooked beaks, sleekly designed for stripping carcasses clean of meat, hung ajar.

"I've never seen so many black vultures in a single place," Josephine said. "What do you think made them gather like this?"

"Probably on their way to a meal, or waiting around for something to die," Emmanuel said. "They're much smarter than they look, you know."

The faint sound of wailing she had heard inside replayed in her mind. Careful not to alarm Emma further, she smiled and nodded before sending her off to play inside. "I heard something in the storage room—it sounded like faint crying, almost wailing. Do you know what could have caused a sound like that?"

Emmanuel opened his mouth to speak.

"And please don't say ghosts," she said abruptly.

"I was going to say residual, spontaneous energy," he replied. "An echo from the past, if you will. It's an old house, and when there's a lot of energy, it's possible for it to be absorbed in the walls and spontaneously repeat itself. It's why some people report hearing music in homes or buildings that used to be bars or dance halls."

She nodded, surprised by his response. "That makes a lot of sense," she said. "Will it continue?"

He shrugged. "Maybe, maybe not. In any case, residual, spontaneous energy is nothing to worry about. It was probably some pre-pubescent kid's room at some point—someone with lots of pent-up emotions, energy that's lingering," he said. "Now, intelligent energy is a completely different story."

Jillian heard the commotion outside and peeked out the window, her gaze falling on the yard next door. The new neighbors were gathered on the front lawn, their mouths agape as they stared at the roof. *Looks like they've met the vultures*, she thought, smiling inwardly. Jillian was a fixture in the neighborhood, her roots running deep. The house she lived in had been in her family for three generations, starting with her grandparents on her father's side, whom she never had the chance to meet—they had passed before she was born.

A strong single mother raising a barely teenage son, Jillian did her best to provide a stable life for them both. She wasn't a nosy neighbor, but she stayed alert, aware of her surroundings, always on the lookout for potential dangers. And though she mostly kept to herself, the sight of what was happening outside often drew her attention. The house next door, after all, had always been an oddity—an attention-getter, but not in a way anyone would brag about. Vacant for years, neglected long before that, it seemed frozen in time, like a forgotten tomb with the ghosts of past inhabitants still lingering within.

It hadn't always been that way. Most of the houses in Hillside were built in the 1940s to welcome soldiers returning from the war, and that's how Jillian's grandfather came across their property—a well-deserved reward for his service. The neighborhood had once been a point of pride, a symbol of hope and renewal. But when the man of the house next door passed away, so too did the widow's pride of ownership. The once open and inviting front yard was soon enclosed by a chain-link fence, its neatly trimmed hedges growing wild, twisted, and gnarled. The lush green lawn, once meticulously maintained, was now tall, wild, and overrun with spiny weeds.

It was hard not to notice the place—it stuck out like a sore thumb compared to the other houses in the otherwise picturesque neighborhood. Jillian's father had often told her not to stare, reminding her that it was impolite. But to Jillian, it seemed the neighbors—the widow and her daughter—were the ones being impolite, constantly peering out through different windows, always watching what was happening outside, yet never stepping out to engage with anyone. Over the years, their behavior made Jillian uneasy.

Now, watching the new neighbors, her eyes softened as she spotted a little girl clutching a stuffed animal. *That's all in the past*, she thought, feeling a pang of sympathy for the family. *I just hope they last.*

Chapter 4

EMMA WELCOMED THE TEMPORARY REPRIEVE from the gloom and solitude that had weighed her down since she first set foot in the new house. For once, the air felt lighter, less oppressive. Laughter bubbled up from within her, filling the room as she lay in bed, chatting away on the phone with her best friend, Brianna, like a girl twice her age. Although they had only met in kindergarten, their bond had been immediate and strong, a friendship that felt pure and ageless. Emma already loved Brianna like family, and she knew the feeling was mutual.

"I miss you, Brie," she said softly, clutching her stuffed puppy, Blue, a little tighter. The warmth of their conversation brought her a sense of comfort, a connection that eased the loneliness she had been feeling.

"I miss you, too. But at least we get to talk on the phone," Brianna replied, her voice cheerful and reassuring.

"My mom said I could talk to you anytime I want, except during meals and at bedtime," Emma said.

"My mom said the same thing," Brianna replied. "Hey, Em, I have a question for you."

"What?"

"Why do you call me Brie?"

Emma had been prepared for the question and answered quickly, a playful smile on her lips. "'Cause you're cheesy and stinky." There was a brief silence before laughter burst through the phone like a bolt of lightning, shattering the quiet.

"I have a question for you, too," Emma said.

"What?"

"Why do you call me Em?"

"Because."

"Because what?"

"Because... Um," Brianna hesitated, as if trying to buy some time. "Because... Your name starts with M?" she said, her voice rising in pitch as she finished her sentence.

"It does not, you silly goose!" Emma exclaimed, erupting in laughter. She gasped abruptly; her laughter extinguished like a flame by a sudden gust of wind.

"Em, what's wrong? What's happening?" Brianna asked, seemingly able to sense her distress over the phone.

Emma's gaze fixed on the silhouette of a young girl that materialized before her eyes. "She's looking at me," she whispered, barely opening her mouth to speak, not wanting to be seen. "What do I do?"

"I wish I were there," Brianna groaned. "I'd march right up to her and pull her hair!"

With her breath caught in her throat, Emma replied, "I don't think that works with ghosts."

"OK, Em. Do what I say. I'll be on the phone with you, so you're not scared. OK?"

"OK," she nodded.

"You know how I always tell you to be brave?"

"Yes."

"Well, be brave."

"OK."

"Now stand up and look at her."

"OK," Emma said, slowly getting to her feet, still clutching her stuffed animal tightly.

She stood face-to-face with the little girl, whose complexion was pale, gaunt, and ghostly. "OK. I'm looking at her."

"Stand up straight," Brianna instructed.

Summoning her courage, Emma took a deep breath, straightened her posture, and squared her shoulders.

"And get right in front of her—look her right in the eyes."

Emma tucked her fine, long brown hair behind her ear and examined the girl's dark, hollow eyes—eyes devoid of any light or life. Completely still, without moving her lips, a chilling and haunting whisper defying all logic escaped the girl's mouth: "Would you like to be my friend?" The voice was high-pitched and eerie, slicing through the silence and sending shivers down Emma's spine. Though the girl appeared innocent enough in her velvet red dress, white socks, and black Mary Jane shoes, Emma was overwhelmed by an unsettling sense of dread, as if she were in the presence of something truly evil.

"Like I said before—NO," Emma said sternly.

"Em, what's happening?" Brianna's voice crackled through the phone.

"She said she wants to be my friend."

"Say, NO, Em!"

"I did!"

"Say it louder. Tell her to leave! Tell her she's not supposed to be here! And say it like you mean it."

Emma's heart pounded in her chest, the relentless thud echoing in her ears as her breath came in short, shaky bursts. The girl in front of her, pale and unmoving, seemed to grow taller, her wide, empty eyes boring into Emma's soul. Trembling, Emma forced herself to step closer, her small voice trembling as she said, "I have enough friends... I don't need another one." She hesitated, but then, channeling the stern authority of her mother, she hardened her tone. "Now, do I make myself clear?"

The air in the room thickened. The girl's face contorted, twisting into a grotesque parody of a frown—an expression not meant for any human face.

Her jaw unhinged, dropping low and impossibly wide, revealing a gaping black void where her mouth should have been. It was a pit of darkness, an abyss that seemed to pull at the edges of reality itself.

Emma's blood ran cold, her hands trembling uncontrollably as the girl began to move in ways that no human body should. From the shadows within her hollow mouth, a sickening, wet sound filled the air, followed by the sharp, skittering noise of tiny legs. Roaches—hundreds of them—poured out from her mouth, crawling over her lips, spilling from her eye sockets, and tumbling down her pale, decayed skin like a living waterfall of nightmares.

The vile creatures swarmed down the girl's body, their antennae twitching wildly, drawn to the light, to the warmth. Emma's scream caught in her throat, frozen by terror as they scuttled toward her, a tide of filth and decay.

Suddenly, the dam of her fear broke, and Emma screamed, louder and more desperate than ever before. She dropped the phone, the harsh thud barely registering through the chaos in her mind.

The door burst open with a violent crash. Her mother rushed into the room, her eyes wide with terror. "Angel! Are you okay?!" she cried, dropping everything—home interior decorating supplies scattered across the floor, forgotten.

Emma shook her head, staring vacantly at the spot where the apparition had stood.

The faint sound of Brianna's voice came through the phone, "Em, are you OK? Should I call 9-1-1?"

Emma's mother picked up the phone. "Brie, Emma is just fine. She'll call you back." She ended the call and gently placed the phone down.

A flicker of movement caught Emma's attention, causing her innocent brown eyes to widen. She turned toward the source and saw a force-field of energy—a rippled, transparent disembodied apparition—hovering through her room. Like a moving mirage, it distorted everything around it, its movement wavering as though caught in a heat haze. She had never seen anything like it. *At least this one didn't stop to talk to me*, she thought, remarkably calm in the face of the strange phenomenon.

"Why did you scream?" her mother asked.

"I saw roaches. Lots of them."

Her mother swept her gaze across the floor. "I don't see anything."

"They came out of the girl's mouth and eyes."

"Angel, you must have imagined it," she said. "Now tell me, do you like the wallpaper I chose for you?" she asked, holding out pink, polka-dot wallpaper.

Emma recognized her mother was quick to change the subject. *It's useless*, she thought. "Yes, Momma," she said unconvincingly, crawling back into bed.

Her mother sat alongside her. "What's the matter, angel? Why are you sad?"

"'Cause you never listen to me," Emma replied without hesitating. "I think you think just because I'm only in the first grade, I don't know things—but I do, Momma. And you never let me talk."

Her mother placed her arm around her. "I'm sorry, angel. Do you want to talk now?"

"Yes," she nodded, wiping a tear from her eye.

"What about?"

Thoughts raced through her mind as she considered where to begin. She had so much to say about their new living situation—her feelings, things she had seen in the house—but it seemed she was never given a chance to say anything. Sometimes they asked for her opinion, but she got the feeling they didn't really want it. It always seemed as though what Emma had to say wasn't as important as what the adults had to say. Not that they would believe her, anyway. As a result, she kept much of what she felt, what she saw, between her, Brie, and Blue. She took a deep breath. "I don't like this house. I want to move back to our old house. I miss Brie."

"You still get to talk to her on the phone, don't you?" her mother said.

"Yes, but I don't get to see her. And she doesn't like this house either."

"And why not?" her mother asked, furrowing her brow.

"She said there's something bad here."

"She's never been here—how would she know?"

"'Cause she knows things. She knows a lot of things. She can feel them, even if she's far away," Emma replied.

"And how is that?" her mother said in a condescending tone that Emma recognized well. She hated that tone, but of course, she would never tell her mother that. It was a tone that screamed, *I'm talking, but I'm not listening!*

She exhaled deeply. "I can't explain it," Emma replied. "But I told her about the bad things I've seen here... At least Brie listens."

"Bad things? What bad things?" her mother asked, leaning in. "And why haven't you told me about this?"

Emma's eyes blazed with annoyance as she vividly remembered frantically telling her parents what she saw the first night in the new house—further proof that her words had fallen on deaf ears. "I have so told you," she said, crossing her arms with a scowl on her face.

"What did you tell me?"

"About Elmo."

"Angel, that doesn't count. That was just a dream."

Emma released an exasperated exhale and huffed loudly. It was clear that no one was listening to her. She looked her mother sternly in the eyes and said, "I never said it was a dream."

Chapter 5

WHEN EMMA TOLD HER SHE WAS SAD because she wasn't being listened to, the words struck Josephine like a gut-wrenching punch, leaving her breathless with guilt. It wasn't just the typical frustration of parenting; it was the kind of hurt that hit her deep, making her feel like both a hypocrite and a failure as a mother. She knew too well the sting of being unheard, the quiet agony of having your voice silenced, of feeling like you didn't matter. Emmanuel had done that to her more times than she could count—more times than she could bear to remember. In the beginning, Josephine had brushed it off, even told herself it was manly, a sign of strength. There was a part of her that had wanted Emmanuel to take control, to lead. But then, what had felt like leadership morphed into something else. He dismissed her thoughts, undermined her opinions, and slowly, insidiously, her voice disappeared. She became an observer in her own life, retreating into silence just to keep the peace.

But the silence came with a price. The resentment festered, growing like a shadow over their marriage, until one day, it nearly broke them. She had thought about leaving, about finding herself again in a world where she wasn't invisible. Emmanuel, sensing the rupture, had promised to change. And to his credit, he had. But it wasn't easy, and it didn't happen overnight.

Josephine fought for her voice, demanding her place in their marriage, standing up for herself in ways she hadn't before. The arguments that followed were fierce and often left the house simmering with unresolved tension. She needed him to know that her opinions mattered just as much as his, that her contributions carried equal weight. It wasn't about control, it was about respect—about being seen, heard, and valued.

She let him lead, but only with the understanding that they were equals. Over time, the balance shifted. Emmanuel had matured, recognizing the damage his behavior had caused, and he worked to right those wrongs. While the old Emmanuel sometimes resurfaced—those moments where he tried to take the reins without consulting her—Josephine was always ready to stand her ground. After eight years of marriage, they had found a fragile peace, a rhythm that worked most of the time.

But hearing Emma say *you never listen*—the same words she had once whispered to herself—was a brutal reminder of the past she had fought so hard to escape. Those words, so innocent yet piercing, reopened old wounds, making her question whether the cycle she had struggled to break was quietly repeating itself in her daughter's life. It was as if all the battles she had fought for her voice, for her sense of self, were suddenly slipping through her fingers, leaving her to wonder if she had truly broken free or if the scars of her silence had been passed down to Emma.

She was determined not to let her past insecurities burden her daughter. Taking a deep breath, she pushed aside the guilt and resolved to make things right. Kneeling in front of Emma, she gently placed a hand on her daughter's shoulder, her voice soft but steady. "Angel, I'm sorry I didn't listen before. I'm listening now." She looked into Emma's wide, tear-filled eyes, searching for the right words to bridge the gap that had formed between them. "I promise, from now on, I'll always be here to listen."

Emma crossed her arms and turned her back on her bed, her expression guarded, as if unsure whether to believe her mother. "Cross your heart?" she said.

"Hope to die, stick a needle in my eye," Josephine said, she said, her voice steady and sincere.

Emma took a deep breath and turned to her. "OK... I saw a girl—my age... When I was on the phone with Brie."

Oh boy, Josephine thought. Here we go. She heard her mention a girl earlier but had chosen to ignore it. There was no escaping it now. She nodded slowly as she thought through how she could continue the conversation without appearing dismissive. "I don't remember having any guests over. What did she look like?"

"A little like me, except her eyes were black, and she didn't blink."

"That's interesting... Did she speak to you?"

"Yes. I think she was spying on me. I think she knows I don't like it here and that I miss Brie."

"What makes you think that?" she asked, bringing Emma close to her chest.

"Because she asked if she could be my friend."

"Oh? And what did you say?"

"No."

"Why is that?"

"Cause Brie told me to, and you told me not to talk to strangers."

"Well, yes—but the stranger rule doesn't apply to little girls your age just trying to make a friend."

"She was stranger than a stranger. I told her she's not allowed to be in the house... I wasn't trying to be mean," she said, looking up at her mother. "Did I do the right thing, Momma?"

Unwilling to validate what Emma said she saw, Josephine contemplated how to respond. For one, she didn't believe in ghosts, and two, she didn't want to give Emma any more reason to be afraid or uncomfortable in their home. With a deep breath, she said, "Well, no one should be in our home unless they are invited. And since she wasn't invited... Yes, you did the right thing."

"Good," Emma replied, inhaling deeply. "She gave me a tummy ache."

Saddened to hear that, Josephine frowned inwardly. *She's too young to be dealing with anxiety*, she thought. She held Emma close and massaged gentle circles on her back as she tried to make sense of what Emma had just revealed to her. She had never mentioned seeing anyone in the house before.

Or had she?

Emma had never given her any reason to believe she had an overactive imagination.

Or had she?

Even if she didn't have one before—this could be new. *She could be developing an overactive imagination*, she thought. She had once read in a parenting magazine at Emma's pediatrician's office that some children escape into an imaginary world when real-life situations get tough, and that lack of social interaction with other kids can lead to over-imagining. Moving into a new house and away from Brianna are certainly reasons enough to explain her sudden change in behavior, she convinced herself. She peered into Emma's eyes, searching for understanding, and said, "Angel, just curious—do you speak to Blue the way you spoke to the little girl you saw today?"

"Of course not," Emma said, her eyes crossed in exasperation.

"Oh? Haven't I heard you speak to Blue before?"

"Yes."

Her patience wearing thin, she took a deep breath and asked, "So how is the way you speak to Blue any different from how you spoke to the little girl you saw?"

Emma crossed her arms and glared at her mother as if the answer to her question were glaringly obvious. Except it wasn't.

"Well?" Josephine said, raising her brows.

"It's *very* different," Emma replied. "Blue doesn't talk back."

Chapter 6

WHY DO YOU ALWAYS DO THIS? Emmanuel thought as the need to relieve himself intensified by the second. *Always waiting until the last minute.* He raced inside the house, through the hallway, and into the bathroom. Shifting from one foot to the other, he unzipped his pants and exhaled a sigh of relief as a forceful stream of urine found its destination.

Suddenly, a searing heat began radiating behind his legs. He turned his head, his heart skipping a beat as his eyes fell upon the shower curtain, fluttering perilously close to the flickering flames of the wall heater. Still urinating, he rushed to pull the curtain toward the toilet, away from the wall heater, narrowly avoiding disaster.

That was close, he thought, rubbing the back of his neck. *Ugh*, he realized, suddenly remembering he hadn't yet washed his hands.

"Honey? Where are you?" Emmanuel called out, turning on the faucet to wash up.

"Just a minute!" she exclaimed from another room.

Josephine poked her head into the bathroom, her face glistening, her brown hair up in a ponytail, moist with sweat. "I was with Emma; in her room. What do you need?"

"Did you just take a shower?"

"Does it look like I just took a shower?" she replied defensively, pulling on her sweat-soiled oversized house shirt. "Why?"

"The wall heater was on... And the shower curtain was bunched up near it—we're lucky I saw it before a fire broke out."

He reached for the pliers he had left atop the sink earlier, along with a box of matches he had used while working on the wall heater. The knob was missing, the screw underneath stripped, so he crouched down and used the pliers to turn off the gas valve. He had tested it earlier, so he knew the pilot light was out, but the gas was working. Using the matches, he got it to turn on just fine. Not that they needed it to work anytime soon—it was summer in Chicago, after all.

Josephine's gaze swung to the box of matches. Shaking her head, her eyes narrowed to slits, she called out for Emma.

"Coming!" Emma's distant voice called back, the sound of tiny footsteps growing louder as she approached.

"Yes, Momma?" Emma asked, clutching her stuffed puppy-dog, Blue.

"Emma, what did we say about playing with matches?" Josephine asked, crossing her arms.

"Never do it," Emma recited.

"And what did we say about you turning on the wall heater?"

"Never do it."

"And why are you never to do those things?"

"Because I could burn the house down," Emma replied as though reading from a script.

"That's right," Emmanuel said sternly. "So then, why did you do it?"

"Do what?" Emma asked, her brows knitted in confusion.

"Why did you use the matches to turn on the heater?" he asked, holding out the box of matches.

Her lower lip jutted out in a pout. "I didn't!" she exclaimed.

"Mija, if I didn't turn on the heater, and Momma didn't turn on the heater, who else could it have been?"

Emma's eyes darted around the room as though searching for an answer. "It must have been a ghost," she said.

Josephine exhaled audibly and crouched down to look Emma directly in the eyes. "You aren't in trouble. We just need you to understand how dangerous what you did is and never do it again. Now, do I make myself clear?"

"But Momma, it wasn't me!" Emma cried, stomping her tiny foot.

"Emma—that's enough. Go back to the living room... We'll talk about this later."

Emmanuel watched with a heavy heart as Emma's face flushed with indignation. She puffed out her lower lip, crossed her arms in defiance, and marched away.

"She gets her stubbornness from you, you know," Josephine said.

"I know," Emmanuel replied. Stubbornness aside, something didn't seem right. Emma didn't have a reputation for lying. Like most kids her age, she didn't exactly confess wrongdoing voluntarily. But when questioned, she always fessed up. *She's an honest kid*, he thought, and he was proud of that. Furrowing his brow, he crossed his arms and studied the shower curtain with piercing scrutiny, his mind filled with questions.

"What's on your mind?" Josephine asked.

He turned his gaze to her and said, "The shower curtain always hangs on the left, alongside the toilet."

"Yes. So?"

"So, if Emma was playing with fire..." He gripped the shower curtain, which had slipped out of its tracks, making it awkward and stiff to maneuver. Heavy and cumbersome, it resisted as he tugged it to the right, the metal rings screeching against the rod. "Why, maybe even how, would she slide the shower curtain clear across the room toward the flames?"

Chapter 7

A WAVE OF SADNESS WASHED OVER JOSEPHINE as she watched Emma sitting on the couch, staring vacantly into the distance, her stuffed animal's blue floppy ear pinched between her thumb and index finger—a self-soothing habit she had developed as a toddler. Josephine had once mentioned the unusual behavior to their pediatrician, who had reassured her that it was normal for children to develop such habits to cope with stress. She thought Emma had outgrown it years ago, but there she was, just as she had been at three years old. But this time, the sweet melodies of her daughter's laughter and the warmth of her smiles were missing. The carefree, innocent giggles that once filled their days seemed more distant with each passing moment spent in that house.

Josephine clung to hope, navigating each day by convincing herself that things weren't as bad as they seemed, that the gloom she felt was only in her mind, and that a mother's love could conquer even the darkest clouds. But deep down, she couldn't ignore the creeping sense that the joy in their lives was slipping away, being sucked into the deepest, darkest crevices and cracks of the home, draining their world of color and light.

"Angel, can you take this box to your room and unpack your toys, please?" Josephine asked, her voice gentle but tinged with quiet desperation. She hoped the task might distract Emma from whatever was weighing on her young heart.

Josephine's heart sank further as Emma shook her head and softly said, "No, thank you." The refusal, so gentle yet firm, felt like a small crack in the already fragile facade she was struggling to maintain. Emma's eyes, usually so full of life, now looked dull and distant, and her rejection of such a simple task was unlike her.

Josephine forced a smile, trying to hide the worry gnawing at her insides. "Are you sure, sweetheart? I thought maybe unpacking your toys might make your room feel more like home," she suggested, her voice trembling slightly with the effort to sound encouraging.

But Emma just shook her head again, more decisively this time. "I don't want to right now, Momma," she said, her voice barely above a whisper.

Josephine sighed, feeling helpless in the face of her daughter's quiet resistance. She didn't want to push her, but the sense that something was slipping away from them both was almost unbearable. "Alright, angel," she said softly, reaching out to gently stroke Emma's hair. "Can you at least tell me why?" Josephine watched her with a heavy heart, wishing she could find a way to reach her, to bring back the joy and light that seemed so far out of reach.

"Momma, it's because I don't want to go to my room."

"I know it's not as big as your old room, but it's more than enough space for a little girl like you," Josephine said.

"It's not that."

"Is it the cemetery across the street?"

"No," Emma replied, shaking her head.

"Well, what is it then?"

"I don't want to be alone," Emma said, crossing her arms. "It's always dark... and cold. And the air feels heavy... and not just in my room—it's the whole house."

Josephine removed her cardigan and wrapped it around Emma's small, thin frame. "Angel, kids are much smaller than grown-ups, so they get cold more easily." She glanced at her wristwatch and turned her gaze to the door, her heart heavy with anticipation. She was expecting Emmanuel to be home any minute now. They had spoken about Emma not adapting well to the move and agreed they needed to do something to help her acclimate. *The solution is on its way*, she thought.

"It didn't feel like this at our old house," Emma frowned.

"Angel, this is an older home, not well insulated. It's normal."

"So, if something is *normal*, does that mean you have to like it?"

Her words hung suspended in the air like a thick fog.

Josephine fell silent as her mind struggled to grasp the depth of wisdom in her young daughter's question. She looked deep into her eyes, aglow with an inner light, and said, "You know the answer to that question. Don't you, angel?"

"Yes, Momma." Caught red-handed, Emma dropped her head.

"Well, what is it then?"

"Normal is not always best," Emma replied.

Josephine nodded and smiled inwardly. *This child is wise beyond her years*, she thought.

The front door swung open. "¡Hola, familia!" Emmanuel said, stepping inside holding a large shoe box peppered with dime-sized holes.

"Hi Daddy!" Emma exclaimed.

"Is that it?" Josephine asked, stepping energetically toward him.

"I have it right here," he replied.

"Have what?" Emma asked, seemingly sensing the excitement rising in the room.

"Angel, we have a surprise for you," Josephine said with a wide, toothy smile.

"A surprise? For me?" Emma asked as Emmanuel placed the box on the floor next to her.

"Go ahead, open it," Josephine said, yearning to witness her daughter's face light up with happiness.

A silence of anticipation settled over the room as Emma crouched down, gripped the box, and removed the lid. She gasped, her eyes wide with amazement, as her gaze settled upon the contents of the box. "Whoa... a puppy." She reached inside and retrieved the pint-sized wonder, its nose sniffing about with curiosity.

"We know you don't care for it here, so Momma and I got her to make you feel more at home," Emmanuel said, placing his hand on Josephine's shoulder.

"Her?"

He nodded. "She's a Chihuahua."

"She's so tiny and so cuuute!" Emma exclaimed, bringing the pup to her chin. "I'm naming her Blue."

"Don't let her size fool you," Emmanuel said. "Chihuahuas are protective, brave, and fearless."

"Wow," Emma said with wide eyes. "Really?"

"Yes, really." He turned to Josephine. "You know, they have a culturally spiritual significance, too."

"Oh, really?" Josephine said, recognizing the sparkle in Emmanuel's eyes. It was a sparkle that conveyed he was well-versed on the topic and had much to say about it. *I'll bite*, she thought. "Why don't you enlighten us?"

"Chihuahuas are a symbol of Native American culture. They were believed to have spiritual powers and were used as servants to shamans and magicians, to guide them," he said. "And the Aztecs believed that Chihuahuas symbolized protection and gave people courage. They were much more than just pets—they were guardians of the home, warding off evil intruders."

Emma's eyes widened. "That's just what I need!" she exclaimed, bouncing with energy. She brought the golden-colored pup to her face and stared intently into its expressive, protruding brown eyes. "Blue, you protect me, and I'll protect you!" she exclaimed, planting a kiss on the pup's forehead.

"How do you know all this?"

"My family had Chihuahuas when I was growing up—lots of them. They reminded my mother of back home. In Mexico, people swear by them," Emmanuel replied, rubbing the pup's silky ear between his fingers. "They're a cure-all, you know."

Josephine scoffed.

"I'm serious," he said. "Here, when your kid gets asthma, you take them to the doctor. In Mexico, when your kid gets asthma, you get them a Chihuahua and the problem is solved."

Emma put the pup down and leaped into Emmanuel's arms with a smile Josephine had not seen since they moved in.

"Hey—what's this all about?" Emmanuel said, embracing her with a smile of his own that extended from ear to ear. "Like I said, she's from both of us—but I'll take it."

They followed Blue with their eyes as she stepped to the center of the room, scanning every inch of the space with an unwavering intensity. Her ears were perked up; she appeared alert and standing at attention, emitting a series of low growls.

Emmanuel threw his head back and erupted in laughter, rooted deep within his belly.

Josephine turned to him and asked, "What's so funny?"

"Now that's a Mexican for you—she just got here, and she's already clocked in and ready to get to work," he said, wiping his watery eyes.

Chapter 8

H E WAS CATCHING UP on paperwork, alone in his office at the church, when he heard the front door swing open. Not expecting anyone, he stepped out to see who had arrived. His eyes landed on the unexpected visitor—his younger sister, Margie—and his jaw dropped as if he had seen a ghost. It had been over five years since he last saw her, and he had resigned himself to the painful reality that he might never see her again. It wasn't easy—losing someone you love never is—but over the years, he had navigated the stages of grief:

Denial. When Margie didn't show up for Christmas dinner, he chalked it up to her usual behavior—flaky, unreliable. She'll come back, he reassured himself, even as she stopped attending family gatherings altogether and ignored his phone calls.

Anger. Margie had always been the rebel, pushing against the grain. But after two children and no signs of maturing, his patience wore thin. One day, he showed up at her house unannounced and let her have it, accusing her of selfishness when he heard she was still out partying until the early hours, leaving her two children—one with special needs—alone to fend for themselves.

Bargaining. He hoped and prayed that it was only a matter of time before she settled down and left her reckless lifestyle behind. He became relentless, calling her repeatedly, trying to convince her to come to his church. *If I could just get her to come, her life would change*, he thought, clinging to the hope that faith might be the answer.

Depression. Many nights, he stayed up long after his family had gone to bed, sifting through old family photos of him and Margie as children—when life was simpler, untainted by the harsh realities of adulthood. They had laughed, played, and watched out for each other back then, before differences in opinions, beliefs, and egos drove them apart. *If only I hadn't been so hard on her*, he often thought, weighed down by guilt and regret.

Acceptance. It took more than two years of complete silence from Margie before he finally came to terms with losing her. He made peace with the situation, but the love he had for his sister never faded. Deep down, he still longed for a chance to speak with the sister he missed so dearly.

And now, it seemed that chance had finally arrived. "I can't believe you're here, hermana," Emmanuel said, his voice thick with emotion as he stood frozen in the doorway, overwhelmed by her sudden presence.

"Hello, Manny," Margie replied, her arms wrapped tightly around her chest, her gaze fixed on the floor, avoiding his eyes.

Emmanuel's mind raced with questions, each more terrifying than the last. Why is she here? Is she dying? Did one of the kids die? He could only imagine that a death of some kind—literal or metaphorical—could have driven her back to him after all these years. She looked thinner now, but not in a healthy way, and her skin bore the wear of more than just the passage of time. Her eyes, once vibrant and full of life, now carried a haunting sadness, a deep-seated pain that seemed to reach into her very soul. Yet despite the changes, the sight of her wavy, jet-black hair and sun-kissed skin brought an odd sense of familiarity, like looking into a mirror reflecting a part of himself.

"How did you know I would be here?" he asked, his voice gentle but tinged with concern.

"I didn't," she replied. "Part of me was hoping you wouldn't be... That way, I could walk away saying at least I tried."

His heart sank into his stomach like a ball of lead. "Well, I'm glad that wasn't the case," Emmanuel said, speaking gently.

"It's not like I had a choice," she said. "I looked for you at your old address. You moved."

"Yes." *It's not like I had a choice either*, he thought. "So, how have you been?"

"Never worse."

It wasn't the answer he expected and surely nothing he had ever heard her admit before. He wanted to know more but resisted the urge to ask. *I don't want to pry—if she wants to tell me more, she can do it on her own*, he thought. "How are the kids?"

"David's fourteen now—sweet as ever." She inhaled deeply. "I don't know how I got so lucky," she smiled.

"And Candy?"

She rolled her shoulders back and shifted her gaze to the church pew. "Can we sit down and talk?"

"Yes," Emmanuel replied, his heart tightening with a sense of dread. "Is Candy OK?"

"She's about the same as when you last saw her—almost eleven now. Except for her special needs, she's your typical eleven-year-old girl... God knows she's got the attitude of one." Margie's eyes darted around the church as if waiting for divine retribution. "Oh shit, is that OK for me to say?"

A gentle smile tugged at the corners of Emmanuel's lips. "It's fine," he reassured her.

"Anyway, she's potty trained now, so that's made caring for her much easier. And David helps a lot," she added, her eyes wide with something close to hope.

"That's great," Emmanuel said, trying to keep his tone steady. "You know, I've never stopped praying for you and the kids."

"Manny, God damn it, this isn't about prayer!" Margie snapped, bringing her hands to her face.

He flinched at her outburst. "I'm sorry... It wasn't my intent—"

"It's never your intent!" she interrupted, her voice thick with frustration. "I know you do a lot of preaching, but I need you to just shut up and listen to me for once." Her eyes bore into him, demanding his attention.

"OK," he said softly. "I'm listening."

"Thank you," she said, her voice dropping to a more controlled tone. "I need to get help, and I need you to watch the kids while I get it."

Emmanuel leaned in, his gaze skeptical. "Why now? I've been trying to get you help for years, and what did you do?" He paused, his eyes searching hers, knowing the answer before she could give it. "You cut me out of your life."

"I'm sorry, Manny. But I need your help now."

"Why?" he asked, the word heavy with years of pent-up hurt.

She turned away, her arms crossing defensively as she shook her head. "It's complicated," she muttered.

"Then dumb it down for me," he pressed, his voice softening. "Por favor."

Margie took a deep breath, her voice trembling as she spoke. "Because if I don't get help, the state is going to take the kids away from me, OK?" she said, rising to her feet in agitation. "And I don't have anyone else—no one who is willing to take them both." She shook her head, her voice breaking. "That's not true. I don't even have a place for David. Not that it matters—those two are inseparable. And I get it," she said, her frustration mounting. "Candy needs to be watched constantly, driven to doctor appointments. But it's you or an institution—those are my choices."

"An institution?" Emmanuel repeated, his voice filled with disbelief. The thought of his niece being left alone with strangers—when she had family—was unimaginable.

"And if I allow Candy to go to the institution... I'm just afraid there's a good chance—once they know how much care she needs—I won't get her back." Margie placed a trembling hand against her forehead, struggling to collect her thoughts. "They stay with you for the summer, or Candy goes to the institution, and David goes..." She took a deep breath, the words catching in her throat. "I don't know where David goes."

Emmanuel's heart ached with compassion. It had been so long since he had seen his sister, and he knew she wouldn't have come to him unless she had no other choice. Maybe, just maybe, this could be an opportunity to mend their fractured relationship. He fixed his gaze on her—forever his baby sister in his eyes. "I'll have to discuss it with Josephine," he said gently. "But it doesn't sound like we have much of a choice, now does it?"

Chapter 9

IT HAD BEEN SO LONG IT HAD BEEN SO LONG since Josephine and Emmanuel last saw their niece and nephew that they almost didn't recognize them. David had grown into a soft, endearing plumpness, his cheeks still holding onto the last traces of childhood. Though tall for his age, there was something about him that suggested he was still on the verge of a growth spurt, teetering at the edge of adolescence. Candy, on the other hand, had shot up dramatically in height. Despite the four-year age gap, she was nearly as tall as David. Thin and lanky, her limbs seemed awkwardly stretched, as though her body hadn't quite figured out how to carry the sudden growth. The contrast between them—the sturdy, rounded softness of David and the fragile, almost clumsy grace of Candy—made the passage of time painfully clear. The contrast between them was striking—except for their reddish-brown hair, which appeared more red than brown in the sunlight, they hardly resembled each other. Yet, there was a shared familiarity in their features, a subtle connection that linked them unmistakably as siblings, even as time and growth had begun to carve out their individual identities.

"Come on in," Josephine said, peeking behind them as they stepped inside. She had been expecting to see her sister-in-law, but there was no sign of her. She closed the door behind the children, masking her disappointment with a smile.

"Can I get you two anything to drink?" she asked, gently ushering them toward the kitchen, her heart heavy with the unspoken question of where their mother was.

"No, thank you, ma'am," David replied, his tone polite and composed.

Candy's eyes fixed on the can of diet cola on the kitchen counter. "Soda," she said, her voice tinged with longing.

"Candy, you know you're not allowed to have soda," David said, wagging his finger at her in a brotherly reprimand. "That's a grown-up drink."

"OK," she replied, a small pout forming as she looked away. "I forgot."

Josephine couldn't help but smile as she watched the siblings interact with mutual respect. David seemed quite comfortable in his role as the older brother, keeping a watchful eye on Candy, who, for her part, seemed content to follow his lead. "I'm impressed," she said. "You're a very good big brother."

"Thank you, ma'am," David replied, standing a little taller, his posture reflecting his pride.

Great manners, too, she thought, smiling inwardly.

"David, remind me, how old are you again?" Emmanuel asked, his gaze shifting to the boy.

"Fourteen, sir," David answered promptly.

Emmanuel then turned his attention to Candy. "And what about you?"

Candy avoided eye contact, her gaze dropping to the floor.

"She doesn't like that question," David said, wrapping his arm around her protectively. "She's ten."

"Oh?" Emmanuel said, raising his eyebrows in surprise. "Why doesn't she like the question?"

"Because she never gets it right."

The air grew heavy with an awkward tension. Josephine sensed the sensitivity around the topic and knew Emmanuel well enough to understand he hadn't intended to make anyone uncomfortable. *Time to change the subject*, she thought. "Do you kids go to church?" she asked, her tone light and conversational.

"Yes, ma'am," David replied, his voice steady.

"Really?" Emmanuel said, his tone tinged with surprise.

"Yes," David confirmed, his eyes scanning the walls.

Josephine narrowed her gaze at him. "Can I help you find something?" she asked, noticing his curious behavior.

"Sorry—no," he replied, though his tone was unconvincing.

She furrowed her brow. "It's OK, David. You can tell us."

"It's just, I don't see any crucifixes hanging on your walls like we have at home."

"That's a good observation, David," Emmanuel said, nodding. "You see, your aunt and I aren't Catholic like you and your mother."

"What are you then?" David asked, tilting his head quizzically.

"Pentecostal," Emmanuel replied.

Josephine noticed a glint of confusion in David's eyes, prompting her to explain further. "We're Christian, David. We love God just like you, and we believe in good and evil."

"So... What's the difference, then?" he asked, his curiosity evident.

She thought back to an analogy she had heard Emmanuel use countless times to explain differences in denominations. While she found it effective, she also felt it was a bit overused. Still, it served its purpose. "Emmanuel, care to explain?" she asked, gesturing for him to take the lead.

"Absolutely," Emmanuel said, turning to David with a smile. "Let me ask you something. What's your favorite car?"

"A Chevy Camaro," David replied quickly, without hesitation.

"I'm more of a Ford man myself," Emmanuel said. "So here's how I like to think of it. You prefer Chevy; I prefer Ford. You might prefer cars; I prefer trucks. You might like black leather interiors; me, I might prefer tan. But whatever the vehicle, whatever your personal preferences, we're all driving on the same highway to heaven."

David's eyes widened with a spark of understanding. "I get it now," he said, nodding.

"Works every time," Emmanuel said with a grin.

"Momma, I want to play outside!" Emma suddenly exclaimed, tugging at Josephine's blouse.

"OK, angel—go ahead," Josephine replied, her tone warm and encouraging.

"Can I bring Blue?" Emma asked, holding up her tiny, four-legged stuffed companion.

"Yes, angel," Josephine said with a smile.

Candy's face fell as she watched Emma run out the back door, her expression a mix of longing and uncertainty.

"Candy, would you like to play outside with your cousin, Emma?" Josephine asked gently.

Candy nodded, her eyes lighting up with hope.

"Absolutely!" Emmanuel exclaimed. "Go on and play with Emma, and we'll keep catching up with David here."

Candy turned to David with a look that only he seemed to understand. "I should go with her," David said, his tone firm but polite. "She shouldn't go alone."

Josephine pointed to the window, through which the entire yard was visible and securely fenced. "That's not necessary—we can watch them from here," she said.

"No, I really should go with her," David insisted, glancing at Josephine for permission. "If that's OK with you?"

She nodded, realizing that he knew his sister best. "Thank you, ma'am," David said, his tone sincere. "When would you like us to come back in?" he asked, checking his wristwatch. "Before sunset?"

Josephine's eyes widened with admiration at his consideration and respect. "That'll be fine," she replied.

"Got it," David said, pressing a button on his watch. "Alarm is set." He reached for Candy's hand. "Come on, Candy. Let's go play outside."

"Oh, and David?" Josephine called after him.

"Yes, ma'am?" he replied, turning to her.

"You can call me Aunt Josie," she said with a warm smile.

"Yes, ma'am—I mean, yes, Aunt Josie," he corrected himself, smiling back.

He turned to Emmanuel. "Sir, if you don't mind me asking—can I call you Uncle Emmanuel?"

"Not a chance," Emmanuel replied, his expression stern.

David's smile faltered. "Yes sir. Sorry, sir," he said, lowering his gaze.

"It's Tio Manny to you," Emmanuel said, his stern expression softening into a grin.

A smile broke across David's face as he followed Candy and Emma out the back door. Josephine watched the children for a moment through the window, ensuring they were a safe distance away before turning back to Emmanuel. "How long will they be staying?"

Emmanuel didn't respond immediately. His attention was fixed on the window, but his gaze was distant, his mind clearly elsewhere. "What's wrong?" she asked, her voice tinged with concern.

"Hmm?"

"What's wrong?"

"Oh, I was just thinking about the window frame," he said, snapping out of his reverie.

Josephine stepped up to the window, examining it closely. The windowsill, once a sturdy piece of fresh pine wood, now bore the marks of a relentless infestation, crumbling beneath her touch. "I thought you replaced it."

"I did," Emmanuel said, inspecting the damage. "Those roaches are something else." He took a deep breath, trying to shake off the unsettling thought. "Anyway, what is it you asked before?"

"How long will they be staying?" Josephine repeated, nervously gripping the gold cross pendant around her neck.

"As long as Margie is going through treatment," he replied.

"And how long is that, exactly?" she pressed.

"For the summer."

Josephine's eyes widened in surprise. This wasn't just a weekend sleepover at Auntie's—this was an entire summer. Three months. Twelve weeks. Eighty-four days. Over two thousand hours of caretaking. Nearly double the meal prepping, grocery costs, cooking, laundry, cleaning—it was enough to make her head spin. She stared blankly in Emmanuel's direction, trying to process the enormity of the commitment. This wasn't a decision Emmanuel should have made on his own—not if he was smart.

"I know it's a big commitment," Emmanuel said, sensing her hesitation.

Through the window, Josephine kept a vigilant watch on the children playing in the yard.

"But it could be good for Emma," Emmanuel added.

He has a point, Josephine thought. With Emma's overactive imagination and her self-soothing habits resurfacing, she could benefit from the company and social interaction. And Emma was still terrified of the house. Having other children around might help distract her and ease her fears. Still, despite the potential benefits, Josephine's mind raced with doubt, worry, and guilt—a gut-wrenching combination of emotions that refused to be silenced. She turned to Emmanuel, her voice tinged with concern. "What if Candy hurts Emma?"

"What?" Emmanuel said, taken aback. He glanced out the window. "Look at them—they're playing so well together. She would never—"

"But what if she did?" Josephine interrupted, her tone sharp.

"She wouldn't... She's only ten years old, for Christ's sake."

"It doesn't matter!" Josephine exclaimed, her anxiety bubbling to the surface. "Things happen, Emmanuel. In the blink of an eye—things happen."

Emmanuel sighed deeply, reaching for her hand. "You're right—I'm sorry," he said, his voice softening.

"Where would they even sleep?" she asked, her mind still racing.

"Emma can sleep with us in our room. Candy can take Emma's room. And David can take the extra room."

"The extra room?" Josephine said, raising an eyebrow. It was so small, almost cruel to have a growing boy sleep in there. Not to mention the so-called echoes of the past she'd heard in that room. She shot Emmanuel a skeptical look.

"What?" Emmanuel said defensively. "If we clean it out, there's enough room for a twin bed and a dresser."

"And nothing else."

"He needs nothing else," Emmanuel insisted. "And there's no need to mention what you heard in the room—unless he does." Their eyes wandered back to the window, where David was playfully chasing Emma.

"You're too fast for me!" David called out, his voice carrying through the yard. "How do your little legs move so fast?!"

"And that kid—I have a good feeling about that kid," Emmanuel said, nodding toward David.

The distant sound of laughter filled the air. Josephine watched as David lifted Emma off the ground with care. He seemed mature for his age, likely less work than Candy and Emma combined. Emma seemed to take well to him, and he could probably help around the house if asked. He also kept a close eye on Candy, which was reassuring. *Maybe he'd be a big help with both of them*, she thought. "I have a good feeling about him, too," she admitted.

"I'm just glad Margie is finally getting the help she needs. And I want to be here for her... For them," Emmanuel said, his voice filled with quiet resolve.

Josephine sighed deeply. "OK," she said.

"OK?" Emmanuel echoed, his tone lifting with hope.

"OK," she repeated, more firmly this time.

"They can stay?" he asked, a note of excitement creeping into his voice.

"They can stay," she confirmed, her gaze narrowing as she added, "But no locked doors."

Emmanuel nodded quickly. "Absolutely."

"And just one more question," Josephine said, her voice softening.

He nodded, waiting for her to continue.

"Where is Margie, anyway?"

Chapter 10

DAVID KNEW THAT STAYING with their uncle was far from his mother's first choice. The tension between them was thick and heavy, like a storm cloud waiting to burst, the bad blood simmering just below the surface. He had often overheard his mother's sharp, biting words, muttered under her breath, about how his uncle thought he was so perfect, dismissing his "holy-roller" persona with a wave of her hand as if swatting away an annoying fly. She would often claim he had skeletons in his closet, just like everyone else, though that was a matter she kept strictly between herself and her brother.

David was nine the last time he saw his uncle. They had never been particularly close, but the memories that lingered were warm and comforting. He remembered his uncle as the one relative who never failed to bring gifts for every birthday and Christmas, even when everyone else seemed to forget. Those small acts of kindness stood out in David's mind like bright spots in the sometimes-overlooked corners of his childhood. And despite the years and the miles that had stretched between them, David missed him—the man who had shown him kindness when it mattered, the one who made an effort even when others didn't.

Of course, he could never tell his mother any of this. To do so would be like throwing a match into a powder keg, sparking a conflict he desperately sought to avoid. So, he kept his feelings buried deep, a quiet yearning for a connection that his mother would never understand or accept.

As he followed his uncle down the short hallway at the end of the house, David's eyes flitted from door to door. "Is this the entire place?" he asked, his voice tinged with curiosity.

"This is it. Not a whole lot to it, I'm afraid," Tio Manny replied with a small shrug.

It wasn't that David was accustomed to large spaces. He just imagined a house was supposed to be… bigger. He had spent most of his life in the Robert Taylor Homes, a sprawling public housing project in the Bronzeville neighborhood on the south side of Chicago. The largest housing project in the United States, it was a maze of 28 virtually identical high-rises, each plagued by more than its fair share of problems—drug dealing, gang violence, and a pervasive sense of danger. The atmosphere was so threatening that even the police feared venturing into the area, wary of being shot at from the towering buildings.

Despite the ever-present danger, David had managed to steer clear of the gang violence that threatened to pull him into the darkness of the housing development. It was his job to care for Candy, and it seemed that even the shadiest figures in the projects respected that unspoken responsibility. Maybe they sensed the goodness in him, or maybe they understood that his little sister depended on him. Whatever the reason, they kept their distance, allowing David to navigate the treacherous environment with a degree of safety that others didn't have.

Candy turned to David, her voice small and hesitant. "Where's my bed?"

"Candy will stay in Emma's room," Tio Manny replied. "Emma will stay with me and your aunt in the next room."

"Daddy, can I show them my secret tunnel?" Emma asked, her eyes wide with excitement.

"If you show them, it won't be a secret anymore," he replied with a smile. "But be my guest."

"Yay!" she squealed. "Come on, follow me," she said, leading the way into her parents' room. She pointed to the closet door with a grin. "There it is," she said proudly.

David opened the door, expecting to see something extraordinary. But inside, he found only a typical closet, filled with coats, jackets, suits, and dresses. "What am I supposed to be looking at?" he asked, tilting his head in confusion.

"Daddy, take them to my room, OK? I'll stay here," Emma said, her tone filled with playful mystery.

Her father sighed deeply. "Mija, that's really not necessary."

"Pleeease," she pleaded, pressing her palms together in a dramatic gesture.

"OK," her father relented. "David, Candy—follow me."

David took Candy's hand and followed his uncle out of the room, curious to see where this was going.

They stopped at the door to Emma's room, just down the hall.

"Go ahead, open the door," Tio Manny said, a hint of amusement in his voice.

David turned the knob and pushed the door open. His eyes widened in surprise, and he let out an audible gasp at the sight before him.

"Tah-dah!" Emma exclaimed, sitting on the bed with her arms outstretched in triumph.

"Whoa! How did you do that?" David asked, his mouth hanging open in amazement.

His uncle chuckled and pointed to the closet door in the room. "It's connected to the closet in the next room."

"Ohhh," David said, realization dawning as the secret of Emma's not-so-magic trick was revealed. "Is this where I'm sleeping too?" he asked, glancing around the room. His eyes landed on the bed—it was twin-sized, definitely not big enough to share with his sister. "I can take the floor."

"Believe me, you do not want to do that," his uncle said, shaking his head.

David shrugged. "It's no big deal." He wasn't above sleeping on the floor. He used to share a bed with Candy, but as they got older and outgrew it, he started sleeping on the floor. He didn't even bother asking his mom for a bed of his own. He knew she was struggling and had more important things to worry about, like keeping food on the table—even if it was him doing all the cooking. All he needed was a bedspread, a pillow, and a blanket, and he'd be just fine. "I'm used to it," he added, following his uncle out of the room.

Tio Manny opened the door at the end of the hall. "You'll sleep in here. It's not much space, but we'll make it work."

David peeked inside the room. *My own bed?* he thought, his heart lifting. It was more than he had at home. "Works for me," he said, a small smile tugging at the corners of his mouth. Tio Manny had covered almost everything. He only had one more question. "Where's the bathroom?"

"Right here." Tio Manny pointed to the final door in the hall. "Aside from no locked doors, we have another rule—and it's important." He gestured toward the wall heater in the bathroom as if it were a hidden menace. "You see that?"

"Yes," David replied, nodding.

"No one is allowed to turn that thing on—that includes you."

"Yes, sir," David said, his tone serious.

"And that shower curtain needs to be pulled to the left, just as it is now, away from the wall heater, at all times, just in case." His stern gaze shifted to Emma, who stood silently, her arms crossed in frustration. "The last thing we need is a house fire."

Emma's eyelids fluttered with frustration; she crossed her arms, her face a picture of stubborn defiance. An awkward silence filled the air as Emmanuel's gaze remained locked on her, as though waiting for her to admit to something.

Suddenly, a bone-chilling scream shattered the silence, piercing the air like a knife. Candy's face contorted in terror as she pointed to the floor, cowering behind David.

"Candy!" David exclaimed in panic. He had never heard her scream like that. "What's wrong?"

The sound of spiny legs scurrying against the white ceramic tiles filled the air. With a sudden burst of movement, a repugnant cockroach boldly emerged from behind the toilet, as if claiming its territory.

"Our unwelcome tenants," Tio Manny muttered, his voice grim. He stomped on the insect with such force that the room seemed to tremble. "Don't worry," he said. They've been served their eviction notice."

Chapter 11

THE SAVORY AROMA OF ITALIAN HERBS and meatballs filled the air, pulling David to his feet like a moth to a flame. He wandered into the kitchen in a trance-like state, his senses captivated by the unfamiliar scent. He wasn't used to the smell of a home-cooked meal unless he was the one cooking it, and something about this meal smelled different—richer, more inviting.

As he entered the kitchen, he found his aunt busy at the counter, her hands deftly slicing through vibrant green leaves. The sweet, pungent fragrance released with each cut filled the room, jolting his senses awake. It was a scent like nothing he had ever experienced before. Intrigued, he inhaled deeply and asked, "What kind of vegetable is that?"

"What? This?" she replied, holding up the bright green leafy stem.

He nodded, curiosity gleaming in his eyes.

"It's an herb... It's called basil. You've never seen fresh basil before?"

He shook his head.

She reached for another leafy green stem, its needle-like leaves reminding him of fresh pine. "What about this? Ever seen this before?"

He squinted at it, trying to place the familiar scent. "There are bushes of that stuff planted around my school."

"It's called rosemary," she said, slicing into the herb with practiced ease.

His eyes widened in surprise. "You mean you can eat that?"

She smiled softly and brushed her hand over his head. "Well, just you wait, kiddo. You're in for a treat."

He returned the smile. "Can I help with dinner?"

She opened her mouth to answer but was interrupted by Emma bounding into the kitchen, clutching her beloved blue-eared stuffed animal, a small notepad, and a crayon.

"David, do you and Candy want to watch my show with me and Blue?" Emma asked, her voice bubbling with excitement.

"What show?"

"Blue's Clues," she replied, proudly holding up her things.

"Isn't that on cable?" David asked, furrowing his brow. With all the talk he'd overheard about saving money, he didn't expect them to be paying for non-essentials like cable.

"Yes, it was hooked up when we moved in," his aunt replied.

"I wanna watch," Candy said from the doorway, her voice soft but eager.

"Is it OK with you, Aunt Josie?" David asked. "Or I can help you with dinner if you'd like."

"No, I have things covered here," she replied. "You go be a kid and relax with the girls."

"Yay!" Emma squealed, dashing into the living room with David and Candy following close behind.

"Sit next to me," Emma said, climbing onto the couch.

"Thanks, Emmy," David replied, taking a seat beside her.

"Emmy?" she echoed, furrowing her brow.

"Yes—is it OK if I call you that?"

She nodded, a smile lighting up her face. "I like it." She turned to Candy, who was seated on the floor between the couch and the television. "Candy, wanna sit next to me, too?"

Candy shook her head, her attention fixed on the screen.

"That's not very nice," Emma whispered, the corners of her lips turning downward in a pout.

"Don't mind her," David said gently. "She isn't trying to be mean… She's just different."

"OK," Emma shrugged, sinking into her spot on the couch.

David watched as the animated show featuring a light blue dog with dark blue spots began, the catchy jingle playing in the background. Emma bobbed her head from side to side, completely immersed in the show. *She's adorable,* he thought, smiling inwardly. Although he loved his sister and wouldn't trade her for the world, he always wondered what it would be like to have a younger sibling who enjoyed playing, watching movies, and having simple conversations. Candy wasn't interested in any of that. "Is this your favorite show?" he asked.

"Yes," Emma replied, flipping open the green cover of her notebook, which was bound with red plastic.

David's eyes sparkled with recognition. "Oh, I see!" he exclaimed. "That must be your handy-dandy notebook, like on the show."

She flashed a wide smile. "Yes," she said, gripping her black crayon.

"What are you supposed to do with it?" he asked.

"Draw the clues, like Steve does."

He observed as Emma mimicked Steve, the show's main character, by drawing a shadow in her handy-dandy notebook. He squinted, trying to see any resemblance between her drawing and the one on the screen. "That doesn't quite look like the shadow Steve drew," he said politely, not wanting to hurt her feelings.

"It's not supposed to."

"Why not?"

"Let me explain," she said, speaking with the maturity of someone much older. "Steve is drawing the shadow Blue is afraid of… I'm drawing the shadow I'm afraid of."

David furrowed his brow, processing her explanation. For someone so smart, she seemed too old to be afraid of shadows. "That's what Momma calls them, anyway," she added with a shrug.

He could tell she wasn't convinced. "You don't think they're shadows?" he asked.

"No."

"Why?"

"A lot of reasons."

"Like what?"

"You want to know my reasons?" she asked, her eyes glimmering with a mix of hope and disbelief.

"Of course," he replied, reaching for her notebook. "I'll even write them in your handy-dandy notebook."

"Really?" she said, her voice rising with excitement.

He smiled and nodded. "What's clue number one?"

"OK. Shadows don't move on their own."

David repeated her words aloud as he carefully wrote them down. "Shadows... Don't... Move... On... Their... Own."

"Clue number two," she said, raising two fingers in the air. "Shadows don't go into and come out of the walls."

"The shadows you see come out of walls?" he asked, his tone more serious now.

She nodded.

His eyebrows shot up. Whatever Emma was experiencing, it was clear this wasn't just a game to her. "Got it," he said, masking his concern as he jotted down the second clue.

"Clue number three," she continued, raising three fingers. "I've never seen shadows like the ones I see in this house in my entire life!" she exclaimed emphatically.

"What do you mean?" he asked, leaning in closer.

She placed one hand on her hip, her expression serious. "I've seen shadows before—lots of them. I'm six years old—not a baby," she said with a touch of sass. "So why do the shadows I see in this house look any different?"

David leaned back on the couch, captivated by the maturity and eloquence coming from his young cousin.

"That's clue number four," she said, holding up four fingers. "Some look like floating bubbles. One looked like a dark storm cloud. Another one looked like a bubble and a rain cloud mixed together. One looked like a little girl," she said matter-of-factly.

David's eyes widened in shock. Surely he hadn't heard her right. "You mean a little girl's shadow, right?"

"No," she replied with unwavering certainty. "I mean... A little girl."

Chapter 12

CANDY'S EYES DARTED AROUND in panic as she bounced in place, tugging urgently on David's shirt. "I need to poop!" she exclaimed, her voice tinged with desperation.

"Candy, wait," David said, without turning to acknowledge her. "Don't worry, Aunt Josie. I'll take good care of them," he assured his aunt as she stood by the front door, ready to leave.

"I won't be long," his aunt replied, keys and purse in hand. "I just need to pick up your sister's medications before the pharmacy closes. It shouldn't be longer than twenty minutes." She stepped outside and glanced back. "I'm not expecting anyone, but if anyone comes by, don't let them in," she warned. "No one is allowed in the house without me or your uncle present."

"I won't," David promised, closing the door behind her.

"Lock the door!" she called out from outside.

David quickly turned the first lock, then the second, and finally the third, securing the door with a metallic click.

Candy tugged on his shirt again, more urgently. "I need to poop!" she repeated, her small voice pleading.

He finally turned to her. "Do you remember how to get to the potty?"

She nodded eagerly.

"OK, go potty then. I'll check on you in a little while."

Candy wasted no time, sprinting out of the living room, through the kitchen, and into the hallway. The short corridor seemed to stretch endlessly as she studied each door, trying to recall which one led to the bathroom. The floorboards creaked under her small feet as she pushed open the first door. Her eyes landed on a bed. "No potty," she murmured, shutting the door with a slight frown. She moved to the door across the hall and pushed it open. Her eyes lit up with relief. "Potty!" she exclaimed.

She stepped into the bathroom, the icy chill of the ceramic tiles bit at her bare feet, sending a jolt of cold through her body. The stark contrast of the room's temperature to the rest of the house made her pause. She hurriedly sat on the toilet, only to feel the frigid seat leeching the warmth from her skin. Shivering, she rubbed her arms for warmth, blinking in surprise as her breath fogged up in front of her.

"Whoa," she whispered, marveling at the sight, the cold now pressing in around her like an invisible force.

The bathroom was silent, save for the steady hum of the house. Until it wasn't. A faint whisper brushed against her ear, almost serpentine in its tone, soft and sibilant. *Are you cold?*

Her breath hitched, but she remained still, her eyes scanning the room. She wasn't frightened, not yet. There was something eerily familiar about the voice, though she couldn't place it.

The whisper grew louder, more insistent. *ARE YOU COLD?*

She nodded ever so slightly, her body reacting instinctively to the voice's demand. Suddenly, the wall heater roared to life with a loud *SWOOSH*, the flames crackling into existence. Candy's eyes widened in fascination, entranced by the flickering firelight that danced on the walls, casting strange, shifting shadows across the room. She gripped the toilet seat, her knuckles white as the fire swayed in time with some invisible force. Slowly, she stood, her curiosity overtaking the rising unease. She peered into the bowl, almost casually, as if the chill had numbed her fear. "No poop," she murmured, shaking her head.

As she neared the sink, her eyes lingered on the faucets, a wary suspicion growing in her chest. The eerie creak of the metal handles turning on their own sent a chill down her spine. They moved with a deliberate, almost sinister grace, as though guided by unseen hands. Candy hesitated, her breath shallow, but the warmth of the water beckoned her like a strange comfort amidst the cold. She tentatively moved her hands under the stream, feeling the warmth spread over her chilled skin.

Her gaze drifted to the mirror, where her breath fogged up the glass in rhythmic puffs. She watched, hypnotized by the mist forming in the reflection. The fog blurred her features, distorting her face, turning her familiar reflection into something unrecognizable.

But then, amidst the haze, something moved—just behind her.

Her heart lurched, and her breath hitched as her eyes narrowed, trying to make sense of the fog that curled in front of her. A shadow—impossibly tall and unnaturally thin—hovered just at the edge of her vision, its flickering form like a glitch in reality, as if it didn't belong in this world. She stood frozen, gripped by an unseen force, paralyzed by the oppressive weight of its presence. Every beat of her heart felt amplified, thudding in her chest as the air thickened around her.

In the mirror, the shadow leaned in closer, its outline sharpening with every passing second. *Leave,* it hissed, the word slithering through the steam, cutting through the silence with a venomous whisper.

A sudden knock on the door shattered the moment. "Candy, are you okay in there?" David's voice called out, muffled but close.

"Yes," she replied, her voice a tight whisper.

"Okay, just checking."

With trembling hands, she shut off the faucets, the sound of rushing water fading into an uneasy stillness. She reached for the doorknob, twisting it first to the right, then the left, pulling harder each time—but the door remained stubbornly locked. Her pulse quickened as her eyes dropped to the knob, watching in horror as the gems embedded in it began to ooze a thick, tar-like substance. The dark liquid pushed through the crevices, writhing and coiling into slick tendrils, as though the door was revealing something grotesque and forbidden.

Just as a cry rose in her throat, the door let out a long, eerie creak, slowly swinging open on its own. Candy stepped into the hallway, her heart still racing, her mind reeling from the strange encounter.

As she passed through the kitchen, her gaze locked onto the soda bottle perched on the counter—the gleaming two-liter of diet cola left all alone seemed almost out of place, a tempting beacon under the harsh kitchen light. Her throat felt dry, her body drawn to it, a desire creeping into her thoughts. A voice slithered into her mind, smooth and honeyed, dripping with something dark. *Do you want soda, Candy?*

Her fingers twitched at her sides as she glanced around, her mind a swirl of conflicting emotions. The voice whispered again, this time more insidious, *I won't tell if you don't.*

Chapter 13

D AVID WAS NO STRANGER to babysitting. Given his mother's condition, he had been born into the role of caretaker. An unspoken understanding had developed between him and his mother: David was the one responsible for his sister, and this duty had become second nature to him. Sure, his mother's revolving door of boyfriends sometimes helped with cooking and cleaning, but they never stayed long enough to be anything more than a temporary burden. So staying with his aunt and uncle, being part of a family without bearing the entire weight of responsibility, felt like a dream come true.

He glanced toward the bathroom. It had been a few minutes since he last checked on Candy, and he could still hear the faint sound of running water. She should be finished by now. "Emmy, I'm going to check on my sister—I'll be right back."

"OK," Emma replied, her eyes glued to the television.

As David stepped into the kitchen, his heart sank at the sight of Candy standing on a chair, guiltily clutching the two-liter bottle of diet cola, with a puddle of soda spilling over the edge of the countertop and dripping down the cabinets. Panic surged through him as he grabbed a kitchen rag. "Candy, you know better," he scolded, frantically wiping up the spill.

Suddenly, a blood-curdling scream tore through the house, freezing him in place.

He gasped, his heart skipping a beat. "Emma!" The fear in her scream propelled him forward, adrenaline surging through his veins. He sprinted into the living room, Candy trailing behind him.

"Emmy, what's wrong? Why did you scream?" he asked, gently gripping her shoulders.

Emma's eyes were wide, her body rigid, as if paralyzed by an unseen force.

"Emmy, what's wrong?" he repeated, his voice trembling with concern.

No answer.

He crouched down to her level, desperately trying to meet her gaze. "Emmy, what happened?"

Still no answer.

He nudged her gently, his voice tinged with urgency. "Answer me, Emmy. Did you see something?"

She nodded slowly, her vacant eyes fixed on the empty wall in front of her.

He followed her gaze, but there was nothing there. "What did you see?" he asked, his voice barely above a whisper.

She was quiet, her small frame trembling.

He took her cold hands in his, shaking them gently. "Emmy? What... Did... You... See?"

"It was... It was a man," she whispered, her voice hollow, as though she were in a trance. "His lips were stitched together."

David's heart plummeted, fear clawing at his chest. He quickly scanned the room, then turned to the front door, checking to see if it was still securely locked. It was. But the possibility that someone—something—was still inside the house sent a shiver down his spine. He turned off the television, straining to hear any sound of movement.

The old house creaked and groaned, the soft whispers of the past seeming to echo through the walls. Did the house always make these sounds? he wondered, dread tightening its grip on him. *There's no time for questions,* he thought, scooping Emma into his arms. Her tiny heart pounded against his chest like a drum. "Come, Candy," he whispered, reaching for her hand. "Hurry."

"But... my soda!" Candy protested, her voice wavering.

"Shh!" David hissed. "No soda for you." He hurried to the door, the floorboards moaning under his weight. His fingers trembled as he fumbled with the locks, one by one—first, second, third—until the door swung open.

"What about Blue?" Emma whispered, her voice tinged with fear.

"Come on, Blue. Hurry!" he called out softly.

The Chihuahua's ears perked up at the sound of its name, and in an instant, Blue darted off the couch and scurried to David's feet.

Outside, David's eyes scanned the unfamiliar neighborhood, searching for a safe haven. His gaze landed on the nearest house, and with long, purposeful strides, he made his way there.

A woman with long, curly brown hair, who looked to be about his mother's age, stood at the threshold of the door, as if she had been expecting them. "May I help you?" she asked, her voice warm and welcoming.

"Hello, ma'am. I'm sorry to bother you. My name is David," he began, his words tumbling out in a rush.

"It's no bother. Is everything OK? Would you like to come in?" she asked, swinging the screen door open wide.

She seemed too eager to help, too friendly. Unsure of whether to trust her, David hesitated, taking a step back. "My aunt and uncle live next door. My aunt stepped out, and my baby cousin here saw a man in the house," he explained, his words almost running together.

"I understand. Come inside—you'll be safe here," the woman urged.

Uncertain, David took another step back, his mind racing with doubt.

A boy, who appeared to be around David's age, stepped up to the door. "Mom, what's going on?" he asked, eyeing the group with curiosity.

"JR—stay inside," she said firmly. "Let's all get inside now."

David still wasn't sure about her, but seeing the boy put him at ease. At least now he knew she had a son, and she seemed genuinely concerned. With Blue in tow, he nodded and ushered Candy inside.

"JR, get me the phone," the woman said. "I'm calling the police."

Chapter 14

J ILLIAN LAID HER EYES on the tiny teacup Chihuahua huddled close
to David's ankles, its little body trembling uncontrollably. *Poor little thing
must be scared to death*, she thought. "May I hold—"

"Her," Emma interjected. "Yes, you can hold her. Her name is Blue."

Jillian crouched down and gently scooped the tiny pup into her arms,
cradling her close to her chest. "Hi, Blue," she murmured softly. "It's OK,
sweet baby." As if reassured by her touch, Blue's trembling gradually subsided,
and the Chihuahua's expressive eyes began to radiate warmth and affection. A
wistful smile spread across Jillian's face, her eyes sparkling with the glow of fond
memories.

Images of her childhood pet, a chocolate long-haired dachshund with fluffy
dark brown fur and long floppy ears, flooded her mind.

Jillian's father had surprised her with the puppy on her tenth birthday, proudly declaring it an expensive breed. Jillian knew nothing about dog breeds and cared little about the cost—she had no concept of such things at that age. But she had fallen in love with the pup instantly and named him Tony. The puppy was perfectly proportioned, save for his oversized ears and courageous spirit, which only added to his charm.

Jillian remembered the worry that crept into her young heart when Tony's growth seemed stunted. Every part of him was growing, except for his short, stubby legs. "Is Tony sick, Daddy?" she had asked, holding the little dachshund close to her chest, her voice tinged with concern.

"No, sweetheart," her father had reassured her with a gentle smile. "Tony is a dachshund—this kind of growth is normal for the breed. That's why they call them wiener dogs."

Jillian had covered Tony's ears protectively. "Daddy, that's not very nice," she had retorted, marching out of the room with a scowl.

Despite his peculiar appearance, Jillian had grown incredibly close to her furry friend. Later, she would realize just how much they had in common, thanks to her older brother, Jerry. Jerry had started dating for the first time, and although Jillian had yet to meet his new girlfriend, her parents were not fond of the girl. They worried about how Jerry had changed since they started dating. He had traded his usual blue jeans, striped collared shirts, and corduroy vests for head-to-toe black clothing and had taken to listening to Black Sabbath and Judas Priest. Her parents labeled the girl a bad influence, saying she was bad for him, but Jerry insisted they were wrong. To prove it, he had agreed to bring her over for dinner, hoping they would see for themselves how great she was.

Jillian was excited about dinner that night. She wanted to see what Jerry's girlfriend looked like, to see what kind of person would want to date her awkward, pubescent brother. *Something must be wrong with her*, she thought. *She probably has a horn growing out between her eyes.* But when his girlfriend arrived, before she even stepped inside, an unsettling feeling washed over her. She hadn't even knocked when Jillian turned to the door and saw two dark shadows peeking in from underneath, even though she came alone. Tony growled like he had never growled before and inched closer to her. Then the lights flickered, but no one else seemed to notice.

There was a knock on the door.

Jillian held her breath and observed from afar as Jerry opened the door.

She released her breath as she caught a glimpse of her for the first time. Except for the fact that she was dressed in all black and had a nose ring—attire not at all common, even jarring, at the time—she appeared relatively normal, but only for a second. She started to change, more like transform, before Jillian's eyes. Her plump, pale skin shriveled, taking on a mucus shade of yellowish-green, and began cracking. Her silver hoop nose ring transformed into a black serpent, slithering in and out through the holes of her all-too-wide, inflamed nostrils. Black maggots bled from her scalp, nesting on her head. Tony began barking incessantly—something uncommon for him, given his temperament—and began making his way to the door. He was a brave little thing. Easy-going, but not one to walk away from a fight, that's for sure. To this day, she didn't know for certain if he was reacting to her fear, or to what she was seeing, but she highly suspected it was the latter. She picked Tony up and retreated to her room, shutting the door behind her.

There was a knock on her door. "Jillian, come out for dinner. Jerry's friend is here," her mother announced.

She would have loved to see how the night unfolded but doubted she could sit at the table without giving away that something was up. If her parents knew she was seeing things, they would surely lose their minds. *No way I'm going out there*, she thought. Her mind was racing as her eyes darted around her room, searching for a way out of the situation. Her gaze settled on the perfume bottle on her vanity.

"Jillian?" her mother said. "Are you in there?"

Jillian picked up the perfume bottle, held her breath, and closed her left eye tightly as she squirted perfume into the other. She winced, her eye burning, as the chemicals in the perfume penetrated it.

"I'll be right there!" she said, rubbing her irritated, watery eye before opening the door.

"Oh dear God," her mother said, flinching. "What happened to your eye?"

She shrugged.

"Looks like you have pinkeye." She drilled her gaze on the dog. "Why all the barking?"

She shrugged again.

"Well, best that you stay in your room tonight—wouldn't want anyone to pick that up. It's infectious, you know. I'll bring you a plate."

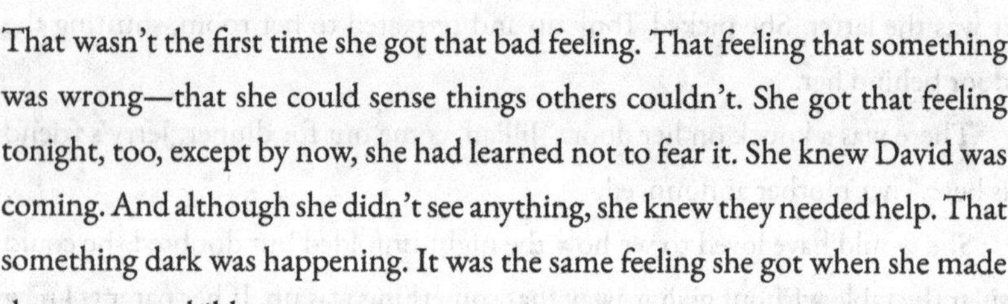

That wasn't the first time she got that bad feeling. That feeling that something was wrong—that she could sense things others couldn't. She got that feeling tonight, too, except by now, she had learned not to fear it. She knew David was coming. And although she didn't see anything, she knew they needed help. That something dark was happening. It was the same feeling she got when she made the news as a child.

They called her a hero in all the headlines and told her she was the bravest, most courageous girl in Chicago. But at only eleven years old, she wasn't trying to be a hero. She was only doing what she thought any normal person in her situation would have done—she spoke up when she saw someone who needed help.

She was grocery shopping with her mother on that summer afternoon, as was common for them to do after attending Sunday morning mass. Her lips were stained red from the cherry sucker in her mouth. As she walked alongside her mother through the produce section, her gaze landed on a pudgy man, no taller than her mother, holding the hand of a young girl who appeared to be around her age. There was nothing particularly unusual about the man at first—middle-aged with blond, thinning hair and a deep dimple on his chin. But then he looked in her direction, and her gaze locked with his in a way that a man shouldn't look at a young girl.

Time seemed to stand still as his eyes remained fixed on her. Jillian saw something she had never seen before. His pupils widened, eclipsing his piercing blue eyes and covering the white all around them. His thin, blond hair, already holding on by a thread, fell from his head, revealing a maze of dark purple boils and wet yellow pus oozing down his temples. The space between his nose and dimpled chin became empty, frozen with a black, hollow otherworldly smile—all too wide and all too long to be human.

Jillian was taken aback, but unafraid. She got a feeling she had never had before—didn't even have the words to describe it. She pulled the sucker from her mouth. "Mom, do you see that man over there? With the girl?" she asked, gluing her eyes on him.

Her mother turned toward Jillian's gaze.

"Yes? Why? Do you know him?"

"No."

"What about him then?"

"He's a bad man," she said, her eyes locked on his every move.

"Sweetheart, it's not polite to stare," her mother said, gripping her by the hand. "Look the other way."

"No, we should tell someone."

"Tell someone what?"

"That he's bad. That girl needs help."

Her mother glanced in the man's direction again. "Why? Because that little girl looks like she'd rather be doing something else?"

"No, I just have this feeling."

"Well, keep that feeling to yourself and leave that poor man and his daughter alone."

Jillian knew that tone. It was the tone her mother used when she had had enough when she stopped listening. "She's not his daughter," she muttered.

"Grab some apples, will you?" her mother asked.

She took a deep breath and stepped toward the neatly stacked crates of apples as she tried to make sense of this feeling stirred up way down within her—a deep need to say something, do something. She tried to ignore it and plucked the apples from the pile, inspecting them for blemishes, but that feeling grew heavier by the moment, like a weight inside of her.

She dropped the fruit. The sound of apples hitting the floor echoed through the produce aisle with a reverberating thud.

It wasn't like her to disobey her mother or run off alone, but she couldn't help it. Her mother may just as well have told her to hold her bladder after having her drink a gallon of water—she had to go. Fast.

She didn't know where she was going, but her strides were long, confident, purposeful, and somehow, she located a police officer right away. "There's a girl in the store—she needs help," she told the officer.

"Which girl?" the officer asked.

"Follow me." She rushed back to the produce section, scouring the store for the man and girl she had seen earlier.

They were nowhere to be seen.

She turned her gaze toward the meat section. "There! There they are!"

Chapter 15

JOSEPHINE'S HEART PLUMMETED into her stomach when she saw the flashing red and blue lights of a police car parked in her driveway. Panic gripped her chest like a vise, tightening with each breath as a thousand worst-case scenarios raced through her mind. "Oh my God," she muttered, her voice trembling with fear. Desperation fueled her actions as she parked her car haphazardly on the street, flinging the door open and jumping out, not even bothering to close it behind her.

"Aunt Josie, we're over here!" David's voice called out from the neighbor's yard, cutting through the haze of fear clouding Josephine's mind.

Her eyes darted to the porch next door, where she spotted the three children huddled together with the woman who lived there. Relief and terror collided in her chest, creating a whirlwind of emotions that propelled her forward. Her heart pounded as she sprinted toward them, her breath coming in ragged gasps. "What happened? Is everyone OK?" she asked, her voice shaking as she frantically patted each child, needing to feel their warmth, to know they were unharmed. "Is anyone hurt?"

The children looked up at her, wide-eyed and pale, but seemingly untouched by whatever had brought the police to her home. Josephine's hands shook as she searched their faces for any signs of distress, the fear still gnawing at her insides, refusing to let go.

"We're OK," David assured her, his voice calm despite the tension that hung in the air.

Josephine let out a shaky breath, but her mind still raced, trying to piece together what could have led to this. She looked into the children's faces, searching for answers.

The woman beside them extended her hand. "Hello, my name is Jillian Russo."

"Josephine Perales," she responded, shaking Jillian's hand. Her eyes flicked to her home, her brows knitting in confusion. *I was gone less than twenty minutes!* "What on earth happened?" she asked, her voice heavy with dread.

"Your little girl saw a man, a stranger, in the house," Jillian said.

"WHAT?!" Josephine's voice was sharp with shock, her eyes wide.

"The kids ran over here, and I called 9-1-1. The police are inside looking for the man now."

"OK. Thank you for your help," Josephine managed, though her thoughts were a chaotic storm. *I checked the back door before I left. It was locked. I heard David lock the front door—three clicks,* she remembered, her mind scrambling for answers. She turned to David, her voice urgent. "When did this happen? I mean, when *exactly* did this happen?"

"Just a few minutes after you left," he replied. "Emma said she saw a man in the living room. She said his lips were stitched together."

"His mouth was stitched together?" Josephine repeated, her confusion deepening. "Did anyone else see him?"

"No, ma'am."

It must be her imagination, Josephine thought, trying to rationalize the bizarre situation. "And where were you? You were supposed to be watching her," she asked, her voice edged with accusation that she immediately regretted.

"I—I was in the kitchen with Candy... cleaning up a spill," David replied, his voice small and guilty. "I heard her scream, and I ran to her as fast as I could."

Josephine took a deep breath, trying to steady herself. "I'm sorry for my tone, David. You did the right thing. Thank you."

"Excuse me, ma'am," a deep, raspy voice interrupted.

Startled, Josephine flinched before turning to see a police officer standing nearby. "Did you find him?" she asked, her anxiety spiking again.

"Is this your home?" the officer asked.

"Yes," she replied quickly. "Did you find him? The man my daughter said she saw?"

"No one is inside the house, ma'am. There's no sign of breaking and entering. We checked every window—they're all secured from the inside." He glanced at the house. "Secured from the outside, too. You know, those burglar bars could be a real issue if there were a fire."

She nodded absently, her mind spinning. "I understand."

"Your daughter—she's young. Your son said—"

"My nephew," she corrected.

"Your nephew told us your daughter said the man's lips were stitched together. It sounds like she imagined it."

"Momma, I didn't," Emma said, tugging on her blouse. "I saw him. He scared me."

"OK, angel. We'll talk about it later." Josephine turned back to the officer. "Are you sure?" she asked, desperation creeping into her voice.

He nodded. "It's a small house—we checked every inch of it."

"OK," she said, her gaze distant, staring at her home as though it had become a stranger.

"We'll be heading out now," the officer said, turning to David. "But I want you to know you did a good thing by coming to your neighbor's house and having her call us. If it happens again, don't hesitate to do exactly what you did."

They watched in silence as the officers got into their patrol cars and drove off.

"Would you like to come in for a moment?" Jillian asked gently. "Until your husband arrives?"

Josephine brought a trembling hand to her mouth and nodded. "Thank you. Just for a few minutes—to collect my thoughts. I don't want to intrude."

"No problem. Let's go inside."

"Come on, kids," Josephine said, following Jillian into her home.

As they stepped inside, Blue darted between Josephine's legs, brushing against her ankles. She gasped. "Sorry," she stammered. "I'm not normally this—"

"Jumpy?" Jillian finished with a sympathetic smile.

Josephine nodded. "I don't blame you. I'd feel the same way if I came home to find my child with a stranger and the police outside my house," Jillian said. "Please, take a seat anywhere you'd like."

"Thank you," Josephine said, settling on the couch as the kids made themselves comfortable in Jillian's son's room. The sound of children's laughter filled the air, but Josephine was lost in her thoughts. *I wasn't gone long. How could someone have gotten in? And why was Emma the only one who saw him? She must have imagined it. It's the only explanation.*

"Can I get you some coffee?" Jillian asked, breaking through her thoughts.

"What?" Josephine blinked, momentarily disoriented.

"Coffee? Can I get you some?"

"No, thank you."

"If you don't mind me asking—what's on your mind?"

Josephine hesitated, unsure whether to spill her worries to a woman she barely knew. But the need to voice her fears overpowered her reservations. She looked at Jillian, her eyes searching for understanding. "It's just that Emma, she's not like other kids. She's honest and smart—very smart. I know every parent says that about their child, so you'll have to take my word for it. And she's never had a wild imagination... At least, she never did before."

She paused, her thoughts tangled.

"I'm sorry, I shouldn't be going on like this. I'm expecting my husband home any minute." She stood up, ready to leave. "Thanks again for your help today."

"Josephine? Before you go?"

"Yes?"

"I know it's none of my business, so what I'm about to say—well, it could go in one ear and out the other."

"Please, go ahead," Josephine said, focusing on Jillian. "I'm listening."

"It's just, in my experience, kids—especially the honest, smart ones like your little girl—don't have a history of imagining things. They don't tend to become liars and start imagining things overnight."

Chapter 16

HE COULD STILL HEAR EMMA'S piercing scream ringing in his ears. Growing up in the projects, violence was a constant presence. Outside, gang fights often erupted in the yards just an eye shot away. Inside, walls would rattle as domestic brawls ensued, accompanied by shouts and screams that became a backdrop to his life. Eventually, he learned to tune out the shouting matches, but he could never block out the news of casualties. It was usually some unsuspecting kid caught in the crossfire, sitting innocently at home in front of the television when an ill-aimed bullet crossed their path. He always knew exactly where it happened, too. Their short, innocent lives were remembered by family, friends, and kind-hearted strangers who left flowers and toys at makeshift memorials. You never get used to that kind of news. So when gunfire rang out, David would calmly escort Candy into the bathroom, where they would lie down in the tub together, shielding themselves from stray bullets. It scared him when he was younger, before he learned to be brave for Candy. Now, it didn't even make him flinch.

But what he heard come out of Emma was different from any scream he'd heard before—fueled by sheer terror. It was something he couldn't ignore if he tried. He didn't see what she saw, but he didn't need to. That scream, the emptiness in her eyes, was more than enough for him to believe she saw someone, or something, that shook her to her core. And although he hadn't known her long, he could tell Emma wasn't one to scream or lie for attention. *Even if she were, no one could make up a scream like that*, he thought.

David sat across from Emma at the kitchen table, watching as she hunched over her coloring book. Her brows furrowed in deep concentration, her tiny hands clutching a blue crayon as she carefully colored within the lines of Blue, her beloved animated dog from the TV show. "What did the man look like, Emmy?" David asked gently.

She shrugged.

"Angel, if you saw him, you must remember something?" her mother coaxed.

Emma peeked her tongue out, focusing on her task, and shrugged again.

David's gaze fell upon her coloring book, and suddenly, an idea sparked. His eyes widened. "Emmy, can I please borrow your handy-dandy notebook?"

She nodded and handed him the notebook.

"And a crayon?"

She nodded again.

David reached into her coloring box for a black crayon and drew three stick figures on the yellow sheet of her notebook, each one taller than the last. "Was the man short, medium, or tall?" he asked, showing her the drawing.

She studied the drawing. "Tall."

It worked. A smile played on his face.

He flipped the notebook to a blank page and drew another set of stick figures, each with circles of different sizes around their midsection. He turned the notebook toward her again. "Was the man skinny, medium, or large?"

She glanced at the page. "Medium," she said, returning her gaze to her coloring book.

He drew another set of stick figures, each with different squiggles on their heads. "Did the man have short hair, medium hair, or long hair?" he asked.

She shook her head without looking.

"Emmy, look here," he urged, tapping the notebook. "Did the man have short hair, medium hair, or long hair?"

"He didn't have any hair," she replied. "None at all."

"That's enough for now. It's getting late, and she needs some time to wind down," Tio Manny said, his voice gentle but firm.

David put down the notebook and leaned back in his seat, convinced that Emma had seen exactly what she claimed. His earlier conversation with her about shadows lingered in his mind. He couldn't hold it in any longer—he had to say something. "Aunt Josie, Tio Manny, can I speak to you... in the living room?" he asked, his tone serious.

"Sure," they replied in unison.

David picked up Emma's notebook and followed them into the living room, where they took seats on the couches.

David leaned in, lowering his voice. "Do you think it's possible that Emma saw a ghost?"

Their responses were immediate and conflicting:

"Absolutely," Tio Manny said.

"Absolutely not," Aunt Josie said.

His aunt turned to his uncle with squinted eyes. "Are you serious?" she asked, incredulous.

"Dead serious," Tio Manny replied. He turned to David with a grin. "See what I did there?"

David scoffed.

"Emmanuel, this is not the time for jokes," Aunt Josie scolded, her tone sharp.

"I'm sorry, but do I really need to point out the elephant in the room?" he asked.

"What elephant?"

"We live across the street from a giant cemetery!" he exclaimed.

"So?"

"So, these things come with the territory."

It was the closest thing to an argument David had witnessed since moving in. His gaze shifted between his aunt and uncle as they went back and forth, their words growing more heated.

"Do you really think spirits don't have anything better to do than hang around their decomposed buried bodies?" Aunt Josie shot back, puffing out her chest.

"I wouldn't—but it's not me we're talking about here," he replied with a smirk.

David smiled inwardly, amused by their disagreement. He could watch them go at it all day, but there was more he wanted to discuss. He cleared his throat to regain their attention.

They turned to him.

"Sorry to interrupt, but has Emma told you about the things she's seen in this house?" David asked.

"What things?" Tio Manny asked.

"Just shadows," Aunt Josie said, waving off the concern.

"They don't sound like just shadows to me," David said, handing Emma's notebook to Tio Manny.

"What's this?" he asked, flipping through the pages.

"Four clues why she doesn't think what she's seeing are shadows—I wrote what she told me."

Aunt Josie shook her head. "David, it's sweet of you to listen to her—I'm glad she has someone else to talk to—just don't let yourself get wrapped up in a little girl's imagination."

"As you can see, your aunt doesn't believe in ghosts," Tio Manny said, raising an eyebrow.

David nodded, then turned to his uncle. "What about you, Tio?"

"Absolutely, I believe in spirits," he said without hesitation. "They most certainly walk among us, but they don't worry me in the least."

He spoke with such confidence that David was taken aback. "How are you so sure?" David asked, curiosity piqued.

Aunt Josie crossed her arms and glared at Tio Manny, clearly unimpressed.

David leaned in, anticipation building. *This is going to be good*, he thought, barely containing his excitement.

"Let's save this conversation for another time," Tio Manny said, rubbing the back of his neck. "The important thing is, there is no reason to be afraid of the dead. It's the living you should be worried about."

Aunt Josie nodded in agreement. "At least we agree on that." She rose to her feet, signaling the end of the discussion.

"Wait," David said, sensing that there was still something left unsaid. Something too strange to ignore.

Aunt Josie sat back down, giving him her full attention.

"The next-door neighbor—the one I went to for help..."

"Jillian?" Josephine asked.

"Yes. Jillian was at her door when we ran over. I didn't even have to knock. It was as though... she was expecting us."

"Maybe it was a coincidence," Tio Manny suggested.

"It's possible. Just thought I'd let you know," David replied. "I'm going to bed now."

"David—before you go, I have a question for you, too," Tio Manny said, his tone serious.

"Yes?"

"I need you to be honest with me... Did you turn on the wall heater today?"

Josephine sat in silence, her thoughts tangled and heavy. *I'm probably overthinking it,* she tried to reassure herself, but the knot in her stomach refused to loosen.

Emmanuel, sensing her unease, turned to her. "Anything on your mind?" he asked gently. "I wouldn't blame you if there was—it's been a night."

Josephine's thoughts drifted back to her quiet conversation with the police officer, the way he had dismissed what happened. *Emma must've imagined it,* he'd said, and Josephine had wrestled with the same thought. But the words of their neighbor echoed louder in her mind: *Honest, smart kids like Emma—who don't have a history of imagining things—don't just start lying overnight.*

"Oh," Emmanuel said, pulling her from her reverie. "Did she say it rudely?"

"No," Josephine shook her head. "That's not it."

"Then what is it?" he asked, his brows furrowed with concern.

She exhaled, her voice quiet but steady. "I never told her I thought Emma was imagining things."

Chapter 17

DAVID HAD NEVER BEEN to any of Candy's doctor's appointments. When it came to his sister, this was the one caretaking responsibility he didn't share. It wasn't that he wouldn't have gone if his mother had asked; he would have, without hesitation. But she insisted on handling it alone, a stance she maintained with a firmness that left no room for discussion. He never questioned why, but deep down, he suspected it was to maintain the illusion that she was the primary caregiver. If David were to accompany them, that carefully constructed facade might easily crumble. Candy would cling to him, treating their mother like a stranger—because, in many ways, she was—and the doctors might start asking uncomfortable questions about Candy's attachment to David instead of her.

He could easily picture himself waiting in the lobby, his legs bouncing nervously as Candy and his mother were called in to see the doctor. He imagined Candy kicking and screaming, fighting tooth and nail to have David by her side, her fear of separation from him palpable in every tear and cry. So when Aunt Josie said she was taking Candy to the doctor, David wasn't surprised that she asked him to stay behind. He assumed his mother had instructed her to do so, probably to avoid dealing with the inevitable outburst. What did surprise him, though, was how easily Candy got into the car with Aunt Josie, without a hint of resistance.

It was as if the usual anxieties had evaporated, leaving David to wonder what had changed. He watched from the doorway as Candy climbed into the backseat, her small frame dwarfed by the car's interior. There were no tears, no pleas for David to come along—just a quiet acceptance that left him standing there, puzzled and a little hurt. It was a moment that felt both ordinary and strange, as if something unspoken had shifted between them, and he couldn't quite put his finger on what it was.

"You be good and do just as Aunt Josie says, OK, Candy?" David said, locking eyes with her through the car window.

She nodded.

He turned to his aunt seated in the driver's seat. "Are you sure you don't want me to come with you?" he asked. "I really don't mind."

"I'm sure," she replied. "No sense in you coming just to sit in the waiting room. Go to Jillian's if you need anything, and don't let anyone in the house."

"I won't." He stepped back and waved as she reversed out of the driveway and drove off.

"Hey David!" JR called out from the yard next door. "Want to come over and hang out?"

He shook his head.

"Why not? I smell bad or something?" JR said, taking a playful whiff of his armpits.

"I need to get permission," David replied. "House rules."

"Oh, well, I'll just come over there then."

"You can't."

"Why not?"

"I need her permission to let you in the house."

"Dude, your aunt and uncle are strict, aren't they?"

"Their house, their rules," he shrugged. He didn't mind. As he saw it, he was already getting more freedom and space than he ever did at home. And after the scare with the man Emma saw in the house—who could blame them?

"Can we at least hang out outside? In your yard?"

David's eyes flickered with uncertainty as he weighed the request. The last thing he wanted was to get in trouble with his aunt and uncle, especially after how generously they had taken him and Candy in. The weight of their kindness pressed on him, a constant reminder that he needed to stay on their good side. His mind raced through the potential consequences, but he quickly rationalized that as long as he wasn't actually in the house, no rules would be broken. It seemed harmless enough, just a small favor with no real risk.

"OK," he finally said, the word slipping out almost hesitantly, as if he was still trying to convince himself it was the right decision.

"Cool!" JR exclaimed, stepping toward David's side of the yard. Eyes wide, he stopped just short of the driveway as if held back by an invisible force field.

"What?" David said, his head moving up and down and side to side, searching for the source of JR's hesitation.

"There's not an electric fence I should know about, is there?" JR asked, dripping with sarcasm.

David rolled his eyes.

"It's a joke, dude!" JR exclaimed, stepping closer. "Boy, are you uptight! Are they beating the shit out of you, or what?" He eyed David up and down as though inspecting his body for signs of injury.

"No—of course not!" David exclaimed, disgusted with the accusation. "My aunt and uncle are really good people. They would never do anything like that."

"OK... Well, what is it then?"

David wasn't stupid—he knew JR was only joking. If he just had a minute to prepare a reaction, he would have laughed off the comment instead of looking at him like he was a complete moron. But he had little experience bantering with kids his age and had no friends outside of school. Even then, he mostly kept to himself. He fixed his gaze on the ground and sat on the grass. "Nothing... I'm just respecting their rules."

JR sat on the grass alongside David.

There was an awkward silence.

"So..." JR said. "Are you living here now?"

"Supposed to be just for the summer."

"Are your parents divorced?" JR asked.

"I never met my father," David replied quietly. "Yours?"

"My dad died when I was nine."

"Oh, that sucks," David said, feeling the weight of JR's loss.

More awkward silence.

"So..." JR said. "Seen any ghosts since you moved in?"

"No. Have you?"

"I wish! We've lived in that house my entire life, and I've never seen a thing." He turned his gaze to the cemetery. "A waste, if you ask me."

David could have left it at that and changed the subject, but he sensed JR's excitement on the topic. This could be his chance to make up for looking at him like he was a moron before. "My baby cousin has seen things, though."

"In this house?" JR asked, pointing to David's home.

He nodded.

"Wait. Your cousin—she's, what... Like five or six?"

"Six."

"And you believe her? Don't kids have, like, have wild imaginations at that age?"

"She doesn't. And she's surprisingly smart for being a little kid. Besides, you should have seen her, heard her scream... You'd believe her, too."

"What exactly has she seen?"

David shook his head, hesitant to say more. It was as if something was telling him that the things Emma saw were not his stories to tell. "It's not just what she's seen," he said. "Weird, unexplainable things have been happening."

"Like what?" JR asked, leaning in.

"We have this old gas heater built into the wall in the bathroom..."

"Yeah, we have one of those, too."

"Well, it turns on... On its own, and the shower curtain always ends up really close to the flames."

"Why don't you just push the curtain to the other end?"

"We do... But somehow, the curtain always ends up back on the other side."

"Are you kidding me?" JR said, his voice rising in pitch.

"I wish," David replied, shaking his head.

"Dude, you definitely have paranormal activity going on in there." A mischievous smile played on JR's face. He turned to David. "I have an idea…"

Chapter 18

JOSEPHINE STEPPED QUICKLY THROUGH the bustling sidewalks of downtown, weaving through the maze of towering buildings and honking horns, tightly gripping Emma and Candy by the hand. "Wait here a second," she said, releasing their hands to dig into her purse. She pulled out a crumpled piece of paper, her brow furrowing as she tried to decipher Emmanuel's handwritten directions to Lurie Children's Hospital of Chicago. "OK, let's go," she said, reaching for their hands again.

Leaving Emma home with David would have certainly freed her up to move faster, but after what Emma had seen the last time she was home alone, Josephine wasn't willing to take the risk. As she assessed Emma's short strides, which threatened to make them late, she urged, "Try to walk a little faster, angel."

"I'm trying, Momma. I have little legs, remember?" Emma replied, her face flushed with exertion.

They stepped through the glass sliding doors of the hospital, greeted by a labyrinth of identical hallways and corridors. Josephine turned to Candy. "You come here with your mother a lot, right?"

Candy nodded.

"Do you know how to get to your doctor's office?"

Candy shook her head.

"Momma, there's a map right there," Emma said, pointing to the hospital directory on the wall.

As Josephine stepped toward the directory, her eyes landed on a sign across the lobby:

The Pritzker Department of Psychiatry and Behavioral Health

"This is it," she said, ushering the children into the waiting room. "Take a seat, girls."

She approached the receptionist, whose fingers were busy clicking away on a keyboard. "Hi, I'm here for—"

Without looking up, the receptionist pointed to a clipboard on the desk.

Josephine sighed, signed Candy's name on the sheet, and then joined the girls.

"Momma, why are we here?" Emma asked, climbing onto the cushioned couch. "I don't feel sick."

"We're here for Candy, not you, angel."

Emma turned to Candy, studying her closely. "You don't look sick. Do you feel sick?"

Candy shook her head.

"So why does she need to see the doctor?" Emma asked, turning back to her mother.

Josephine gazed into her daughter's wide, innocent eyes, struggling with how to answer. She knew Emma was bright enough to understand Candy's condition if she took the time to explain, but she wasn't sure where to begin. Selfishly, she hoped Emma might figure it out on her own. *That's a lot to expect from a child*, she thought. She decided she would explain later, in private. Now, in front of Candy, just didn't feel like the right time. "Candy is just here for a checkup," she said gently.

The waiting room door swung open. "Candy Perales?" the nurse called.

"That's us," Josephine said, getting to her feet. They approached the nurse.

"Hello," the nurse greeted them with a smile. "And you are?"

"Josephine Perales—I'm Candy's aunt."

"Okay," the nurse said, "follow me this way. The room is just around the corner."

Josephine gripped the girls' hands as they followed the nurse.

"Here we are," the nurse said, opening a door to a small exam room. "The doctor will be right in."

Emma's eyes widened with excitement as they stepped inside. The room was unlike any exam room she had seen before. Children's drawings adorned the walls, and colorful toys and stuffed animals were scattered across a red cushion mat, creating a welcoming atmosphere despite the faint scent of antiseptic. Candy, however, was drawn to a beige metal filing cabinet along the wall. With a sense of purpose, she reached for the drawer and began to pull it open.

"Candy, don't touch that," Josephine said quickly, her voice gentle but firm.

But Candy ignored her, reaching deeper into the drawer.

"Candy isn't a good listener," Emma whispered to her mother.

Josephine rose from her seat. "Candy, stop that right now," she said firmly. Candy continued to ignore her commands. "I said stop!" Josephine exclaimed, her voice rising in frustration.

Emma's face lit up as Candy's hands emerged from the drawer. "Oooh, puzzles!" she squealed.

Josephine let out a sigh of relief. "I'm sorry, Candy," she said, feeling a pang of guilt. She realized Candy probably knew where the puzzles were kept from previous visits.

There was a knock on the door. "Knock, knock," a voice called from outside. A woman dressed in plain clothes, holding a medical chart, stepped into the room.

"Yes, everything is fine," Josephine said, turning to the woman. "Just some confusion about the puzzles."

"Hello, I'm Dr. Hart," the woman introduced herself, extending her hand.

Josephine shook her hand. "I'm Josephine Perales—Candy's aunt."

"I'm surprised to see Candy without her mother. I hope everything is okay?"

"Yes, her mother is away—Candy is staying with me for the summer."

Dr. Hart flipped through the medical chart. "It says here Candy's mother granted an Emmanuel Perales permission to bring her in."

"That's my husband—Candy's mother is my sister-in-law. Is that a problem?"

"Yes and no," Dr. Hart replied. "I can see Candy today, but I must request that you and…" She glanced at Emma.

"My daughter."

"… that you and your daughter wait outside."

"That won't be a problem," Josephine said, though her tone suggested otherwise. "It's just, I was hoping to get an update on Candy's condition. Will that be possible?"

"I'm afraid not," Dr. Hart replied. "Not without the signed consent of Candy's mother."

"I understand," Josephine said. "We'll leave you two to get started then." She took Emma's hand and led her out. As they walked back to the waiting room, Josephine knew it was time to talk to Emma about Candy's condition. "Angel, I want to talk to you about something."

"Okay, Momma."

She took a deep breath as they sat down, searching for the right words.

"Why does Candy's doctor have all those toys?" Emma asked.

Josephine exhaled and smiled gently. "Remember, I told you Candy is here for a checkup?"

"Yes."

"Well, different doctors treat different conditions."

"I know."

Her brows shot up. "You do?"

Emma nodded.

"Give me an example."

Emma's eyes rolled upward, as though searching her mind for an answer. "Like a dentist is a tooth doctor, and a vyna-col-jist is a doctor that delivers new babies."

Close enough, Josephine thought with an irrepressible smile. "Yes, well, do you know not everyone learns the same way?"

Emma nodded again.

"How do you know?"

"In kindergarten, the teacher split the class into groups 'cause she said we learn differently. Me and Brie and three other kids were Peacocks because the teacher said we were the fastest learners... And the others were Blue Jays or Redbirds."

Impressive, Josephine thought. "Do you know Candy learns differently, too?"

"Yes. I know. And sometimes she does things that seem mean or naughty, like ignoring me or not following the rules, but she isn't doing it on purpose."

"Did you figure that out on your own?"

"No—David told me."

Josephine let out a deep sigh. *Of course he did.*

"I want soda," Candy said in a flat tone, staring vacantly into the distance.

"Are you allowed to have soda at home?" Dr. Hart asked.

Candy shook her head.

"Oh, I see. You're trying to see what you can get away with now that you're alone with me, aren't you?"

Candy didn't respond.

"Are you enjoying your summer with your aunt and uncle?"

Again, no answer.

"Are they nice to you?"

Hesitantly, she nodded.

"I'm glad," Dr. Hart said, her voice warm. "How have you been feeling lately?"

A low humming sound filled the room, breaking the silence. Candy's eyes darted around, searching for the source of the noise. Her gaze settled on the fluorescent ceiling light above her, its soft buzz the only sound.

"Have you had any more difficulty telling between what's real and what's not?" Dr. Hart asked gently.

Candy kept her gaze fixed on the ceiling light, her silence heavy.

"Candy? Can you hear me?" Dr. Hart's voice was soft, but concerned.

Suddenly, a voice from within pierced Candy's thoughts, deep and raspy, commanding, *Look at her!*

"Candy? Are you okay?" Dr. Hart's concern grew as she leaned forward.

Look at her! the voice insisted again. Slowly, as if pulled by invisible strings, Candy shifted her gaze from the ceiling light to Dr. Hart. *Now, say yes,* the voice commanded.

"Yes," Candy replied, her voice flat and mechanical.

Dr. Hart's eyes widened slightly, impressed by the unexpected response. "I love your eye contact," she said encouragingly. "What about your concentration? Are you having any trouble concentrating, you know, thinking, Candy?"

No, the voice whispered, guiding her.

"No," Candy echoed, the words leaving her lips with the same vacant detachment.

Dr. Hart's eyebrows shot up in surprise. "I think this is the first time I've been able to get two words out of you," she said, scribbling notes with renewed interest. "Last time you were here, you said you stopped hearing voices. Is that still the case?"

Yes, the voice whispered again, its control tightening.

"Yes," Candy responded, her gaze empty, unable to break free from the voice's influence.

"Oh, very good!" Dr. Hart exclaimed. "I thought you were answering 'no' to all my questions, but you're not one to fall for tricks, now are you?"

Say no, the voice instructed.

"No," Candy repeated, her tone devoid of emotion.

Chapter 19

I N THE WAITING ROOM, Josephine stole a glance at Emma, who was deeply engrossed in coloring. Her small face was etched with a focus and determination rarely seen in children her age, the tip of her tongue peeking out slightly as she concentrated on staying within the lines. The sight brought a brief sense of calm to Josephine, a reprieve from the tension that had been building all day.

Sensing this moment of peace, Josephine decided it was the perfect time to escape into a bygone era. She reached into her purse and pulled out the leather-bound diary that had become her constant companion. The soft, worn leather felt familiar in her hands as she opened it, readying herself for the world around her to blur and for her reality to momentarily fade into the background.

As she began to read the diary entries, the words on the page seemed to lift her out of the present and transport her to a different time. Josephine could almost see the girls described in the entries, their hair styled in elegant waves that framed their faces, each strand perfectly in place, adorned with delicate ribbons that radiated a timeless sense of style and grace. She could hear their laughter echoing through the hallways, feel the rustle of their skirts as they moved through rooms now empty but once filled with their youthful energy. The past felt alive in her hands, as if those who had once walked through her home were now whispering their stories directly to her.

There was Mousy Madeline, the diary's author, who revealed little about herself beyond a short-lived crush on Michael D. This left much to Josephine's imagination. She pictured Madeline as a petite girl with long brown hair cascading down her back, her delicate face partially hidden by bangs and oversized glasses. Madeline seemed to blend into the background, much like a mouse hiding in the shadows, hoping to go unnoticed.

Then there was Julianna, also known as Princess Jewels, described as the prettiest and most popular of the group, with a chameleon-like personality that allowed her to adapt seamlessly to any social situation. And finally, there was Sophia, affectionately nicknamed Sophia the Siren, a nod to the captivating allure that preceded her wherever she went.

As Josephine continued to read, she could almost see Madeline, Julianna, and Sophia, their youthful energy palpable as they gathered at soda shops, exuding a charm and camaraderie unique to their time. The diary's pages brought to life their pivotal moments, from light-hearted sleepovers filled with laughter to serious conversations about the looming impact of the Second World War. Josephine felt a deep connection to these girls, their friendship immortalized in the delicate script of the diary, and she found herself lost in their world, if only for a little while.

They were lucky, Madeline wrote. Each of their fathers had managed to make it back home alive, but their mothers warned them they'd be different on account of what they called shell shock. It was such a big deal, they even learned about it in school. They were told when a person is subjected to a life or death situation, like their fathers were, a chemical reaction occurs inside the body that heightens awareness, numbs pain, and triggers the body's fight or flight response—preparing the body for escape or imminent attack. Symptoms include denial, numbing, intrusive images and thoughts, and nightmares. According to Madeline, Julianna's father never had a drink in his life, but now her parents were fighting all the time because he had turned into a belligerent drunk. Sophia said her dad had nightmares—waking up the whole house with his screaming almost every night. But it seemed to Madeline that her own father came back the worst. She wrote about how her father acted much like Julianna and Sophia's fathers, then some. She said he always thought he was being watched, followed, and imagined things.

Poor things, Josephine thought, *being torn from their families at such an impressionable age, then having to deal with the aftermath*. It seemed they coped by forging unbreakable bonds of friendship—a true testament to the resilience and strength of their generation. She turned to the dog-eared page and continued to read where she had left off:

> *October 12, 1946*
> *Today, Sophia has proved herself worthy of being in our group. Michael David, that scumbag, asked her to the Halloween dance. She said no, but it begs the question: has he no shame? It got worse... Sophia said he knew I liked him, but he never liked me, so he told her she shouldn't feel bad about going with him to the dance. He said, "I can't help it if I'm good-looking and girls like me." UGH! I've never been so angry! When she told me, I felt like I was going to explode! One thing's for sure... I don't know how (yet), but he will pay.*

Michael David. It was the first time Madeline had revealed his full name. She couldn't place it, but it sounded familiar somehow. And then there was the matter of Madeline, the teenage girl, out for revenge. *Scandalous*, Josephine thought, eager to read on.

"Mrs. Perales?" Dr. Hart called out, her voice amplified by the silence in the waiting room.

Immersed in her reading, Josephine's body jolted at the sound of her name. She turned her gaze to Dr. Hart.

"She's ready for you."

She got up and stepped toward her. "Thank you, doctor," she said. "I know you're not supposed to say anything, but I hope everything went well."

"You're right, I'm not supposed to say anything," Dr. Hart said. "So... I'll just say how good it makes me feel when I see my patients making significant, sometimes even miraculous, progress." She turned to Candy, flashing a wide smile and a subtle wink. "Generally speaking, of course."

Chapter 20

AT CHURCH, EMMANUEL MAINTAINED an open-door policy. All who stepped inside were welcome—no one was ever turned away. It was a place of worship and also his workplace, where he navigated the complexities of dealing with unique personalities, issues, challenges, and the occasional confrontation. Whatever the day might bring, he faced it with readiness.

But when his workday ended, like anyone with a demanding job, he longed for the comfort and solace of home. His home was his sanctuary, a place of peace and refuge, a beacon of tranquility amidst the chaos of the outside world. Protecting that peace was paramount, so he was careful about who he allowed into his home. Strangers were considered cautiously, and not just anyone crossed his threshold. For Emmanuel, maintaining the sanctity of his personal space was as vital as the work he did within the church.

"JR? Is that the kid from next door?" Emmanuel asked.

"Yes," David replied. "Jillian's son."

"What will you be doing while he's here?"

"Hanging out in my room—playing games."

"What kind of games?"

"Board games."

Since when do kids their age hang around playing board games anymore? he thought. "What kind of board games?"

"Just whatever JR has lying around."

"Give me and your aunt some time to discuss. We'll let you know," he said.

"OK, I'll be outside with Emma and Candy," David said, stepping to the back door.

The bang of the screen door springing shut echoed throughout the home. Josephine turned to Emmanuel. "So what do you think?" she asked.

"You know I don't like strangers in the house—you never know what you're letting in," Emmanuel said.

"I know—that's why I'm leaving this decision up to you."

Emmanuel took a deep breath, crossed his arms, and leaned back in his seat, watching David and the girls play through the kitchen window. He was convinced that David wasn't just a good kid—he was an exceptional one. Despite everything, David had taken on responsibilities that would overwhelm most adults, and he had done so without complaint. Emmanuel knew that when the summer was over, David would return to those burdens. The least they could do was give him some space to be a kid while he was under their roof.

With that thought in mind, Emmanuel stood up from his seat and stepped toward the screen door. "David!" he called out, his voice carrying across the yard.

David sprinted to the back door, a look of curiosity and concern on his face. "Yes, Tio Manny?" he asked, stepping inside, his energy still buzzing from the outdoor play.

"Your friend can come over, but we have rules. Do you understand?" Emmanuel's tone was firm but not unkind.

David nodded eagerly, sensing the importance of the moment.

"First, this is not an open invitation," Emmanuel began, his gaze shifting briefly to Josephine, who watched silently from the kitchen table. "This is a one-time invitation. We'll see how it goes and take it from there."

"I understand, Tio Manny," David replied, his voice steady, though a hint of excitement sparkled in his eyes.

"I'm not finished," Emmanuel continued, his voice taking on a more serious edge. "No overnight stays under any condition—not like we have the space, anyway."

"Got it—no problem," David answered quickly, his eagerness palpable.

"And last—your aunt and I will try to give you some space, but just remember—" Emmanuel started to say, but before he could finish, David cut in with a knowing grin.

"No locked doors," he said, completing the sentence as if it were a mantra he had memorized long ago.

Emmanuel's stern expression softened into a small smile. "Exactly. No locked doors."

If JR had any hope of them becoming friends, even if only for the summer, he needed to convince his mother that David wasn't a bad influence. Thankfully, it wasn't hard. He told her that David's uncle was a pastor, deeply religious—a detail that he knew would sing to his mother's heart—and that his aunt was a stay-at-home wife, seemingly overly protective of David considering his age.

"Thanks for having me over, sir," JR said as he stepped inside the Perales's home, lugging a black Jansport backpack so full it looked like it might burst at any moment.

Emmanuel eyed the bulging bag with curiosity. "What do you have in there?"

"David said he didn't have any board games, so I brought a bunch for us to choose from," JR replied, running a hand through his thick, bushy hair.

Emmanuel shot him a skeptical look but nodded.

"Tio Manny, is it OK if JR and I go to my room now?" David asked, his voice tinged with excitement.

"Go ahead," Emmanuel agreed.

JR followed David through the living room to his bedroom at the far end of the house. As he entered the dimly lit room, he hesitated, taking in the sparse furnishings—a tiny dresser and a mattress set directly on the floor. "You don't have a bed?" he asked.

"It's on my uncle's list," David shrugged. "The mattresses are plenty comfortable for now."

JR glanced around the room, noticing the feeble glow of the ceiling light struggling against the oppressive darkness. "Why is it so dark in here?"

"Bad lighting, I guess," David replied, closing the bedroom door behind them.

JR reached instinctively for the door lock.

"Don't!" David exclaimed, his voice sharp.

"Why not?" JR asked, his hand pausing mid-air.

"House rules," David explained.

"I thought we were going to play with the Ouija board?" JR said, his brows knitting together in a frown.

"We will," David reassured him. "But we'll have to do it with the door unlocked. The floors are creaky, so we'll hear if anyone's coming."

Dissatisfaction furrowed JR's brow. He considered the suggestion for a moment. "I can ask my uncle if I can go over to your house, and we can do it another time."

"No!" JR blurted out, eyes wide with panic. Doing this at his house was not an option. David's aunt and uncle had their house rules, and JR's mother had hers—rules that strictly forbade playing with spirit boards. As a devout Catholic, she believed the Church's warnings: don't give the devil a foothold. To her, a spirit board was akin to a gateway drug. But JR wasn't planning to cross over to the dark side or become some kind of devil worshiper. He just wanted a chance to communicate with his father—ask him how he's doing, tell him he misses him. *What harm could that do?* "It's fine," JR finally said, dismissing his worries.

With a determined expression, JR unzipped his backpack and carefully retrieved a box concealed within.

David's eyes narrowed as he focused on the box. "Checkers?"

JR pried open the lid, revealing an immaculate, untouched set of checkers nestled inside. But then, with a surreptitious smile, he moved the checkerboard aside to reveal the hidden treasure beneath.

"Sneaky," David remarked, a hint of admiration in his voice. "Why'd you hide it?"

"Are you serious?" JR asked incredulously.

"Are we doing something illegal or something?" David questioned, his tone tinged with uncertainty.

JR scoffed. "Dude, I bought this in the toy aisle at the grocery store. I just assumed your uncle would disapprove of us playing with it."

"Why?" David asked, genuinely curious.

"Because a lot of parents don't—especially religious ones," JR explained. "Have you ever used it before? Do you even know what you're doing?"

"No," JR admitted, "but I've seen it used in movies. It's not rocket science." He placed the board on the bed and held up a small, triangular-shaped object. "This is called a planchette," he said, showing David the mysterious game piece, which had a small, transparent window at its center. "Do not leave the planchette on the board unattended—ever. If the planchette is on the board, make sure one of us is holding it at all times."

"Okay," David agreed.

"And always say 'goodbye' at the end of a session. We need to make sure the planchette moves to 'goodbye' as well," JR added.

"Why?" David asked, his curiosity piqued.

"If you don't, it's like setting a phone down without hanging up. The spirit could linger on the other line."

"Got it," David replied, feeling a mix of anticipation and unease.

"Now, we each hold one end of the planchette over the board, ask a question, and watch the magic happen," JR said, his excitement palpable.

"That's it?" David asked, still a bit skeptical.

"That's it," JR confirmed with a sly smile.

Chapter 21

THE INSTRUCTIONS JR EXPLAINED sounded simple enough. David placed his fingers over the cold, smooth surface of the planchette, ready to begin. "What should we ask?" he said, fixing his eyes on JR.

"You go first," JR replied.

David paused, searching his mind for a question. "What color is the sky?"

JR rolled his eyes and scoffed. "No, dummy," he said. "Ask something you want to know about someone who's dead."

"Oh, let me think," David said, trying to come up with a relevant question. He didn't know anyone who had died—except for his father. But dead or alive, he wasn't interested in communicating with him anyway. His eyes suddenly lit up. "I know what to ask," he said. He set his gaze on the board and asked, "Did Emma really see the ghost of a bald man in this house?"

As their fingers rested on the planchette, the object seemed to lighten. They watched as it glided from the center of the board over to the word *Yes*.

"You totally guided it there," David said, unconvinced it had moved on its own.

"Dude, I did not," JR replied, his wide eyes betraying his sincerity. "Ask it something else."

David sighed. "Fine," he said, returning the planchette to the center of the board. "Is a ghost responsible for turning on the wall heater in the bathroom and moving the shower curtain?" He watched, expressionless, as the planchette moved again, settling on *Yes.* "I knew it," he muttered.

"Let me try," JR said. They returned the planchette to the center. "Is the bald man Emma saw the same ghost responsible for turning on the wall heater and moving the shower curtain?"

David turned away, his fingers still on the planchette.

"It says *No*," JR said, a note of worry in his voice. "There's more than one ghost in the house."

They brought the planchette back to the center.

"How many spirits are in this house?" JR asked.

David watched as the planchette spelled out: *M. A. N. Y.*

He immediately released his grip on the planchette.

"What did you do that for?" JR asked.

"This is boring—let's play something else."

"Are you kidding?" JR said, glaring at him in disbelief. "This is the coolest thing I've ever experienced!"

"You're just moving the planchette to creep me out," David said. "It's not working, so let's play something else."

"I'm not moving it, and I'll prove it to you."

"How?"

"Ask it something that's not a yes or no question."

David sighed, clearly annoyed. "You're just going to move it again."

"Ask it something I couldn't possibly know."

David narrowed his eyes, considering the challenge. JR knew about the bald man Emma saw, the wall heater, and the curtains. He could guess questions about his sister, uncle, aunt, and cousin. But then, David realized JR knew nothing about his mom. "I got it," he said, feeling confident.

They returned the piece to the center of the board. "What kind of illness does my mother have?" David asked.

JR furrowed his brow, surprised by the question. "You didn't tell me your mom was sick," he said.

The air seemed to crackle with an electric charge. The planchette moved, almost as if possessed, spelling out:

M. E. N.

In a surge of anger and fear, David released the planchette, his heart pounding.

JR stared at the board, astonished. "Dude, don't even worry about it," he said, placing the planchette back on the board and looking at David. "Whatever your mom does, it's none of my business."

JR paced the room anxiously, his mind racing to understand what had just happened. He had seen the fear in David's eyes, watched his face go pale when he released the planchette. Whatever had caused that reaction must have been bad. Real bad. "Talk to me, dude," he said, turning to David.

David crossed his arms, clearly wrestling with his thoughts.

"Look, if the Ouija board is freaking you out, we never have to play it again," JR said, hoping that wasn't the case.

"It's not that," David replied.

"What is it then? Is it because the board called your mom a whore? Is that, like, news to you or something?"

David shot him a disgusted glance.

"Ghosts are just like people," JR continued. "Some of them can be real jerks."

"Shhh. Dude, if my aunt or uncle hear you talk like that, they'll never let you visit again."

"Sorry," JR said, relieved that David still wanted him to come back.

"Besides, the only jerk here is you. My mother is not a whore—she has a mental illness."

M. E. N. T. A. L. I. L. L. N. E. S. S.

JR's eyes widened as he connected the dots. "Ohhh, I'm sorry, I had no idea," he said.

"It's OK," David replied. "Not even my uncle knows about my mom. He thinks she's away in rehab." He took a deep breath, as if preparing to say more. "She, she—" But his words faltered, his hesitation clear.

JR saw the turmoil on David's face, the way his shoulders slumped as if burdened by the weight of unspoken thoughts. "What is it?" he asked gently.

David shook his head, the silence between them heavy. "Nothing."

"Is this about the board getting it right? About your mom?"

"No, but if the board got that question right, it makes me believe the other answers were right too."

JR sat down beside him. "You're afraid, aren't you?"

"Wouldn't you be?" David asked incredulously.

He was right. The house was across the street from a cemetery, and his little cousin was seeing things. Now, the board was telling them there were many spirits in the house, at least one of which might be trying to burn it down. "Damn," JR said, shaking his head. "You're right—that sucks."

David rubbed his face with his hands, clearly distressed. "I should just tell my uncle," he said.

"No—you cannot tell your uncle."

"Why do you care?"

There were many reasons JR cared. If David told his uncle about the Ouija board, JR knew he might never be allowed to come over again. Plus, the thought of his mother finding out he had defied her sent shivers down his spine. But JR wasn't about to admit that. He needed to make this about David. "Your uncle's a pastor, right?" he asked.

"Yes. Why?"

"Religious people don't like Ouija boards. If you tell your uncle you played with it, he'll probably kick you out."

"Ugh, you're right," David groaned, burying his face in his pillow.

JR smiled inwardly, but he needed more reassurance. Something that would keep this between them—and he knew just how to do it. "And where would that leave your sister?" he said, pressing the point.

David lifted his head. "OK, I get it. But what am I supposed to do? Just live here while some ghost tries to burn the place down?"

Some ghost? David's words sparked a thought in JR's mind. *Ghosts are just like people.* "I might have an idea," JR said. "Hear me out."

"OK."

"Ghosts are just dead people, right?"

"I guess," David shrugged.

"And not all people are bad."

"Yeah. What's your point?"

"So all we need to do is call a good ghost and ask it to protect you, Candy, and the house... Maybe even ask it to kick the bad ghosts out while we're at it."

David took a deep breath, his gaze distant.

"What do you think?" JR asked, his excitement growing. "Good idea, right?"

Chapter 22

WHEN EMMANUEL GOT WORD that Ben Evans, a renowned pastor and televangelist, was coming to town to give a seminar on spiritual gifts, he seized the opportunity without hesitation. Walking into the bustling Hilton Hotel in downtown Chicago, his heart raced with anticipation, eager to soak up the wisdom that awaited him. *This must be it,* he thought, as he moved toward the low hum of voices—men in suits and ties, congregating like a herd around the entrance to the conference room. He stepped inside, his eyes scanning the crowd for a familiar face.

"Cap, over here!" Daniel, his trusted companion, called out from the front row.

Daniel was like a brother to Emmanuel in more ways than one. Always willing to help and with a sunny disposition, he was among the first and most loyal congregants of the church, eager to contribute and grow the congregation in any way he could. Whether it was picking up a mop or leading a prayer service, Daniel lived by the motto, "All for the grace of God." His enthusiasm and dedication were met with Emmanuel's unwavering support.

Over the years, their bond deepened, forged in shared faith and mutual respect. Emmanuel had stood by Daniel through thick and thin—celebrating with him during the joyful moments, such as serving as the minister at Daniel's wedding, and offering counsel and comfort during the darkest times, especially when Daniel's marriage crumbled despite his best efforts to save it.

Still, Daniel always found a way to stay positive, and Emmanuel found that kind of energy contagious. Daniel was the type of person who radiated warmth and optimism—someone Emmanuel wanted to have around, a radiator, not a drain. Emmanuel appreciated that Daniel, despite the challenges that naturally came with their work, was incredibly uplifting and rarely exhausting.

Their relationship went beyond the walls of the church; it was a brotherhood rooted in loyalty, trust, and a shared commitment to their spiritual journey. Emmanuel knew that no matter what challenges arose, he could always count on Daniel, just as Daniel knew Emmanuel would always be there to guide and support him.

As Emmanuel made his way through the packed room toward Daniel, he felt a sense of gratitude wash over him. "Thank you, brother Daniel. Glad you made it," he said, settling into the seat Daniel had saved for him.

"I got here early to secure a spot," Daniel replied, glancing around at the packed room. "It's a full house."

"I expected as much," Emmanuel said, his gaze sweeping the room before locking onto the stage.

"Oooh, there he is," Daniel whispered, his excitement barely contained. "He looks just like he does on TV."

"Maybe even better," Emmanuel agreed, as his eyes fixed on the tall, clean-shaven man stepping up to the podium, not a hair out of place.

The room fell silent, the whispers dying down as Ben Evans took his place at the podium, his presence commanding the attention of every soul in the room.

"Well, good morning, family!" he exclaimed. "It is just a joy and honor to be with you this morning," he said, speaking in a strong, welcoming Southern accent.

"Good morning!" the group of mostly men replied in unison.

"I have a very important topic to discuss today—one that is dear to my heart," he said, placing his hand over his chest. "I'll be talking about unleashing the divine power of spiritual gifts."

The eager group prepared to immerse themselves in note-taking, filling the room with the sound of shuffling paper.

"Now, I could have selected from many topics to discuss, but I chose this one because it's something we don't talk about enough, and yet it is of utmost importance in our work."

Silent nods filled the room.

"Today will be more about teaching and less about preaching. So, who's ready to get started?" he said with a wide, toothy smile, his arms outstretched.

"Amen!" the group erupted.

"That's what I was hoping you'd say." He removed his dark purple suit jacket and placed it over the podium. "Woooo, you know Pastor Ben is ready to get serious when he removes his jacket," he said.

Quiet laughter rippled through the room.

"Now, if the tie comes off, I may have to ask one of you to fetch me some sweet tea."

"I love this guy," Emmanuel whispered, leaning toward Daniel.

Pastor Ben stepped toward the whiteboard at the front of the room as he began his lecture. "Spiritual gifts are noted throughout the New Testament. When the various lists of spiritual gifts are put together, there are twenty-three. They are as follows," he said. He un-capped a dry-erase marker and pressed it against the board.

The room grew quiet as the group sat at the edges of their seats, waiting for him to continue.

"Now, you didn't really think I was going to stand up here and write all twenty-three gifts on the board, did you?" he said, turning around to face the group.

There was silence.

"Come on, people—it's the '90s! We have modern technology!" he said, picking up a stack of papers from the podium. "I brought handouts!"

Laughter bubbled up again.

"He is good," Daniel whispered to Emmanuel, as the handouts made their way around the room.

"Now, as I was saying," Pastor Ben said, fixing his gaze on the handout. "The spiritual gifts are: Apostle, Prophet, Teacher, Miracles, Healing, Evangelist, Pastor, Exhorting, Giving, Ministering, Helping, Ruling, Tongues, Showing mercy, Interpretation of Tongues, Word of wisdom, Marriage, Word of Knowledge, Celibacy, Faith, Hospitality, Discerning of spirits, and Administration." He inhaled deeply. "Boy, is that a mouthful!" he exclaimed. "Now, who can tell me who gives these gifts?"

A flurry of hands rose across the room.

"You there—what's your name?" he asked, pointing to a man seated in the back row.

"Jason," the man replied.

"Brother Jason, it's a pleasure to meet you. Now tell me, who gives these spiritual gifts?"

"The Holy Ghost," Jason replied.

"That's absolutely right. And where is this said in the scripture?"

Jason's eyes widened, clearly unprepared for the follow-up question.

"Anyone?" Pastor Ben said, his gaze sweeping the room.

An awkward silence settled in as he searched for a single raised hand.

"Bueller? Bueller?" he said with a wide smile.

Laughter filled the room.

"Sorry gentlemen, sometimes I just can't help myself."

Emmanuel cleared his throat and raised his hand.

"Oh thank goodness," Pastor Ben said. "I was starting to get worried. You, there—what's your name?" he asked.

"Emmanuel."

"Brother Emmanuel, it's a pleasure to meet you. Now tell me, where in the scripture does it say that the Holy Ghost gives spiritual gifts?"

"1 Corinthians 12:11," Emmanuel replied.

"Very good," Pastor Ben said. "Extra credit—what exactly does the scripture say about it?"

"It is the one and only Spirit who distributes all these gifts. He alone decides which gift each person should have."

"Well, OK then," Pastor Ben said. "The Holy Spirit decides which gift you get—a gift is given to all children of God, by the way—but it's up to us to decide when we will use it," he said, moving his gaze around the room. "Show of hands—who here believes the spiritual gift can be taken away if unused or used improperly?"

Emmanuel crossed his arms and watched as hand after hand rose.

Pastor Ben's gaze once again turned to Emmanuel. "Brother Emmanuel," he said. "You are the only one in this entire group of what, fifty individuals, that does not agree that a spiritual gift can be taken away. Why is that?" he asked, furrowing his brow.

Aware that all eyes were on him, Emmanuel cleared his throat. "Romans 11:29 tells us that the gifts and the calling of God are irrevocable."

Pastor Ben's eyebrows shot up, impressed. "Huh, you don't say?" he said. "Well, I guess it's pretty clear what your gift is, now isn't it?"

"Yes, sir."

"What would that be exactly?"

Suspense hung heavy as the group waited for Emmanuel's answer.

"Knowledge."

"Well, let me tell you, I agree with that," Pastor Ben said, stepping up to the podium. "Oh, and brother Emmanuel, beautiful name you have, by the way. It means God is with us." He smiled. "But something tells me you already knew that, didn't you?"

Chapter 23

DAVID DIDN'T KNOW MUCH about spirit boards. He'd never watched horror movies, mainly because Candy was always with him, and he didn't want to give her nightmares. The little he knew came from JR, who had explained it in a way that made it seem harmless enough. "It's just a dumb toy," he had told himself. But now, sitting face-to-face with the board, a sudden wave of dread washed over him, chilling him to the bone.

I'd rather be doing anything else, he thought, but the board had already confirmed what he feared ever since Emma mentioned the shadows: the house was haunted. The eerie sense of being watched, the unsettling flicker of the wall heater, the strange, oppressive energy that seemed to cling to every corner—it all pointed to something malevolent lurking just out of sight. And with the heater acting up, it felt like whatever was haunting the place had every intention of burning it to the ground.

The stakes were too high—Candy, Emma, Tio Manny, Aunt Josie—everyone he cared about was at risk. He couldn't just sit back and do nothing, even though every instinct screamed at him to leave the board alone. He took a deep breath, his hands trembling slightly as he reached out to touch the planchette. Whatever this was, it was far more than a game.

Taking a deep breath, he asked, "How do we summon a friendly spirit? And how can we be sure it's friendly?"

"We could ask my dad to help," JR suggested, his voice tentative yet hopeful.

"Your dad?" David's skepticism was evident, his eyebrows furrowing.

"What's wrong with my dad?" JR shot back, defensive, his eyes narrowing in challenge.

"Nothing, but... isn't he, like, in heaven? Do you really want to bother him with this?"

A flicker of disappointment crossed JR's face, softening his expression into something more vulnerable. "I hadn't thought of it like that," he admitted, his voice subdued, almost apologetic.

David could see the sadness in JR's eyes, the weight of it settling between them like an unspoken burden. He's probably been thinking about his dad this whole time, David realized, his heart sinking. JR hadn't just wanted to play with the board—he'd wanted to talk to his father, maybe even without fully realizing it. But something about the idea didn't sit right with David. That's why I asked Tio Manny about this, he reminded himself, recalling their conversation.

His uncle had gently explained that there's a reason people say 'rest in peace.' He'd told David that, as much as it hurts, we have to let the dead rest, likening it to the ultimate retirement. "They've done their work on Earth and now get to enjoy eternal peace in heaven," his uncle had said, his voice carrying the wisdom of someone who'd seen the impact of disturbing that peace.

David's heart ached for JR, understanding the longing behind his friend's suggestion. But he knew he had to say something, to gently steer JR away from a path that might lead to more pain. "I get it, JR," David began, his voice soft. "I know you miss your dad. But maybe... maybe we should let him rest, you know? It's like what my uncle said—he's in heaven, and he's finally at peace."

JR's eyes glistened with unshed tears, and for a moment, David feared he'd pushed too far. But then JR nodded slowly, the tension in his shoulders easing slightly. "Yeah... yeah, you're right," JR whispered, his voice tinged with both resignation and relief. "I just... I miss him, you know?"

"I'm sorry, dude. I really think it's for the best," David said gently. "Do you have any other ideas?"

JR nodded slowly. "Hold the planchette," he instructed, his voice lacking its usual confidence.

Eager to get it over with, David did as JR said.

"Close your eyes." David released an audible exhale and closed his eyes.

"Oh otherworldly spirits, we are here to call upon the friendliest of spirits. The best protector of spirits," JR intoned, trying to sound authoritative but only succeeding in making David more anxious. Unconvinced by JR's approach, David peeked out one eye. "Evil spirits go away. We are summoning good spirits only," JR continued, his voice wavering. "Do you understand?"

A shiver ran down David's spine as the planchette hovered over the word *Yes.*

"It's working," JR said, his voice tinged with both awe and fear. They returned the planchette to the center of the board. "Are we speaking with a friendly spirit?" JR asked. The planchette moved so quickly across the board that they nearly lost their grip. They lowered their eyes to the board.

"We have a good one," JR said with a subtle smile, but there was a nervous edge to his voice.

"Now what?" David asked, trying to steady his breathing.

"It needs an invitation."

"An invitation?"

"I think that's what they called it in the movie... Or maybe a permission slip?"

"A permission slip?" David said incredulously.

"It doesn't matter—just tell it what you want it to do."

David took a deep breath. "Hello, good, friendly spirit. Please come into my home and protect me and everyone and everything in this home," he said, his voice trembling slightly. He fixed his eyes on the planchette. *Why isn't it moving?* he wondered, his anxiety growing. "Why isn't it moving?" he whispered.

"You didn't ask it a question," JR replied, his voice barely above a whisper.

He cleared his throat. "Hello, friendly spirit. Will you please come into my home and protect me and everyone and everything in this home?"

Suspense hung heavy in the air as they waited for the planchette to respond.

David released an audible gasp as the planchette jerked from the center of the board over the word *Yes,* causing him to lose his grip.

Silence settled in the room.

David fixed his eyes on JR—it was unlike him to have nothing to say. JR's eyes were wide, as though frozen in perpetual shock. "What are you staring at?" David asked, turning toward JR's gaze. The planchette was still hovering over the board.

JR moved his hands in front of his chest and said, "No hands."

Emma said, pulling the refrigerator door open with her four-legged friend in her arms. She reached into the fridge for a single slice of Kraft cheese, swiftly removing the plastic wrap. As she shut the refrigerator door and brought the cheese slice to her mouth, she noticed a sudden change in her pint-sized companion—Blue's tiny body was trembling, and a series of low growls escaped her throat.

"What's the matter, Blue? Are you hungry?" she asked, bringing the cheese closer to the pup's mouth.

But Blue's attention was fixed elsewhere. The little dog turned its gaze toward the hallway and released a single high-pitched yelp.

"But you never say no to cheese," Emma said, frowning. A flicker of realization crossed her eyes. "You never bark like that, either." She followed the pup's rigid gaze toward the hallway. "Do you see something?" she asked, taking a cautious step forward. Blue's body stiffened; muscles tensed.

She stopped, her own fear mounting. "Blue, are you afraid of something?" she whispered. Another step forward. Fur standing on end, Blue began barking nonstop, like an alarm being set off, its high-pitched yelps reverberating through the quiet house. Emma's eyes locked onto David's bedroom door, her heart pounding in her chest as a dark, tar-like substance began to seep out from underneath, like a sinister blob threatening to consume the house and everything in its path. Breath caught in her throat, she muttered, "Blue, are you seeing this, too?"

Chapter 24

S CREAMS ERUPTED THROUGH THE HOUSE, reverberating off the walls and sending shockwaves through every room. A thunderous crash followed as David's bedroom door slammed open, nearly tearing it from its hinges as he barreled out, eyes wide with fear. Panic surged through him like a wildfire, propelling him down the hallway at breakneck speed. His heart hammered in his chest, but in his blind rush, he almost trampled over little Emma, frozen in terror.

But he couldn't leave her behind.

With his heart racing and adrenaline coursing through his veins, he scooped her up without missing a step, clutching her tightly against his chest. "Come on, Emma—I got you," he gasped, his voice trembling as much as his hands. He held her close, desperate to shield her from the chaos behind them.

"Move out of the way!" JR's voice echoed through the hallway, panic-stricken. "COMING THROUGH!"

Their adrenaline surged as they bolted for the living room, their screams filling the house with a cacophony of terror.

"Boys! Calm down!" Tio Manny's voice cut through the chaos. "What's wrong?"

David skidded to a halt, setting Emma down as he tried to catch his breath, his hands on his knees. The fear constricting his chest made it hard to speak.

"Did someone get hurt?" Aunt Josie asked, her eyes scanning Emma for injuries.

David pointed shakily toward his room, gasping for air as he tried to explain the terrifying creature they had just escaped. "It was huge... came out of nowhere," he managed to gasp out.

"Stay here," Tio Manny ordered, his face set in determination as he cautiously approached David's room. The others huddled together, watching from a distance as he nudged the door open with his foot. A loud gasp escaped him, and he slammed the door shut, sending a shockwave through the house. "¡A la fregada!" he cursed in Spanish, shaking his hand as if it had been burned. With long, hurried strides, he retreated to the living room.

Aunt Josie stumbled back, her hand flying to her mouth. "Oh my God," she muttered, her voice trembling.

"Did you see it?" David asked, his chest rising and falling with quick, shallow breaths.

"I saw it," his uncle replied, his eyes wide.

"Should I call the police?" Aunt Josie asked, her voice laced with panic.

Tio Manny shook his head slowly. "The police can't help us," he said, his gaze dropping to the floor.

"Oh my God," she repeated, her voice barely above a whisper. "What is it?"

He exhaled deeply, shaking his head. "That is the biggest flying cucaracha I have ever seen!"

"A flying cockroach?" Aunt Josie said incredulously, turning to David. "That's what all the screaming was about?"

David nodded, still trying to catch his breath.

She scoffed and rolled her eyes. "Aunt Josie, you don't understand—you didn't see it!" David exclaimed, his voice desperate. "It attacked us—flew right at us—both of us! Didn't it, JR?"

JR nodded vigorously, his face pale. "It was huge—as big as a bat!"

"What a bunch of babies," she replied, shaking her head.

"It's OK, boys—I get it," Tio Manny said, patting David's shoulder. "She's never been alone in a room with one of those things. They are ter-ri-fy-ing."

Aunt Josie shook her head, disapproval gleaming in her eyes. "The foggers aren't cutting it—I'm calling the fumigators first thing tomorrow," she said, stepping toward David's room.

"Hey! Hey! What do you think you're doing?" Tio Manny asked, raising his eyebrows.

"I'm handling it," she said, scoffing as she marched forward.

Chapter 25

AFTER A LONG EVENING OF ENDURING the overly dramatic antics of Emmanuel and the boys, Josephine slipped into bed, craving some quiet time for herself. Over the past week, she had been completely absorbed in the lives of Madeline, Julianne, and Sophia, feeling as if she had come to know them intimately. With a mix of anticipation and a touch of sadness, she reached for the old diary on her nightstand, aware that her journey with these newfound companions was nearing its end.

Settling into the covers, she flipped open the diary to the dog-eared page where she'd last left off, eager to dive back into the unfolding teen drama centered around the elusive Michael D. Would he really pay as Madeline had ominously suggested? And what did 'paying' even mean to a group of teenage girls in the 1940s? Josephine's mind raced with possibilities. Maybe they would toilet paper his house or egg his car—did teenagers even drive cars back then? she mused.

She devoured page after page, searching for any hint of Michael D.'s fate, only to find the focus had shifted. Madeline's entries now detailed the deepening bond between her, Julianne, and Sophia. The mystery surrounding Michael D. remained just that—a mystery—as the girls' friendship blossomed on the worn pages. Just one entry remained. Her eyes widened as they landed on the name Michael D. She smiled inwardly, thinking, *Surely a final parting gift from Madeline herself.*

> *November 1, 1946*
> *I had the girls over to play Truth or Dare last night. We turned off the lights. Momma lit candles. They were scared at first. I assured them there was nothing to fear as long as they played by the rules. They were a couple of chickens, though. No one chose dare, only truth. I asked them the same two questions. "Do you have a crush on Michael D?" They both said NO. Believe me, I would know if they were lying. Then I asked, "Have you ever had a crush on Michael D?" And guess what? They both said YES! You would think I'd be upset about it, but I'm not. It actually makes perfect sense when you think about it. The three of us like the same things... Makes sense that we would have a crush on the same boy. Anyway, that's in the past. What matters is, we all despise him now. Especially since he's going around with slutty Linda like some puppy dog all madly in love. He even calls her the "love of his life" and goes around bragging about the promise ring he bought her—says he's going to marry her one day. We all think it's pretty pathetic. Disgusting, really. Besides, a love like that is bound not to last.*

Josephine furrowed her brows. It wasn't the ending she had hoped for. The tone felt off, far too angry for the sunny teenage girls she had imagined, the kind who would gush over one another while sipping root beer floats and strawberry malts at the local soda shop. The diary's final entry unsettled her. *She sounded angry,* Josephine thought, her mind racing with possibilities. Did they egg Michael D.'s car? Toilet paper his house? Tell Linda what a creep he was, convince her to dump him, and then initiate her into their group? The questions swirled in her mind, each one more unsettling than the last.

She flipped through the remaining blank pages, one by one, searching for anything more to satisfy her need for closure. Just as she was about to close the diary for the last time, something caught her eye. She gasped audibly, her heart skipping a beat as she discovered a short list of words scribbled on the back of the last page. Unsure of what to make of the list, she turned toward Emmanuel, eager to show him. But his slow, steady breathing signaled that he was fast asleep.

Josephine hesitated, considering whether to wake him, but ultimately decided against it. *Perhaps it's for the best*, she thought, trying to convince herself. *Maybe I've become too invested in Madeline's life, making a bigger deal out of this than it really is.*

But the unease gnawed at her, refusing to let go. She couldn't stop herself from reading and re-reading the words, hoping that some new understanding, some hidden meaning, would reveal itself. But it was useless. *There's only so much meaning that can be gleaned from just eight words*, she thought, frustration mounting. What had once been a portal to a nostalgic, bygone era had transformed into a doorway to something darker, something twisted. The air around her grew heavy with a sense of dread as she snapped the diary shut and tucked it away in the drawer of her nightstand, attempting to seal it away from her thoughts—at least for the night.

But peace eluded her. The mystery gnawed at her, refusing to be silenced, even as she tried to push it away. She tossed and turned, two questions weighing heavily on her mind: *Why would a young girl write something like this? Why would anyone write these words?*

Chapter 26

"MOMMA, HAVE YOU SEEN BLUE?" Emma asked, clutching her handy-dandy notebook.

"She's right next to you," her mother replied, following the pint-sized pup with her eyes, its paws pitter-pattering against the floor at Emma's feet.

"No, I mean my stuffy, not the real one! I can't find it anywhere!"

"Emmy, hurry! Your cartoon is about to start!" David exclaimed from the living room.

"Momma, I need Blue! My show!" she cried.

"I'm sorry, angel... Momma has her hands full. We have company coming over today."

"Emmy! It's starting!"

"Momma! Please!" she cried. "You know I can't watch Blue's Clues without Blue!"

"OK, OK, let me think," her mother said. She brought her hand to her head as though searching hard for an answer. Her eyes sparked with realization. "I placed it in the toy chest in your room."

"OK, thanks, Momma!" Emma replied, skipping away to her room. She turned the knob, but it did not give. "Candy, we're not supposed to lock doors!" she yelled, knocking hard.

"Emmy... You're missing it!" David called out from a distance.

Her eyes widened, struck by a grand idea. With her pup by her side, she ran to her parent's room next door and into the adjoining closet. Blue's tiny legs moved quickly, struggling to keep up. "Come on, Blue," she said, picking up her furry friend. "I need to get my other Blue." The pup cocked its head to the side, looking confused. "You know what I mean." With the pup in her arms, she stepped through the closet, pushing aside the hanging garments in her way, and opened the door on the other end.

As she emerged from the other end of the closet she gasped, startled by Candy's towering presence.

"Leave," Candy said, standing over her, as though she knew she was coming.

"I just need my—"

In a swift motion, Candy wrapped her hands around Emma's fragile neck and lifted her up. Emma released the pup from her grip. Her feet dangled in the air as Candy moved her to the bed. She opened her mouth, struggling to breathe as Candy's grip tightened around her. Candy's lips curled up, her face contorting into a monstrous, barely recognizable version of herself.

Blue's bark cut through the silence in the room like a knife, her repetitive yelps unwavering in rapid-fire succession.

"Emmy? Candy? Are you in there?" David said from the other side of the door. Candy turned her gaze to the doorknob, her hands still firmly gripping Emma's neck.

Her heart racing, Emma tried to scream for help, but not a single sound could escape Candy's deathly grip.

David's instincts were in high gear. *I have to get in there*, he thought. The sound of splintering wood echoed through the house as David delivered a powerful kick to the door. The door's aged, rusty hinges groaned in protest, not giving in.

"David? What's going on over there?" his Aunt Josie, called out from the kitchen.

He stepped back and propelled himself forward, slamming his shoulder into the door. Still, it did not give. *Emma's secret tunnel*, he thought. With bated breath, he sprinted into the next room and plunged through the depths of the adjoining closet, his body contorting to fit the small space. Time seemed to slow as the darkness swallowed him whole, but he pushed through, crawling with a speed fueled by fear. He emerged on the other side to find his sister's hands wrapped tightly around Emma's tiny neck. "Candy, Stop! Let her go!" he shouted as his aunt pounded on the door demanding to be let in.

Candy released her grip.

Emma laid on the bed, desperately gasping for air. David unlocked the door.

"Oh my God," Aunt Josie said, stepping quickly to Emma. She appeared weak, her face pale. "Angel, are you OK?"

Emma inhaled deeply, struggling to fight back tears, and nodded.

Aunt Josie turned to David. "How did you know?" she asked.

He shrugged.

She locked eyes with him with a piercing gaze. "Two minutes ago, Emma was in the kitchen with me, searching for her stuffed animal. I didn't hear a thing. How did you know she was in danger?"

"I don't know," he replied. "It's just, Emmy didn't come when I called her... And I know how much she loves her show... And I didn't know where Candy was, and sometimes she doesn't know her own strength... And then I heard Blue barking... And the door was locked," he said, his words tumbling out in a rush as panic crept into his voice. "I'm sorry, Aunt Josie. I'm really, really sorry."

"Don't be. You just saved my baby's life," she said, squeezing Emma in an embrace.

David turned to Candy, his heart racing. Her breath came in heavy, ragged gasps, her eyes locked onto Emma with a chilling intensity, as if she were contemplating her next move. "Candy, don't you—" he began, but before he could finish, Candy's lips curled into a feral snarl. With a guttural groan, she lunged at Emma with lightning speed, making it abundantly clear that the battle was far from over.

On high alert, Emma let out a bone-chilling scream and bolted from the room, her feet pounding the floor as she fled from her attacker. Panic surged through David as he shouted after Candy, "CANDY, STOP! LEAVE EMMA ALONE!"

The chaos erupted further as the steel screen door slammed shut with a metallic clang, echoing through the house as the chase spilled into the backyard.

"David, stop her!" Aunt Josie's voice rang out, laced with desperation.

"I'm trying!" David yelled back, darting out the back door. Candy was thin, her legs long and lean, and she was fast—much faster than him by a long shot. But David was determined. He sprinted after her, his heart pounding in his chest, every muscle in his body straining as he pushed himself to close the gap.

Emma reached the corner of the yard, her back against the fence. With nowhere left to run, she spun around just in time to see Candy bearing down on her, a blur of fury and speed. A gasp escaped Emma's lips, her eyes widening in terror. But just as Candy was about to strike, she suddenly collapsed onto her back as if she'd been slammed by an invisible force, her body hitting the ground with a sickening thud.

"CANDY!" David shouted, his voice cracking with a mix of fear and relief as he sprinted toward her.

But something was wrong. As he closed the distance, he noticed an abrupt change in Emma's demeanor. There was a strange, almost unsettling spark in her eyes—one he had never seen before. She looked laser-focused, her gaze steely and cold, a determination that bordered on vengeful. *Why is she looking at me like that?* David thought, his confusion mounting.

"Angel, stop!" her mother's voice cried out from a distance, but Emma was already moving. She ran toward Candy, who lay sprawled on the ground, her small fists clenched, her steps purposeful and unwavering.

David's eyes bulged in panic as he realized Emma was barreling straight toward him, her pace relentless, with no sign of slowing down. His heart raced as he swerved to the right, then to the left, trying to dodge her. "NO, EMMA! STOP!" he shouted, his voice cracking with desperation. But it was no use. Emma was like a force of nature—unstoppable. Their bodies collided with a heavy thud, and David was sent stumbling backward, crashing hard to the ground.

Gasping for breath, Emma's mother finally reached them, her face flushed with exhaustion and confusion. "What has gotten into you?" she demanded, her wide eyes fixed on her daughter, staring at her like she was a stranger—someone she no longer recognized.

David, his chest heaving, struggled to regain his bearings. His eyes darted toward Candy's motionless body, still sprawled out on the ground. A fresh wave of adrenaline surged through him. Pushing himself to his knees, he crawled quickly to his sister's side, his mind racing with fear. *Please be okay*, he thought, his trembling hands reaching out to her, desperate for any sign of life. Candy lay on the ground, devoid of any signs of life. Her eyes were wide open, vacant, like they were staring at everything and nothing all at once. Blood stained the earth beneath them as it poured out of her neck through a long, narrow like a nightmarish fountain. His eyes widened as he examined his hands and knees, caked with burgundy-tinged blood.

With furrowed brows and tightly pressed lips, Aunt Josie fell to her knees and brushed her hand against Candy's pale, stony face.

Her silence confirmed what he already knew. He tried to get on his feet, but his trembling knees collapsed beneath him. His heart pounded violently in his chest as he took in the chilling details of the horrifying scene, trying to piece together what happened. She was running at full speed one moment, down on the ground the next—like she slammed into a brick wall. He shook his head. It made no sense.

As the world held its breath, a solitary droplet descended from above, landing on David's cheek with a silent splatter. He turned to Aunt Josie, horror washing over her face as though she were staring at the face of death. The droplet ran down his face slowly, warm and sticky, but he didn't touch it. Instead, his eyes rolled skyward to the line of dark crimson blood, thick and haunting, suspended in the air—a long-forgotten clothesline hung taut over Candy's body.

Chapter 27

H E DIDN'T WITNESS firsthand, but he didn't need to. The weight of what had occurred was enough to shake Emmanuel to his very soul. The mere thought of it twisted his stomach into a sickening knot. No one should ever have to endure such horror, let alone witness it. Emmanuel couldn't begin to fathom the depths of David's grief—losing his sister in such a brutal, unimaginable way. The pain must have been like a living, breathing entity, clawing at him from the inside, a wound so profound it seemed beyond healing.

And then there was Emma, so young and fragile, her innocence shattered by a tragedy she couldn't possibly comprehend. The horror of it lingered in her wide, bewildered eyes—those once bright, trusting eyes that had seen the world as a place of wonder and safety, now clouded with confusion and fear. It was as if the world had betrayed her, its cruelty seeping into her tender heart, leaving a scar that time alone could never erase.

Emmanuel felt an urgency welling up inside him, a desperate, gnawing need to act before the unbearable weight of it all crushed them. Every second felt like a lifetime, the pressure mounting, suffocating. They couldn't afford to wait.

"Thank you for seeing us on such short notice, Dr. Hart," he said, his voice steady despite the storm of emotions raging inside him. He sat between Josephine and David, a protective presence, while Emma played quietly on the floor mat behind them, her small hands moving with a mechanical precision that belied the turmoil in her young mind.

Dr. Hart's eyes softened as she turned her attention to David. The boy was trying so hard to hold it together, but she could see the cracks in his façade, the grief threatening to swallow him whole. "I'm so sorry for your loss," she said gently, her voice thick with empathy, a depth of understanding that came from her own encounters with grief. "Candy was my patient for many years."

"We know, and that's why we're here," Josephine interjected, her voice trembling with the desperation of a mother who didn't know where else to turn. Her eyes, usually so full of warmth, were now clouded with worry. "We can't find Candy's mother—we were hoping you might help."

Dr. Hart opened Candy's patient file, her fingers hesitating before she picked up the phone. The room held its collective breath as she dialed. A moment later, she lowered the receiver, regret settling on her face. "The phone line is no longer in service," she said quietly.

Disappointment etched itself across their faces. They had exhausted every lead. The number and address Emmanuel's sister had provided for the treatment facility were fake. They had searched for her at her apartment in the projects, but no one answered the door, and through the broken blinds, Emmanuel could see the place was abandoned. They had called everyone they knew and visited her last known workplace—no one had heard from her since she handed the kids over to Emmanuel.

"You're wasting your time," David said, his voice flat, emotionless. "I told you, she's not coming back."

An unsettling silence filled the room.

"Did your mother tell you that?" Dr. Hart asked gently.

"Yes," David replied.

"Why didn't you tell your aunt and uncle?"

He crossed his arms defensively. "She made me promise not to say anything."

Emmanuel dropped his head, a heavy sigh escaping from deep within. He had sensed from the start that it would come to this, but the thought of turning his sister away had been too unbearable—he couldn't risk losing her again.

Yet, here he was. *I lost her anyway*, he thought. If someone would have come to him in his shoes, he would have told that trying to hold on too tightly, especially when it came to matters of love and family, never grant control—only chaos. He had learned that bitter lesson years ago, when his marriage had nearly crumbled. That was before Emma, before the ministry, back when he was a different man—an unemployed, jealous drunk, undeserving of Josephine. Back then, he tried to control everything—what she wore, where she worked, even if she could work—believing it would keep her close. But all it did was push her away, sending his life spiraling out of control.

And now, despite everything, he was falling into the same trap again.

His chest tightened with the weight of regret. He turned to Josephine, meeting her eyes with a mixture of sorrow and humility. "I'm sorry," he murmured, his voice thick with emotion. "I should have known better."

Josephine met his gaze, her expression softening with understanding. "It's not your fault," she reassured him gently, her voice a soothing balm against the storm brewing within him. But the urgency of their situation quickly resurfaced, and she turned to Dr. Hart, her voice heavy with desperation. "What should we do?"

"Do you mind if David waits in the lobby with Emma for a few minutes?" Dr. Hart asked, her tone calm yet authoritative.

"Of course," Emmanuel replied, his voice steady but tinged with the weight of the moment.

David stood from his seat, extending his hand toward Emma. "Let's go, Emmy," he said softly, his voice gentle, almost protective. Emma, her focus still on the puzzle pieces scattered in front of her, looked up at him and nodded. She set the pieces aside and walked with him out of the room, her small hand grasping his.

Dr. Hart rose from her desk and quietly closed the door behind them. She took a deep breath, her demeanor shifting to one of professionalism laced with compassion. "Listen, I realize this is a horrendous situation you're in," she began, her voice measured, "but it's been three days since Candy's passing, so I have two pieces of advice for you." She sat back down, and Emmanuel and

Josephine leaned in, eager for guidance. "First, I recommend you move forward with guardianship proceedings so you can begin the long process of funeral planning."

"How long will that take?" Josephine asked, her voice trembling with the weight of the unknown.

"There's the initial filing, then an investigation and evaluation, followed by court hearings and proceedings—you're looking at a few months, minimum." Dr. Hart's voice was steady but carried the weight of inevitability.

Emmanuel's shoulders slumped, his head dropping as her words pressed down on him. The idea of waiting months just to begin the legal process felt unbearable, like a heavy stone lodged in his chest.

Dr. Hart continued, her tone gentle but firm, "Who knows? Maybe Candy's mother shows up before it gets to that point."

"And if she doesn't?" he asked.

Dr. Hart paused before responding, her words careful, "Short of finding the money for what I imagine will be a mountain of legal expenses just for a shot at expediting the process, I'm not sure there's anything you can do but wait."

A wave of nausea washed over Emmanuel at the thought of waiting so long to lay Candy to rest. The time stretched before him like an endless tunnel, and the pressure of financial strain tightened around him like a vice. They had already exhausted all financial resources—there was nothing left to sell, nothing more to downsize, and no savings left to tap into.

"We'll use this time to save up for the funeral and burial," he said, his voice heavy with resignation.

"I think that's a good idea," Dr. Hart replied, her voice soft, though the bleakness of the situation remained unspoken between them.

"What's your second piece of advice?" Josephine asked, her voice barely above a whisper, as if speaking too loudly would shatter what little composure she had left.

"Move on as best you can and be present for your children—David, especially."

"What about Emma?" Emmanuel asked, his brow furrowing in surprise. Emma was so young, and David seemed to be handling things better than expected, given the circumstances.

"I have a feeling that Emma is not the one you need to worry about. She's young, and kids are resilient." Dr. Hart shifted her gaze to Josephine, her eyes softening. "On the phone, you mentioned that Emma saved David's life—is that right?"

Josephine nodded, tears welling up in her eyes as she relived the memory.

Dr. Hart exhaled deeply, the weight of her words evident in her tone. "Survivor's guilt is a beast in kids who have witnessed death, let alone those who survive it," she said. "It can manifest in several ways—nightmares, irritability, anger. My advice is to be ready."

"I understand," Emmanuel replied, rising from his seat, the grief clinging to him like a heavy cloak. "Thanks again for seeing us, doctor." He turned to leave, but a gnawing question held him back. He hesitated at the door, then turned back to Dr. Hart. "Is there any way we could have prepared for this? Anything in her file, her history that could have flagged Candy having any aggressive or violent tendencies?"

Dr. Hart tilted her head thoughtfully, considering his question. "It's possible that Candy felt threatened by your daughter, given how close she and David were—but no, nothing in her history suggests any inclination toward aggression or violence."

He nodded, but her words offered him no solace, no relief from the tormenting question of why.

"Mr. Perales," Dr. Hart said gently, her voice layered with empathy, "with all due respect—please don't blame yourself. It's horrible, but sometimes... things like this... just happen."

Emmanuel scoffed, bitterness lacing his voice as he responded, "With all due respect, doctor, but I believe... they just don't."

Chapter 28

E MMANUEL WAS JOLTED AWAKE by the sudden sound of banging echoing through the house. His eyes shot wide open, the white around his irises visible, as he lay still in bed, listening for the disturbance.

He gasped, his muscles tensed. *There it is again*, he thought. He turned to Josephine and Emma, both sound asleep, and quietly pushed himself out of bed to investigate.

"Emmanuel, what are you doing?" Josephine asked in a loud whisper.

He flinched. "I thought you were asleep," he said. "Do you hear banging?"

"Yes," she replied. "It's just the wind slamming the back screen door. I must have forgotten to lock it."

But I didn't, he thought. "OK, go back to bed. I'll take care of it."

There was nothing unusual about the weather that night. No violent winds, just a quiet stillness like the night before, and the night before that. He moved cautiously through the bedroom, unwilling to disturb the silence by turning on the lights, navigating the darkness with only memory to guide him. Each step sent the floorboards creaking beneath his bare feet, the sound amplified in the quiet house.

When he reached the back door, he carefully disengaged the locks, each click echoing in the stillness. His hand hovered over the doorknob, but he recoiled as the screen door suddenly slammed against the metal door frame, sending a violent shiver through his body.

The air around him grew thick, weighted with an unsettling presence. He took a step back, his heart pounding in his chest, as the banging grew louder, more insistent, as if something—or someone—was demanding to be let in.

Josephine rushed out of their bedroom into the kitchen. "Emmanuel, for crying out loud, would you just lock–"

"Shhh," he interrupted. "Get back in the bedroom."

She scoffed and begrudgingly did as he said.

He set his gaze on the doorknob, his breath quickening, and without hesitation, reached out to turn it. Now face-to-face with the screen door, he moved to grasp its handle. Just as his fingers brushed the cold metal, the door violently swung open and slammed shut with an ear-shattering crash, mere inches from his face.

He froze, heart pounding, his hand still outstretched as if ready to tame a wild animal. Determined not to let it escape his grip again, he lunged for the door's handle, gripping it tightly as he planted his feet firmly on the ground. He braced himself, expecting the door to resist, to pull back with the same force that had thrown it open.

But there was only silence.

He waited.

Silence.

Tentatively, he jiggled the handle—it was locked. Slowly, he released his grip and stepped back.

More silence.

This couldn't be a dream. This is happening, he thought. The darkness around him was thick, but his experience was crystal clear. Unlike his daughter, who often spoke of vivid dreams, he had never had one in his life—or at least, none that he could remember. His doctor had once explained that he suffered from something called Charcot-Wilbrand syndrome, a rare condition that robbed him of the ability to recall or visualize images from his dreams.

His eyes remained fixed on the door, watching it like a prison guard monitoring a notorious fugitive. Finally, he pulled out a chair from the kitchen table and sat down, never breaking his gaze. The door was solid iron, easily weighing two hundred, maybe even two hundred fifty pounds. The lock was engaged, sturdy and secure. There was no logical reason for it to swing open like that, and even less reason for it to slam shut with such violent force.

The quiet darkness whispered a lullaby, and his eyelids grew heavy. As sleep began to overtake him, one final thought drifted through his mind... *I hope this was a dream.*

Josephine walked into the kitchen, her footsteps soft against the tile. She was startled to find the back door wide open and Emmanuel slumped over the table, fast asleep with his arms crossed. Concerned, she stepped over to check the screen door—it was locked—before gently nudging him awake.

He flinched, eyes blinking rapidly as he came to. "You slept here all night?" she asked, her voice a mix of worry and disbelief.

"Yes," he replied with a groggy yawn, rubbing his eyes and wiping away the drool that had pooled at the corner of his mouth. Slowly, he lifted his head from the table, still heavy with sleep.

She reached for the coffee can from the counter. The deep, rich aroma of coffee grounds filled the room as she pulled back on the lid. "Why didn't you go back to bed after you locked the screen door?"

"It was locked," he replied, rolling his neck to ease the stiffness.

"It must have been the wind then."

He gazed at her intensely, his expression stern. "That was no wind," he said.

Here we go again, she thought, recognizing his tone. She knew where this conversation was headed. As his wife, she had always supported him whole-heartedly, believing in their shared mission—the church and their roles in it. But when it came to unexplainable situations, Emmanuel was quick to jump to conclusions and attribute them to the supernatural. She inhaled deeply. "Sometimes strange things happen, Emmanuel," she said, handing him a cup of coffee.

"We both heard the banging, so we know we didn't dream it up," Emmanuel said, sipping his steamy beverage.

"Yes, I know." She also knew he didn't dream.

"Are you talking about the banging from last night?" David asked, stepping into the kitchen.

"Emmanuel, let's talk about this later," Josephine said, not wanting to alarm David.

"No, I think David is old enough to hear this," Emmanuel insisted.

"Hear what?" David asked, taking a seat across from his uncle at the table.

"The banging last night—when I opened the back door, the screen door slammed right in my face."

"So?" David said.

Josephine was taken aback by David's response. It wasn't just the word, but the tone—short and a little rude. *Strange,* she thought. *Maybe it's the beginnings of the survivor's guilt Dr. Hart warned us about.*

"So... The screen door was locked," Emmanuel said.

David scoffed.

"What?" Emmanuel replied, glancing at David sideways. "Do you have something to say?"

"Apparently it wasn't," David replied, his tone dismissive.

Josephine's eyes widened. There it was again—that tone. Unwilling to hold her tongue, she asked, "David, is something bothering you?"

"No," he replied flatly.

"It was locked," Emmanuel insisted. "I checked after it slammed on me."

"Maybe the wind made it rattle," Josephine said, crossing her arms.

Emmanuel shot her an incredulous glare. He stood from his seat and walked to the back door. "This isn't your typical screen door," he said. "This is a custom-built iron door—the Alcatraz of screen doors." He pulled the door handle back and forth. "Do you hear anything?"

"No," David replied. "So what?"

"So, there's no give—it's built solid." Emmanuel eyed the door from top to bottom. "Never seen anything like it used in a home like this. Who would want a screen door like this?"

Josephine rolled her eyes. *He's fishing for an answer,* she thought. An answer like, *'Someone that's hiding from the boogie man.'* But she wasn't going to give it to him. To her, the answer was obvious. "A little old lady concerned for her safety—that's who," she said. "Probably the same little old lady who had the burglar bars installed on every window in the house."

Emmanuel shook his head, dissatisfaction creasing his brow.

Josephine knew where this was headed. Emmanuel wanted to pin the banging on something paranormal or supernatural—something she didn't believe in. And she knew if they continued this conversation, it would likely get heated, and now, in front of David, wasn't the time. Whatever Emmanuel had to say would have to wait. She turned to him with a forced smile. "Now, who wants some breakfast?"

Chapter 29

T HEY MET WHEN THEY WERE just seventeen, and by the time their eighteenth birthdays rolled around, they were already married. Emmanuel's parents were fully supportive, but Josephine's parents had their reservations, insisting they were too young. Despite their objections, the young couple forged ahead, bound by a love they believed was stronger than any doubts. Emmanuel often joked that she couldn't resist his stunning, Ponch-like looks—a nod to the popular television series *CHiPs*. And she didn't deny it. If it hadn't been for the show's popularity, she might never have given him a second look.

Emmanuel was born and raised in Chicago, the son of a Mexican immigrant mother, and Spanish was his first language. He spoke with a slight Spanish accent, something Josephine found endearing from the start. Over time, Emmanuel realized there were many things she found charming about him—his taste in music, his dancing, his love of food. To her, he was... exotic.

Of course, they had their differences—Emmanuel was fascinated by the supernatural, drawn to the ethereal and unseen, while Josephine found no appeal in such things. But these differences only added depth to their relationship, never driving them apart. Not at first, anyway.

That morning, Emmanuel stepped into the bedroom and saw Emma, sound asleep in bed. "She's still asleep?" he asked, a hint of regret in his voice. He wished he had the chance to say goodbye before leaving for work.

"She's exhausted, poor thing," Josephine replied, putting folded laundry in the dresser drawers.

"She's wiped out," he said.

"She sure is. There's a lot more activity in the house since David and Candy moved in."

"David and Candy—right," Emmanuel muttered, removing his shoes.

She narrowed her gaze on him. "Do I detect a hint of sarcasm in your tone?"

"No," he replied. "It's much more than a hint."

She rolled her shoulders back in a stretch, already burdened by the weight of the conversation. "Go ahead," she said. "Say what you have to say."

"The screen door slammed shut right in front of my face—why can't you just accept that spirits are real?" Emmanuel said, wasting no time leaping into the crux of the conversation.

"I know they are," she replied. "But ghosts hanging around our house pranking the living? That's a completely different story."

He released an audible sigh. "It bothers me that we aren't on the same page."

"About ghosts?" she said incredulously.

"This isn't about ghosts," he replied. "It's about me dedicating my life to something and feeling like my wife doesn't support me."

"WHAT?!!" she shouted.

"Shh!" Emmanuel exclaimed, fixing his gaze on Emma. "You'll wake her."

"What?!" she repeated in a loud whisper. "How could you say that, Emmanuel?" She pronounced his name with proper Spanish pronunciation—*Eh-mah-nwel*, not like she usually did—*Eee-man-well*, signaling he had struck a nerve. "Especially after all we've done, the sacrifices we've made to keep the church open."

He shook his head as he meticulously adjusted the length of his tie, ensuring it hung just right against his crisp white shirt. Yes, she didn't give selling the house a second thought for the sake of saving the church. And, yes, she had put her pride aside when she asked her sister to let them stay in her home until they got the church finances in order. And, yes, when it came to all things spiritual, there was nothing else they disagreed on. Still, this wasn't a minor disagreement he could easily move past. Especially not now, given his growing concerns about the activity in the house. "I know what you've sacrificed. Being a pastor's wife is not easy—I know that," he said. "I'm just not sure you know what it means to be a true believer."

Josephine fell back onto the bed as though she had just received a gut-wrenching blow. He hit another nerve. A big one. She gritted her teeth and flayed him with her eyes. He covered his face with his hands, immediately regretting his choice of words. "I'm sorry!" he exclaimed, recognizing how condescending he must have sounded. "That's not what I meant."

"Please tell me what you really meant then, *pastor*," she replied, emphasizing the word with an icy tone that sent shivers down his spine.

He shook his head. "Who's being sarcastic now?"

"What do you want from me? *I. Have. Never. Seen. A. Ghost*," she said, punctuating every word with the weight of her frustration. "Therefore, *I. Don't. Believe. They. Exist.*" She crossed her arms and exhaled sharply. "Is this what they call an irreconcilable difference? Should we just agree to draw up the divorce papers and call it a day?"

He knew she was angry, that she was being sarcastic, but her words triggered memories of the worst day of his life to come flooding back—the day Josephine handed him divorce papers. *We moved past that*, he thought. "Please don't say things like that. I know you're angry, and I know you don't mean it, but it's hurtful—it just hits too close to home."

Her face washed with regret, as if the weight of her ill-chosen words settled on her conscience. She inhaled deeply. "I'm sorry. I know that was a low blow," she said. "But unless you can accept that this is where we differ, I'm just not sure what else we can do."

Emmanuel wasn't sure either, but he was never one to walk away from a tough problem. "I'll be at the church. I'll pray on it," he said, picking his keys up from the nightstand. He stepped up to Josephine for a kiss on the lips.

She turned her face.

A kiss on the cheek would have to do. "I'll see you later. Call me at the church if you need anything. I love you."

Chapter 30

I T WAS A SMALL, MODEST building on Chicago's south side, but it was the pride and purpose of Emmanuel's life. He pulled into the church parking lot, breathing in the smell of freshly poured asphalt—a major improvement from the uneven yard that had previously surrounded the home he had renovated and converted into a church. Stepping out of his car, he paused to take in the sight of the freshly painted, pure white exterior of the building before heading inside.

The air inside the church was always different—lighter, purer, and still with a serene calm that seemed to settle Emmanuel's thoughts the moment he crossed the threshold. He inhaled deeply, letting the peace wash over him, easing the tension that had been building inside his chest. Here, in this sacred space, his mind felt clearer, and for a brief moment, the weight of his burdens seemed lighter. But even within these walls, the disagreement with Josephine gnawed at him, heavy and unrelenting. This wasn't a simple lover's quarrel, some minor difference of opinion he could let go of. No, this felt deeper—darker. Something sinister lingered in their home. Emmanuel couldn't see it, but he could feel it—an oppressive presence lurking in the shadows, feeding off the discord between him and his wife.

A priest in Mexico had once told him that luck didn't exist, that what people called good luck was simply a blessing from God. And what they considered bad luck—flat tires, rain on a wedding day—was often just chance. But when true misfortune struck, the kind that shook your soul, it wasn't luck at all. There was always something darker, an unseen force pulling the strings.

Emmanuel couldn't shake the feeling that such a force had taken hold of their lives, weaving itself into their home. He believed it was behind Candy's tragic death, feeding off the division it was creating between him and Josephine. And unless he could convince her of the reality of these evil spirits, it would only continue to thrive, spreading its darkness through their lives.

He couldn't blame her for being skeptical, given how he had behaved early in their marriage—arguing for the sake of arguing, refusing to admit when he was wrong. He was the stereotypical hot-headed, machismo Chicano—aggressive, dominating, proud, controlling, determined never to show weakness, and sometimes even violent. His behavior had devastated her, almost ended their marriage. But he had learned the error of his ways and worked hard to change. Now, somehow, he needed to convince her that this wasn't the old Emmanuel slipping back into his old stubborn ways. They needed to fight this thing—together.

His eyes locked onto the large wooden cross hanging on the wall, draped with a velvet purple sash, its presence commanding the stillness of the church. Emmanuel's heart felt heavy as he gazed at it. "I could use your guidance right about now," he murmured under his breath, bowing his head in prayer. In that quiet moment, he asked for knowledge, wisdom, and revelation—anything that might help him show Josephine that the supernatural world wasn't just a belief, but a reality that coexisted with theirs, influencing everything around them.

He glanced at his wristwatch. An hour had passed, and he was no closer to an answer than when the conversation with her that morning left him searching for more. His gaze returned to the cross, lingering there, his mind desperate for clarity.

If I could only make her understand, he thought, dropping his head in frustration.

Then, as if struck by divine intervention, a revelation hit him like a bolt of lightning. His eyes widened with realization. Without a second thought, Emmanuel stepped up to the podium, retrieving his Bible. He rushed down the hallway to his office at the far end of the church, his heart pounding with a mix of excitement and determination.

The moment he reached his desk, he swept the clutter away with one arm, sending papers fluttering to the floor in a storm of urgency. He sat down, rolling his neck to ease the tension, his fingers trembling with the weight of what he was about to do. He cracked his knuckles and grabbed a pen. The pieces were starting to come together.

She needs a teacher, not a preacher, he thought.

What Emmanuel lacked in formal education, he made up for with an insatiable passion for learning and a relentless thirst for knowledge. With a pen and notebook in hand, he settled into his chair and opened his Bible. The soft flutter of pages filled the room as he flipped back and forth, searching for answers like a student racing to complete an open-book test before time was called. With each piece of information he extracted, he scribbled in his notebook in a shorthand only he could understand, focused on crafting the perfect lesson plan, choosing every word carefully.

He knew what he had to do, and more importantly, the exact words he needed to get his message across. He turned to a blank sheet of paper and wrote neatly:

Stages of Demonic Activity:

1. *Invitation*

2. *Infestation*

3. *Oppression*

4. *Possession*

5. *Death*

Chapter 31

JOSEPHINE HEARD THE FRONT DOOR swing open from the kitchen. She took a deep breath and rolled her eyes, trying to shake off the frustration that simmered inside her. She wasn't looking forward to facing Emmanuel again, especially after their last conversation about ghosts. They had never agreed on the subject—not since they started dating—and she knew they wouldn't start now. He had been at the church all day, well into the evening, even missing dinner. Not that she minded; in fact, she hoped the time away had given him a chance to move on and focus on something more pressing, like starting the guardianship process for Candy. But he had been stubborn about that, too, insisting on giving his sister more time to come back.

When Emmanuel stepped into the kitchen, Josephine tried to keep her tone light. "Did you have a good day?" she asked, her eyes searching his face, hoping to see any sign that he'd let go of his earlier obsession.

He kissed her cheek. "Josephine, perdóname... please."

"I forgive you. Let's just drop it, OK?" she replied, scrubbing dried pasta sauce from a dish under the running water.

"I know I handled the conversation wrong before," he said.

Is this the beginning of an apology? she wondered. She placed the dish in the sink, turned off the faucet, and faced him. "You have my attention," she said, crossing her arms.

"I should never have spoken to you the way I did. It was my ego telling me that, because you are my wife, you should just listen to me without questioning."

"Yes… it was," she replied.

"I'm not perfect."

"Amen to that," she quipped.

"I just need you to hear me out, really hear me."

She narrowed her eyes, leaning back against the kitchen counter. "Fine. I'll sit, and I'll listen," she said, pulling out a chair and sitting down. "But if your ego takes over, this conversation is over."

"That's fair," he said, taking a seat across from her. He cleared his throat. "Let's start with what we agree on."

What we agree on? What would that be exactly? she thought. She was ready to push back already, but he seemed to be trying hard, so she decided to give him a chance. "OK," she replied.

"Scripture says God created all things, including physical and spiritual beings. Do we agree on that?" he asked.

"Absolutely," she said.

"And all of God's creatures were made good, but some fell. So, the spiritual world has both holy beings and fallen, evil beings," he continued. "We agree so far?"

"Yes."

"The holy beings work with God and help humanity, but the fallen ones are set on evil, death, and destruction. Right?"

"Right."

"And the fallen ones are what we know as demons."

She nodded, finding him a bit long-winded. "And almost everything true of angels is true of demons, except demons are evil, serving Satan, while angels are good, serving God," she said, hoping to move things along.

"Exactly," Emmanuel said. "And you were right about ghosts—there is no such thing."

She leaned in, incredulous. "Emmanuel, are you feeling OK?" she asked, her eyes wide.

"I'm fine," he said.

"So, let me get this straight," she said, scratching her head. "You spent all day at church, digging through the Bible, and now you're telling me there aren't any ghosts in this house?"

He nodded. "I should've been clear before. Ghosts don't exist—at least, not in the form of the dead."

"What are you saying?" she asked, confused.

"I'm saying there are no ghosts here. No dead people playing tricks on us."

Josephine sat back, trying to connect the dots. He had just gone on about angels and demons, and now he was telling her there were no ghosts—something she believed all along. What's the connection? Her eyes widened as it suddenly clicked. "They're not ghosts... they're demons." The familiar warmth in her eyes vanished, replaced by a cold, creeping fear as the weight of her own words settled in. She turned to Emmanuel. "Are you sure? That there are demons? In our house?" she asked, her voice barely a whisper.

"Yes," he replied, solemn.

She took a deep breath, grappling with the new information. Ghosts were never a concern of hers—she might as well have believed in unicorns. But demons... demons were real.

"There's only one mention of a disembodied soul on Earth, and that's in 1 Samuel 28:7-21," Emmanuel continued. "Even then, it's shown as unnatural and evil." He handed her his Bible. "I bookmarked it—it's high-lighted—read it for yourself."

She didn't need to. She knew he wouldn't make this up. Still, questions swirled in her mind. People talk about seeing ghosts all the time—spirits of deceased loved ones. I never believed it, but all those people can't be wrong. She began pacing the room. "What about all those late-night infomercials?" she asked. "You know, the Psychic Friends Network? Dionne Warwick and all those people who claim to speak with the dead? They're everywhere."

"They're seeing and communicating with demons," Emmanuel said firmly. "Luke says demons are intelligent and can communicate with humans. They're deceptive and can take on any form, including that of a deceased loved one."

Josephine rubbed her temples, struggling to process everything. Emmanuel had been a pastor since before Emma was born, and they'd argued about this for years. Why hadn't he told her all this before? "Why are you just now telling me this? If what people think of as ghosts are demons, why didn't you tell me earlier and end this disagreement?"

"Language barrier," he said.

She scoffed. "That's ridiculous."

"I'm serious," he said sternly.

She stared into his eyes, sensing his sincerity but still confused. They'd never had major communication issues before—or had they? Small misunderstandings over the years popped into her mind, things Emmanuel had often attributed to Spanish being his first language. "So... like when you say you're having Cheerios, but you really mean cereal?"

"Yes!" he said, relieved. "Exactly."

Surprisingly, she began to understand. He'd been unintentionally saying 'ghosts' when he meant evil spirits, just like how people often used the words 'ghosts' and 'spirits' interchangeably. "Or like that time at my cousin's baby shower when you told her, 'The embarrassment is making you glow.'" She smiled inwardly, remembering how Emmanuel had mixed up the Spanish word for pregnant, embarazada, with embarrassed.

He looked at her blankly, then smiled. "Yes. Newsflash—you married an idiot."

Chapter 32

HE BREATHED A SIGH OF RELIEF, grateful that he had finally managed to convey his message without slipping back into old habits.

For the first time in a long while, they seemed to be on the same page. *That's progress,* he thought. But even as a small sense of accomplishment settled in, he knew there was still so much left unsaid—questions he couldn't yet answer, explanations that would have to wait. "I'm sorry for the misunderstanding," he said softly, reaching across the table to take Josephine's hand.

"How many demons are we dealing with here?" she asked, seemingly having moved past their disagreement.

"It's hard to tell," he replied. "There's not exactly a sign-in sheet for this."

She glared at him, clearly unamused by his sense of humor. "Give me a number. Ballpark—how many?"

He inhaled deeply as he considered how to answer her question. "Between what Emma has experienced, the banging, the wall heater, Candy, and likely even the roach infestation—"

"What do the roaches have to do with anything?"

"Roaches—particularly the kind that can eat through a newly replaced window frame overnight—are a symptom of diabolical infestation."

She placed her hand over her mouth.

He continued, "Roaches are creatures of darkness, thriving in places where there is neglect and chaos, much like how demonic forces are believed to inhabit spiritually corrupt environments."

She placed her other hand over her stomach. Emmanuel imagined the weight of his words moving through her intestines like a lead balloon. "How did this happen?" she asked.

"I don't know exactly, but this sort of thing doesn't happen on its own," Emmanuel replied. "*It was invited.*" A flurry of questions remained: Who invited it? By what means was it invited? When? And for what purpose? One thing he knew for sure was that demonic activity followed a clear pattern of events, which he needed Josephine to understand. He took a deep breath as he settled on where to begin. "There are five stages to demonic activity. It starts with an invitation, also known as permission or encroachment, then progresses to infestation, oppression, possession, and finally... Death."

The color drained from Josephine's cheeks, leaving her already pale complexion ghostly. Her forehead wrinkled with anguish and disbelief, as if unable to digest the magnitude of Emmanuel's words.

Emmanuel knew it would be a lot for anyone to take in. He opened his notebook, prepared to walk her through each of the stages. "I listed the five stages here," he said. He read from his notes:

Stages of Demonic Activity:
  1. *Invitation*

  2. *Infestation*

  3. *Oppression*

  4. *Possession*

  5. *Death*

"Oh boy," Josephine said, her eyes fixed on the notebook. "Start at the beginning."

"It was invited—given permission to be here, communicated with, or summoned somehow," he explained. "The invitation could have been direct or implied."

"Direct or implied? What's the difference?"

"It was given a direct invitation, meaning it was directly summoned through the occult—Ouija board, spells, curses…" He imagined the vacant home being occupied by squatters or ignorant thrill-seeking teenagers toying with dark forces on Halloween night, given the house's proximity to the cemetery. *Naive kids have no idea what they're toying with when they play with these things,* he thought. *I sure didn't.* "No telling what's happened in this house in the past fifty years."

"So what's an implied invitation?"

"Invited indirectly—by temptation, for example."

She shook her head. "I still don't understand."

He thought back to how he reconciled the information when he first learned it years ago. "Think of it this way," he said. "A demon will come if you call." He brought his hand to his ear and pressed his thumb to his temple as if speaking into a phone.

"Through a spirit board, spell, or curse," Josephine said. She locked eyes with Emmanuel as though struck by a realization. "What if Madeline and the girls she wrote about in the diary used a spirit board in the house? They lit candles. Madeline said they were scared."

"Anything is possible," he said. "But demons can also gain entry by simply knocking on the front door and tricking someone into letting them in, usually by offering something they know the person wants. Think of it like a child predator baiting their victim." This was the type of invitation that Emmanuel was more concerned about, given the children in the house and demons' propensity to manipulate the young and vulnerable.

"So if a child falls for the trick by taking the bait, the invitation is implied."

He nodded, "Exactly." He suddenly noticed the color drain from his wife's face. "What is it?"

"Maybe Candy took the bait," she said with wide eyes.

He shrugged his shoulders. "It's possible," he said, maintaining his gaze on her. He sensed there was more to her concern. "There's more, isn't there?"

She nodded slowly. "Emma said the little girl asked her if she wanted to be her friend," she said, swallowing hard. "Was that an invitation?"

"What little girl?" he said, his expression a mix of anger and confusion.

"Emma said she saw a little girl in the house. She said the girl asked to be her friend."

Emmanuel's eyes widened. It was the first he'd heard of this. "What did Emma say?"

"She said no. She definitely said no. She even demanded the girl leave."

He rolled his eyes skyward. "I wish you'd tell me these things." He shook his head. "I wish she'd tell me these things."

"Why is Emma the only one seeing these things, anyway? Does she have the gift of discerning spirits?"

"Demons prefer to go unseen, to remain undetected while wreaking havoc, but they have a way of revealing themselves to the young." Emmanuel saw the worry etched across her face. The creases in her forehead ran deep. He understood this was a lot for her to take in and knew she only wanted the same thing he did—to protect their daughter, their family. "The gift of discerning spirits is rare—in all likelihood, she will outgrow what she is able to see."

She nodded slowly. "OK, tell me about the next stage."

"Infestation," he said. "The demons are among us—co-existing with us in the house."

"Can they hurt us?"

"No. They cannot hurt believers. The demons may be in the house, but the people in it—we belong to God."

"In that case, why bother?"

"They want to evoke fear and push their limits. So they rebel and control whatever they can—the banging, the wall heater—all because they cannot control, possess, what they want the most: us." His own words made his heart race with fury; his chest tightened with each rapid beat. The thought of demons being in their home. Toying with their things. Trying to manipulate their little girl. *The cowards!* With a sudden burst of fury, he propelled his clenched fist down, stopping just short of pounding the surface of the kitchen table. He squeezed his eyes shut and took a deep breath, forcing himself to swallow the anger that was simmering in his soul. "I know it isn't easy, but we must resist dark emotions," Emmanuel said. "Anger, fear, anxiety, depression... These are all a part of the third stage—oppression. The demon seeks control of the mind because demons are mischievous, and the devil seeks to devour believers by scheming, using our own thoughts against us."

She nodded. "I understand."

"After oppression comes the fourth stage, possession. The demon invades the body, bringing it closer to what it's really after—the soul."

"Enter stage five," Josephine said.

"Yes, well—I believe that part goes without saying," he replied.

"How do we stop it?"

"I don't know yet," he replied. "But first, we need to get to the bottom of it."

Chapter 33

EMMANUEL SET OFF ON HIS MISSION with a determined resolve, much like a doctor probing for the root cause of a mysterious illness. He understood that to address the demonic activity plaguing the house, he first needed to uncover its origin. His initial step was to delve into online city records, where he quickly discovered the names of the previous occupants: *Randolph and Gloria Lennard*. The names stirred a vague sense of familiarity, but they offered no immediate answers.

To broaden his investigation, Emmanuel turned to the county deed records, meticulously combing through each property on the street. He was particularly interested in learning more about the neighborhood's history, especially about any long-term residents who might have observed or experienced unusual occurrences. It was during this search that he learned Jillian had lived in the area for quite some time, longer than most of the other residents.

Recognizing that Jillian was the only neighbor they had started to build a rapport with, Emmanuel decided to begin his investigation close to home. He hoped that Jillian might have some knowledge of the Lennards or, at the very least, be able to provide some context about the neighborhood's past. With this in mind, he approached her, his curiosity mingling with a sense of urgency. He needed to piece together the puzzle before whatever was lurking in the house could cause further harm.

He walked over to the chain-linked fence that separated their properties, where Jillian was on her knees, pulling weeds. "Hello, I'm Emmanuel," he called out as her gaze met his. "I believe you've met my wife."

"Oh, hello," she said, rising to her feet. She was an attractive woman, with a beauty that was both subtle and striking, like a gem half-buried in the earth, waiting to be fully uncovered. She brushed the dirt from her gloved hands. "I'm Jillian. It's a pleasure to meet you."

"I'm sorry we haven't introduced ourselves properly sooner—things have been... hectic since we moved in."

"Hectic?" she asked, her brow furrowing in concern.

"Yes," he replied, choosing his words carefully. "I was hoping you might have a moment to talk."

"Sure," she said, removing her gloves. "Are you searching for something?"

Confused by her response, he tilted his head slightly. '*Are you searching for something?*' he thought. Any number of responses would have made more sense, given the context of the situation. *What about? How can I help?* Even a simple *Yes?* But, '*Are you searching for something?*' seemed presumptuous, yet not entirely far-fetched. He put his thoughts aside. "I was hoping you could tell me what you know about this place. Have you lived here long?" he asked.

"My whole life—I inherited the house from my folks. My grandparents lived here before that."

"So the house has been in the family a long time."

She nodded. "Three generations."

"Is there anything you can tell me about the people who lived here before? Anything unusual or strange about them?"

She scoffed. "Isn't that the sort of thing you should have asked before you bought it?"

"I didn't," he said. "It belongs to my sister-in-law. She got it for a steal—paid only ten grand."

Her eyes widened, her face contorting with surprise and disbelief.

"I know," he said. "Makes me wonder, what's the catch?"

"Yeah, right," she scoffed. "You couldn't pay me enough to buy that house."

He furrowed his brow. "Oh, really?"

"Really."

"And why is that?"

She inhaled deeply. "I don't know. A bad feeling?"

"About the house or the people who lived there?"

She shrugged, "Both, I guess."

"Can you tell me anything about them?"

"Not much. Just that an old woman and her elderly mother lived there—always had. They never had visitors and rarely left the house. I didn't even know either of them had died until the house got put up for sale by the city."

"Interesting."

"Never saw the mother—guessing she was too old to get around. I assume she was the first to go, but I didn't hear word of her passing."

"What about her daughter?"

"She was in her sixties, or seventies maybe? I don't know, but she had a full head of white hair—been that way ever since I could remember. And she was always peeking through her windows like she was hiding from something." Her eyes darted around nervously. "She had the palest skin I've ever seen, and these eyes... They seemed to look right through you, like you failed to exist." She flinched, as though the thought of the woman sent a shiver down her spine.

It seemed to Emmanuel she had much more than a bad feeling about the women and the house. The way her eyes were darting around—it was as though she was avoiding something. And her flinching—her body's involuntary reaction to some uncomfortable emotion. Although years had passed since they died, the thought of them and the house obviously still bothered her. "Did you ever speak to either of them?"

"Never cared to. I suspect the feeling was mutual."

He shifted his gaze to her perfectly manicured lawn stretched out before him like a flawless canvas, each blade of grass trimmed to perfection. "Gorgeous lawn you have there," he said. "You must spend a lot of time outside. Strange that you didn't speak to them all those years."

She fixed her gaze on the buzzing bees and butterflies surrounding the daylilies and coneflowers neatly planted at the front of her yard. "I stayed inside mostly. Anything to avoid catching them watching from out the window. I guess they gave me the creeps."

"I'm sorry. That's no way to live." His eyes landed on the gold crucifix pendant hanging from her neck. "I hope you don't mind me asking—are you a spiritual person?"

"Oh yes," she replied. "I attend the Queen of All Nations Catholic Church here in Hillside."

"And do you get these 'bad feelings' often?"

Her eyes darted nervously from side to side, a telltale sign of her anxiety. She stepped back, as though trying to shrink away from the conversation. "Uh, not, not, not often," she stuttered. She cleared her throat. "Why do you ask?"

"Just wondering," he replied, unwilling to stir her up further. "I appreciate your time."

She nodded.

He turned to walk away, but a nagging question tugged at the corners of his mind. "Jillian, just one more thing," he said.

"Yes?"

"Earlier, you said, 'Are you searching for something?'"

"I did?"

"Yes. You did," he said. "Do you know what it is I should be looking for?"

She shook her head. "Sorry, I don't know what you're talking about."

She was lying, and he knew it. But he couldn't force her to talk. He dropped his head.

"But I just remembered something—something you might be interested in knowing... About the previous tenants."

He lifted his head.

"My parents told me the man of the house died there, outside in the yard. They said it happened before I was born," she said. "Something about a vicious dog attack."

Emmanuel felt a cold chill run down his spine. The pieces were starting to come together, but they painted a picture he wasn't sure he was ready to see.

Chapter 34

JILLIAN'S MOTHER ALWAYS PUT ON A SMILE on a smile when the cameras came around, a perfect mask of pride and maternal warmth. She would stand tall, her voice steady as she spoke to the reporters, calling Jillian her brave little girl, her pride and joy. She'd tell them she always knew there was something different about Jillian, something special. But the smile was brittle, a facade that cracked at the edges when the cameras were off. Her father, on the other hand, avoided the spotlight altogether, retreating into the shadows whenever the news crews arrived. He'd mutter under his breath about how he didn't like the attention, didn't like Jillian having it either. "You never know who's watching," he'd warn, his voice tight with unease.

But behind closed doors, away from the prying eyes of the world, their true feelings simmered just beneath the surface. They were angry—furious, even. Angry at Jillian for what she'd done that day in the grocery store. Angry that she hadn't just looked the other way like her mother had told her to, like her father had taught her to.

In her heart, Jillian knew she'd done the right thing. Even as a child, she understood that some things couldn't be ignored, that there were moments when you had to stand up, no matter the cost. She wouldn't have changed her actions for all the money in the world. But she also understood that her parents' anger wasn't really about her; it was about their own fears and insecurities, their unresolved grief that had festered for years.

Her father, especially, carried the weight of the past like an anchor around his neck. When he was young, a car accident had claimed the lives of his entire family, a tragedy so profound that it had made headlines, shattering the small, close-knit community of Hillside. His grandparents had taken him in, raising him with the kind of love that only those who have experienced deep loss can offer. But they, too, were taken from him—his grandmother passing first, followed by his grandfather the very next day. The doctors had called it Broken Heart Syndrome, explaining that his heart had simply given out, weakened by the overwhelming grief of losing his wife.

Her father believed his grandparents had hung on just long enough to see him through to adulthood, enduring their pain so he wouldn't be left alone in the world too soon. But their deaths had left him with a deep, unhealed wound, one that never truly closed. He would often tell Jillian that he couldn't afford to let himself experience that kind of loss again, that if it happened, he wouldn't survive it. And so, he kept his family close—maybe too close. The fear of loss had wrapped itself around his heart like a vise, tightening with every passing year.

Jillian understood that now, in a way she hadn't as a child. She could see how her father's grief had shaped him, how it had cast a shadow over their lives. And though she loved her parents, she couldn't help but feel the weight of that shadow, the suffocating fear that had been passed down to her like an unwelcome inheritance.

But in that grocery store, in that moment of crisis, Jillian had made a choice. She had chosen to act, to do what she knew in her heart was right, even if it meant defying the fear that had governed her family for so long. And for that, she would never apologize.

Jillian understood this impulse, recognizing that if the situation were reversed, she might not have fared any better. Still, whatever genetic darkness had burrowed itself into her father's DNA, she believed she had managed to escape it—or so she thought. But in the end, what she believed didn't matter. It was her parents' thoughts that shaped her reality, especially in moments like this, seated between them in her behavioral therapist's office.

Jillian took a deep breath, fighting the urge to mimic her mother's words, which she had heard so many times they were now etched into her memory.

"What if he had hurt you?" her mother said, her voice trembling as tears welled up in her eyes. "The poor child he took prisoner was your age—he could have just as easily taken you, too."

Jillian exhaled deeply, trying to remain calm. "Everyone said I did the right thing. Everyone called me a hero."

"You disobeyed your mother!" her father exclaimed, his voice sharp with anger and fear, the weight of his past losses looming over them like a shadow.

Dr. Robinson interrupted, "Let's focus on Jillian's feelings, what was going on internally, and put her actions aside for a moment."

"Fine," he replied.

"Do you remember what you felt that day?" Dr. Robinson asked.

"Yes."

"Tell me about it."

"When I saw him, I knew I had to find help for the girl."

"How? Did you hear a voice?"

"No." She turned to her mother. "For the hundredth time, I do not hear voices in my head." She shifted her gaze back to Dr. Robinson. "It was just a feeling... Like that feeling when you need to use the restroom or sneeze. Something stirring up that I needed to let out."

"How did you feel after you told the officer?"

"Instant relief—like how you feel after you've been holding it and finally get to the toilet."

"Has this ever happened before?"

"No."

"Has it happened since?"

"That's what I'm afraid of, doctor. What if it happens again? What if next time there's no police officer?" her mother said. "What if next time she's not so lucky?"

"I understand your concern, but before we get there, let's allow Jillian to answer the question." She turned to Jillian. "Has it happened since?"

She gazed at her mother, a shell of the woman she was only a couple of months ago. Before she became a 'hero.' Her mother was thin to begin with, but judging by her gaunt cheeks and protruding collarbone, she had grown noticeably thinner. Her hair, typically done up, now appeared ragged and disheveled. Her face had aged, etched with lines of worry. Except for the facade she put on for the reporters, she couldn't remember the last time she had seen her mother's toothy, vibrant smile. Then, there was the arguing that had become her parents' nightly ritual. He argued that her mother should have kept a closer eye on her. He said if anything ever happened, Jillian's blood would be on her mother's hands. They had never argued before. It pained her to see them this way.

"Jillian?" Dr. Robinson called out.

"Yes?" she replied, lost in her thoughts.

"Has it happened since?"

She gazed deep into her mother's hollow eyes, glinting with a haunting sadness, then turned to her father, perpetually angry and popping Rolaids like an addict. She didn't have a doubt they loved her, and although she didn't agree with them, she didn't want them to lose any more sleep over this. She took a deep breath and said, "No. It hasn't happened since."

Chapter 35

J ILLIAN DIDN'T TELL EMMANUEL what he should be looking for. In fact, she insisted she didn't know what he was talking about. But she had slipped, and Emmanuel caught it. Like an investigator reading a witness, he noticed the subtle shifts in her body language—the slight hesitation, the way her eyes darted away from his. She was hiding something.

But what?

And why?

The aroma of smoked meat and eggs filled the air. "Back to square one," Emmanuel muttered, biting into a strip of crispy bacon.

"Where do you go from here?" Josephine asked, handing him a steaming cup of coffee.

He shook his head, staring into the cup. "I don't know."

David shuffled into the kitchen, his gaze fixed on the floor, as if the world around him was too much to bear.

"¡Buenos días!" Emmanuel greeted him with forced cheer, expecting a reply. But David silently took a seat at the table without a word. Emmanuel's eyes narrowed, noticing the dark purple circles under his nephew's eyes—like week-old bruises against his tan skin. "Did you get any sleep?" he asked, concern creeping into his voice.

"Yeah," David muttered.

His sluggish movements and refusal to meet his uncle's gaze cast an unsettling shadow over the room. "What's the matter? ¿Estás crudo?" Emmanuel prodded, trying to lighten the mood.

"What?"

"Are you hungover?" Emmanuel clarified, leaning in to catch a whiff of David's breath. The sour stench made him recoil. "Good God, when was the last time you showered?" he asked, waving his hand in front of his nose.

David shrugged, indifferent.

"You don't know the last time you showered?" Josephine asked, incredulous. "That's a problem in and of itself."

"What's the point?" David replied flatly. "I'm just going to be accused of turning on the wall heater and trying to burn the house down."

Emmanuel and Josephine exchanged uneasy glances. "Have some bacon," Josephine offered, sliding a plate toward David.

"I'm not hungry," he said, pushing the plate away.

Emmanuel's concern deepened. Even in grief, David never passed up food. "Is everything OK?" he asked cautiously.

David abruptly stood, his chair scraping loudly against the kitchen floor. "I'm done. I'm going over to JR's."

He's done? Emmanuel thought, alarmed. David hadn't touched his plate. The tension thickened as they watched him leave the kitchen, silence hanging heavy between them.

The slam of David's bedroom door reverberated through the house like a gunshot, sending a jolt through Emmanuel's chest.

"Where is this attitude coming from?" Josephine asked, her voice tight with worry, her eyes searching Emmanuel's for answers.

"I don't know," Emmanuel replied, crossing his arms as he leaned back in his chair. Something was off—something dark. David's appearance, his smell, the way he spoke; it was as if he had become a different person overnight. Emmanuel recalled his mother's warning: sudden, negative changes in behavior, especially with dark circles under the eyes, were signs of dark magic at work. Could the answer to the demonic activity he'd been searching for be right under his roof?

"We should give him some space," Josephine suggested, her voice soft but laden with concern. "He's probably going through the survivor's guilt Dr. Hart warned us about."

"No... That's exactly what it wants us to think," Emmanuel said, shaking his head, his voice barely above a whisper. He reached for his coffee cup, but as his fingers brushed the mug, a cold wave of dread washed over him. The mug flew from his hand as if ripped away by an unseen force, slamming against the wall with a violent crash. Coffee splattered across Emmanuel, the cabinets, and the floor.

Josephine stumbled back, gripping the counter for support, her eyes wide with shock. "What the hell was that?" she gasped, her voice trembling. "An echo from the past?"

Emmanuel nodded slowly, his heart pounding, his gaze locked on the wall now dripping with black coffee. "You could say that."

"What's that supposed to mean?" Josephine asked, her voice barely a whisper, fear creeping in.

Emmanuel took a deep breath, his mind flashing back to a long-buried memory. "It means... this isn't the first time a glass has flown out of my hand like that."

Emmanuel remembered the details of that night vividly, even after so many years. He had been at his tía's house when he and his cousins, Jesse and Lucy, decided to toy with the spirit world. He was eleven years old, his cousins twelve and fourteen, and they were bored, searching for something to do while their mothers prepared tamales for Christmas that evening. They made a makeshift spirit board using cut-out letters from an old magazine, glue, and a piece of cardboard. Lucy and Jesse began the ritual, sitting around the coffee table and inviting a spirit to join them, using a glass as a planchette, while Emmanuel and Margie observed from the couch.

"Are you sure you know what you're doing?" Emmanuel asked, a note of apprehension in his voice.

"How hard could it be?" Jesse replied with a shrug. "If there is a spirit out there, please come to my house," he said, holding the glass over the board.

"You're inviting it here?" Emmanuel said, his tone incredulous.

"I don't mean literally," Jesse replied, rolling his eyes. "I just want it to talk to us."

To their shock, the spirit revealed itself through the board, spelling out its name: Damien.

"Manny, are you going to play or not?" Lucy asked, her voice tinged with impatience.

"I want to play," Margie said, her eyes wide with curiosity.

"No! You're too young!" Emmanuel exclaimed, a protective instinct kicking in. Even then, he sensed something wicked about the board, something he needed to shield his little sister from. "I'll do it," he said, rising to his feet.

He stepped up to the table, his heart pounding with a mix of fear and doubt about whether their homemade creation would actually work. He reached for the glass, and as soon as his fingers made contact with it, the glass shot across the board with terrifying force, smashing violently against the far wall.

Their eyes were glued to the spot, their faces etched with horror and disbelief, hearts racing as they struggled to comprehend what had just happened.

"What is wrong with you, man?!" Jesse exclaimed, his voice shaking.

"I didn't do it!" Emmanuel fired back, his voice rising with fear. It was the scariest thing he had ever experienced, and every fiber of his being wanted to stop there, but he couldn't convince his cousins that he hadn't thrown the glass.

"Come on, Margie, let's go," he said, grabbing her hand and dragging her out of the room.

His cousins, undeterred, continued without him. Later that evening, Emmanuel's mother received a frantic call from her sister, demanding to know what they had done and what he had seen that night. She explained that after Emmanuel and Margie had left, the kids began screaming uncontrollably, hysterical with fear, forcing her to drive them to the first Catholic church that would take her call.

She handed the phone to the priest, who asked Emmanuel to explain what had happened. Emmanuel recounted how he had stopped playing after the glass hit the wall. But he would later learn that this was only the beginning. His cousins had continued to invite the spirit and taunted its presence. He was told that every piece of glass in the house shattered that day—picture frames, windows, lightbulbs, mirrors—all reduced to shards. In a desperate attempt to end the torment, they tore up the board into pieces, but to their horror, the pieces mysteriously reassembled themselves.

"My primos were never quite the same after that night," Emmanuel said, his voice heavy with the weight of the memory. But there was something else that happened, something Emmanuel had never told a soul. "I remember feeling this lingering heaviness in my chest, like I couldn't breathe. It started the moment the glass hit the wall," he began, his eyes distant, lost in the past. "Then suddenly, I saw this bright light—warm, glowing—and a woman."

"Your guardian angel?" Josephine asked, her tone a mix of curiosity and disbelief.

"I believe so," he said, his voice tinged with awe. "She had her arms extended in front of her like she was pushing something back. She said, 'Leave, he's not yours.' And then, just like that, the heaviness in my chest was gone." He shook his head, still grappling with the significance of the moment. "We opened a portal that night. Maybe it was me that set the demon off—caused the glass to fly. Maybe it recognized me, knew who I was—who I would one day become," Emmanuel said, his voice dropping to a near whisper. "Maybe it's been watching, waiting, all along."

Chapter 36

EMMANUEL SENSED THEY WERE dealing with an intelligent spirit, not residual energy. The way the glass flew out of his hand and the precise time he was talking about the demon—it was no coincidence. "A portal must have been opened." Without another word, he rose to his feet and strode out of the kitchen, his steps long and purposeful.

"What are you doing?" Josephine asked, rushing to keep up.

"Searching David's room," he said, not bothering to ask for permission or give it a second thought. Privacy was a luxury they couldn't afford when evil forces were involved. They tore through the room, pulling drawers from the dresser, flipping the mattress, leaving no corner untouched.

"How will we know if we've found it?" Josephine asked, rummaging through a pile of clothes on the floor.

"A spirit board, or any evidence of witchcraft—black magic, spells, curses." Emmanuel's eyes landed on a black and red cardboard box. Strange. David hadn't mentioned having checkers, and given how close he and Emma were becoming, it seemed odd that he wouldn't have asked her to play. He pried open the lid, and there it was—the board he knew as a gateway to hell. "A Ouija board." He stared at it, disgusted by the deceptively harmless-looking game that had been linked to so much darkness. It was said to be so sinister that it was responsible for the untimely death of William Fuld, the owner of the Ouija board company, in 1927. The story went that the Ouija board had allegedly recommended that Fuld build a particular factory to expand production. While walking on the roof of this factory, Fuld leaned on a support that gave way, causing him to lose his balance and plunge to his death.

Emmanuel's glare drilled into the board, his hatred for it palpable. "What are we going to do with it?" Josephine asked, her voice trembling slightly.

Emmanuel ripped the board from the box, his grip tight, his expression fierce. "We burn it... Right now. Let's go."

They stepped out of the room and into the backyard, their steps hurried and filled with purpose. Emmanuel grabbed a shovel leaning against the house and marched to the far end of the yard. "I need you to do exactly as I say," he said, driving the shovel into the ground. "Do you understand?"

"Yes," Josephine replied, her voice steady.

"It's not enough for us to burn it," he said.

"We bury it?"

He dropped the shovel to the ground, beads of sweat forming on his brow. "First, we anoint it." He pulled a small glass bottle from his pocket, twisted the cap off, and poured the anointing oil over the board. "Now we pray."

Josephine nodded and bowed her head.

"Satan, you have no power over us. You have no power over this home," Emmanuel declared, his voice firm and resolute. He retrieved a lighter from his pocket. "We are children of God, and we bind you from this home and everyone in it!" There was a sharp click as he flicked the lighter, igniting a flame. "In the name of the Father, the Son, and the Holy Ghost." With a swift motion, he brought the flame to the board, releasing it from his grip and dropping it into the freshly dug hole. They stepped back, watching as the board erupted in flames, the fire consuming it with a fierce intensity.

The flames crackled and roared, the darkness of the night illuminated by their light. As the board burned, a sense of finality washed over them. But deep down, Emmanuel knew this was just the beginning.

Next door, the sound of Alanis Morissette's *Ironic* filled the living room, its familiar tune creating a cozy, almost nostalgic atmosphere. David and JR were glued to the TV screen, their attention wholly absorbed, oblivious to the world around them. The soft glow of the screen bathed them in flickering light, casting shadows that danced across the room.

Without warning, David rose from his seat, his movements slow and deliberate, as if he were in a trance. The couch beneath him held a deep impression—a silent testament to hours spent sitting there, lost in thought. He walked past JR, his steps steady but detached, as though he were being summoned by an unseen force.

"Dude, what's the matter with you?" JR asked, his brow furrowing in concern. His mouth twisted into a grimace as a chill of unease settled over him. David didn't respond. His eyes were wide, his stare vacant, as he moved toward the window. He gazed out, seemingly lost in another world, and then, as if suddenly released from an otherworldly grip, his knees buckled, and he collapsed to the floor.

"Dude, you OK?" JR shouted, rushing to his side, panic rising in his voice. He knelt beside David, his hand on his friend's shoulder, trying to rouse him from whatever had just overtaken him.

David's head dropped, his voice a low mutter. "They found it."

Chapter 37

THE PILE OF ASHES by the Ouija board brought Josephine little comfort. The sound of Emma's heart-wrenching scream in the distance only confirmed what she already feared—whatever malevolent force they were dealing with, the demonic activity in the house, was far from over. Her muscles tensed, her eyes widened in terror as she sprinted toward the house, shouting Emma's name. "ANGEL! ANGEL! MOMMA'S COMING!" she cried. Under any other circumstance, Emmanuel would have easily outrun her, but not today. Adrenaline surged through her veins, propelling her forward with a speed she didn't know she possessed.

She grabbed the screen door, but it wouldn't budge. Panic set in as she yanked and yanked again. "You locked it?" she asked incredulously, her voice laced with fear.

"No," Emmanuel replied, just as bewildered.

Emma screamed again, her voice piercing through the house. "Momma, momma, help!" The desperation and dread in her cry sent chills down Josephine's spine.

"Let me try," Emmanuel said, reaching for the door handle.

Josephine watched in disbelief as he effortlessly pulled the door open. It was as though whatever malevolent presence had seized the house sensed her fear, her vulnerability as a mother, and was toying with her, exploiting her every weakness. It's toying with me, she thought, a chill running down her spine.

They rushed inside, ears straining to locate Emma's cries. "She's in the bathroom," Emmanuel said. Josephine moved as fast as her legs could carry her. The sound of shattered glass crunching underfoot echoed through the hallway as they reached the bathroom. The mirror lay in shattered pieces on the floor, reflecting a hundred tiny versions of the chaos around them.

Josephine's gaze locked onto Emma, sitting on the toilet, her bare feet dangling above the floor, her face streaked with fear-filled tears. "I didn't do it," Emma whispered, her voice trembling as she looked up at her mother, eyes wide with terror.

"It's OK, momma's here, angel," Josephine whispered, lifting Emma gently from the toilet seat. She held her daughter close, murmuring words of reassurance as she felt Emma's small heart pounding against her chest, the rhythm a stark reminder of the terror that had just gripped her.

Emmanuel crouched down to examine the fragments of glass scattered across the floor. Hundreds of broken pieces lay in disarray, as though the mirror had been shattered in a violent outburst, the destruction seemingly fueled by an unseen rage.

"It didn't work," Josephine said, her voice tinged with despair.

David burst into the bathroom, breathless. "Is Emma alright?" he asked, panting.

Emma nodded, still clinging to her mother.

"I heard a crash and her screaming from next door. I got here as fast as I could," David said, his voice strained with worry.

Josephine noticed something different about him. The surly teenager who had stormed out earlier seemed to have vanished. There was a new energy about him—his eyes were clearer, the dark circles that had once marked his exhaustion had faded, and the unpleasant odor that clung to him before was gone. "We found the Ouija board," Josephine said sternly. "We burned it."

David's face flushed with guilt. "I'm sorry, Aunt Josie. I didn't know they were bad, and we must have left the line open when the giant flying roach attacked us. I promise, I'll never touch one of those things ever again," he said, speaking so quickly that his words tumbled over each other.

Josephine could sense the sincerity in his apology, the regret in his voice unmistakable.

"And then I invited a good spirit to protect us and the house."

Emmanuel's eyes widened. "You did what?"

"I invited–"

"No, I heard you," he interrupted. "I just can't believe what I'm hearing. Never, ever invite a spirit into your presence. Do you understand?"

"Even a good one?"

Emmanuel dropped his head. "Mijo, there are no good ones."

"Oh. I'm sorry, Tio," he replied. "But the house was haunted before I played with the Ouija board, I swear."

Josephine recalled Emma saying she was seeing things well before David moved in. The wall heater had been acting up since we moved in, too. "He's right. Something else is going on in this house."

Wide-eyed, David bobbed his head vigorously.

Josephine observed Emma's facial expression. Her eyes were shut tight, as though she was trying to drown out the world around her. My poor baby shouldn't be going through this, she thought. Her patience expired, she turned to Emmanuel and said, "Let's move. Today."

"No, that's what they want," Emmanuel replied without hesitating.

"They? Who's they?"

"The demons. They want to see this so-called man of God get bullied out of his home."

She recognized a glint of pride in his eyes. There's more to it, she thought. "You're worried about what the congregation will think, aren't you?"

He gave no response.

"No one needs to know. It's no one's business but our own," she said.

"But I'll know!" he exclaimed, looking at his fragmented reflection in the broken mirror. He inhaled deeply and turned to her. "I know you think this is my pride getting in the way, and I would be lying if I said it has nothing to do with it. But this is about more than pride—it's about fulfilling my duty—my Godly purpose."

She crossed her arms.

He continued, "This is not the first time evil has attacked, and it won't be the last. What are we supposed to do? Run away when things get hard?"

She scoffed.

"No, absolutely not. Because when we do, the enemy wins. The fact is, we are protected by God, and they hate us for it," he said, his eyes moving around the room as though his words were directed at the walls."

He paused.

"So we leave—then what? We let your sister deal with this?" he said incredulously.

She took a deep breath as she imagined the worst—her sister all alone in this house? She couldn't fathom the idea. "No," she said. "But what are we supposed to do?"

"Burning the Ouija board and the deliverance prayers should have stopped the activity in the house, and it didn't," he replied. "There must be another source. We need to find it."

Josephine thought back to what Emmanuel said when they were searching David's room—they should be searching for any evidence of black magic, witchcraft, spells, curses. Her eyes widened with realization. "David, take Emma to the living room," she said, handing Emma to him. She turned to Emmanuel. "I think I can help. Follow me." She stepped into their bedroom and pulled the diary from her nightstand. "Turn to the last page," she said, handing it to Emmanuel.

Emmanuel's face contorted into a twisted mask of revulsion as he read the list of items written in the leather-bound diary. *"Grave dirt, menstrual blood, human bone dust, feathers...* Why didn't you show this to me sooner?""Why didn't you tell me sooner?" he asked, his voice laced with urgency.

"We had a lot going on—didn't seem all that important," she replied, her tone defensive but tinged with guilt. "Do you know what it means?"

He nodded slowly, his mind racing to connect the dots. "It's no grocery list, that's for sure. They're ingredients... For a spell."

"A spell?" Josephine's eyes widened in shock. "Do you think it's related to the activity in the house? And do you think Madeline—the girl from the diary—conjured it?"

"It's possible... I don't know," he shrugged, the weight of uncertainty heavy on his shoulders. "But it's a lead—definitely worth investigating." Emmanuel's thoughts churned, trying to piece together the puzzle. Even if he could confirm that a spell was involved, it was far from enough. He needed to know what kind of spell it was, who conjured it, who the spell was targeting, and for what purpose. It wouldn't be easy. Curses and spells have been around since the beginning of time, practiced in various cultures across the world. Identifying the exact nature of this one would be like finding a needle in a haystack.

"Is there anything else you found that might help?" he asked, his eyes narrowing with intent.

She nodded. "In the pine chest, there was a newspaper article. It said something about a gravesite disturbance. I remember it was dated 1940-something..."

"Did you keep it?" His voice was tight with hope, hanging on the possibility of another clue.

She shook her head, her expression apologetic. "No. I only read the headline."

Emmanuel rattled off questions like an investigator interrogating a key witness. As far as he was concerned, she was one. Though she didn't have all the answers, every piece of information was valuable. Like a puzzle, he would use it to piece together the source of the demonic activity. He already knew graveyard dirt was commonly used in black magic and rituals, so it wasn't a stretch to connect the items listed in the diary with the newspaper article. "Do you remember anything else?"

"The chest contained mostly clothes," she said, her face scrunching up in concentration. Then her brows shot up as a memory surfaced. "There was a small burlap pouch. It contained charcoal, I think."

"Charcoal?" Emmanuel repeated, his mind sifting through everything he knew about rituals and spells. It didn't immediately resonate with anything he was familiar with, but it certainly wasn't a common find. "It must mean something," he murmured, more to himself than to Josephine.

Josephine could see the gears turning in his mind, and she felt a surge of hope. If anyone could figure this out, it was Emmanuel. "What do we do next?"

"We need to find out what kind of spell these ingredients were used for," he said, his voice steady despite the uncertainty they faced. "And we need to figure out who performed it—and why."

"But how?" she asked, the enormity of the task beginning to weigh on her.

Emmanuel glanced at the diary in his hands, then back at Josephine. "We start by digging deeper into the people that used to live here and the history of this house. There's something here, some connection between the past and the present. We just need to find it."

Chapter 38

I**T IS A COMMON MISCONCEPTION** that there exists a one-size-fits-all approach to dealing with demonic activity. Confronting such malevolent forces requires skill, preparation, and a deep understanding of the enemy. In many cases, no amount of prayer, crucifixes, or holy water will suffice if the origin of the dark force—or forces—remains unknown. Like a seasoned commander preparing for battle, one must clearly define objectives, gather intelligence, assess resources, and forge alliances with those who share common goals and can offer support when needed.

For Emmanuel, burning the Ouija board was a small victory—a necessary step in his strategy—but it was only the beginning. Much work remained. He enlisted his trusted friend Daniel, bringing him up to speed on the scant information he had pieced together.

As Emmanuel stepped into the lobby of the Chicago Public Library, he spotted Daniel waiting near the entrance. "Thanks for meeting here," Emmanuel whispered as he approached.

"I arrived early and got a head start," Daniel replied.

"Find anything?"

"Oh yeah," Daniel said, a hint of excitement in his voice. "Follow me."

He led Emmanuel to the public computer section, where they sat down. Daniel handed him a printout. "I found the article your wife mentioned, dated 1946, about the gravesite disturbances. But I also found another, more interesting one, dated February 6th, 1947."

Emmanuel read the headline aloud, *"Police suspect Hoodoo in Al Capone gravesite disturbance."* He looked up at Daniel. "Hoodoo? Is that the same as Voodoo?"

"No," Daniel clarified. "Voodoo is a religion. Hoodoo is the magic derived from it. Historically, it was used during the enslavement era around the Mississippi Valley for curative and protective purposes, and to communicate with ancestors. Over time, it expanded to include spells for justice or revenge."

"Give me a moment," Emmanuel said as he read the article:

According to Hillside police, the grave of notorious Chicago gangster Al Capone was disturbed last week at Mount Carmel Catholic Cemetery in suburban Hillside, where the Capone family is buried. The disturbance, part of a series of similar incidents, occurred during late-night hours. Cemetery maintenance workers noticed disturbed earth among rows of graves at the back boundary of the cemetery, along with unusual objects scattered over and around several grave sites. One grave had been partially disinterred, with holes as deep as three feet. Objects found included black chicken feathers, black candle wax, coins, strips of black cloth, unidentified blood, red pepper pods, and empty black pepper packets. Workers also discovered jars filled with an unrecognizable liquid substance deposited at the bottom of the dugout area over a casket.

Hillside law enforcement has partnered with forensic anthropologists at the University of Chicago to investigate the disturbances. Initially, authorities believed these activities to be the work of teenage pranksters. However, after consulting with forensic anthropologists who used forensic archaeology and cultural anthropological knowledge of African American traditions, it was revealed that hoodoo practices are to blame for the disturbances at the grave sites.

Emmanuel stared at the article, trying to connect the information to the disturbances in the house. The timing seemed right; the ingredients matched the list in the diary, and the cemetery was right across the street. He turned to Daniel. "Did you find any other reported gravesite disturbances related to hoodoo?"

Daniel shook his head. "Not a single report in the entire state since then. If you ask me, the article your wife found in the chest was a keepsake."

"Assuming it was a keepsake, why disturb another grave so soon after?" Emmanuel asked.

Daniel shrugged. "Beats me."

Emmanuel typed "Al Capone burial date" into the search bar. The library filled with the cacophony of screeches, beats, and static as the internet came to life. He leaned in, squinting at the screen. "Al Capone was buried on February 4, 1947."

"The grave was fresh. They must have targeted it," Daniel said. "But why?"

"I don't know." Emmanuel leaned back in his seat. "What about the jars filled with an unrecognizable liquid substance? Any idea what that could mean?"

"Not yet," Daniel replied. He placed a book on Emmanuel's desk.

Emmanuel read the title aloud: "Hoodoo, Conjuration, Witchcraft, and Rootwork." He shifted his gaze to Daniel. "Looks like I have some reading to do."

Daniel dropped four more lengthy books on the desk with a thud. "Volumes one through five," he said with a wry smile.

"Anything else I should know?" Emmanuel asked.

Daniel's smile faded. "Maybe," he said. "I found something else that happened in the area around the same time. I don't know if it's relevant, but it sure is interesting." He handed Emmanuel another printout.

Emmanuel's eyes scanned the bold letters of the headline:

HILLSIDE FAMILY ELECTROCUTED IN CAR:
YOUNG CHILD IS LONE SURVIVOR

A gasp escaped his lips. "Oh my God."

Daniel shook his head. "Gruesome, isn't it?"

"It's the stuff of nightmares," Emmanuel said, his voice barely above a whisper.

Daniel leaned in. "And one more thing—I did some research on the amethyst from the doorknobs."

Emmanuel looked up, intrigued. "And?"

"I think there's a connection." Daniel handed him another sheet of paper. "See for yourself."

Chapter 39

H E HAD NEVER SMELLED BURNT FLESH, but Emmanuel imagined it was something putrid and nauseating, like the smell of leather being tanned over a flame, and he couldn't shake off the stench. It was a horrendous scene his imagination had concocted, one he desperately wanted to purge from his mind. He had likely spent too much energy on that damn article—reading and re-reading the account of what had happened to those people just down the road all those years ago. Mike Marino, his wife Jane, their sixteen-year-old son Mike Jr., and his girlfriend, Linda, all died that night. Emmanuel assumed, or perhaps hoped, that the sheer volume of research he had done during the day would be enough to push the details of the article out of his mind. But it was the middle of the night, and here he was, tossing and turning, the gruesome images playing on a loop in his mind. He could picture it all so clearly. And when he finally drifted off to sleep, he had his first dream. The details largely mirrored what he remembered from the article, but where the article left gaps, his imagination filled them in. Having never dreamt before, he didn't know what to expect, but it felt as though he was a spectator, watching a haunting movie unfold.

The nightmare unfolded in Hillside, in the spring of 1947, near Emmanuel's home. The small town's high school was alive with the buzz of anticipation for the Spring Fling that night, but winter had stubbornly refused to loosen its icy grip. A fierce storm loomed, threatening to derail the evening's plans. A last-minute decision was made: Mike Jr. and Linda, who had hoped to attend the dance unchaperoned, were met with a firm denial from his parents. Mr. Marino argued that Mike was just a kid, inexperienced in navigating the treacherous winter roads, and liable to get both himself and Linda killed. The parents decided it was too dangerous—not worth the risk for a school dance—and told him he couldn't go. But Mike Jr., determined and relentless, had spent months planning the evening with Linda and knew she would be heartbroken if he didn't take her. Finally, they relented on one condition—Mr. Marino would drive them to and from the dance—and though frustrated, Mike Jr. agreed.

When the time came, Mrs. Marino and their younger son joined the drive as chaperones. The article hadn't provided the finer details, but Emmanuel's mind filled in the blanks. He pictured Mrs. Marino as the typical overzealous mother, eager to capture memories of the stunning young couple with her camera. In the backseat, he imagined the youngest son, sitting awkwardly, squeezed into the corner as far from the two lovebirds as possible, who were cozied up to one another, holding hands and exchanging smiles.

Emmanuel saw the icy roads just as the article had described, the car's tires struggling for traction as it descended a steep hill. The vehicle began to slide, the world outside the windows blurring as gravity took control. No one in the car was particularly alarmed—this was Hillside, after all, and sliding on ice was as common as breathing. "Keep the steering wheel straight and ease off the accelerator. Hard braking or swerving will only make it worse," Mr. Marino said calmly, repeating the same advice Emmanuel's father had once given him during his own driving lessons on Chicago's treacherous winter roads.

Mr. Marino managed to regain control of the car, bringing it to a stop at the bottom of the hill. The tension in the vehicle was palpable, the kind of tension that clings to the air like fog after a storm. Then, suddenly, they heard it—a deafening crack that shattered the stillness of the night, reverberating through the cold air like the shot of a rifle. Eyes wide with fear, they scanned their surroundings, hearts pounding in their chests, silently praying they were safe. A moment later, a thunderous crash echoed through the night as a tall birch tree, burdened by the weight of the storm, toppled fifty feet ahead of them. Nervous laughter and sighs of relief filled the car, but the moment of respite was fleeting.

Overhead, a power line, sagging under the relentless weight of snow and ice, snapped free from its post. Emmanuel watched in horror as the line whipped wildly through the air like an enraged serpent, its sparks lighting up the night like a Fourth of July firework. The car's occupants were frozen in fear as the cable slashed back and forth across the road, its movements erratic and deadly. Finally, the line lay still, a sinister, dormant threat stretched across the width of the road, glowing faintly in the dim light of the storm.

The dream lingered with Emmanuel, a haunting reminder of the fragility of life and the thin line that separates safety from disaster. It was as if the nightmare had imprinted itself on his very soul, leaving behind an indelible mark that he could neither shake nor fully understand.

It seemed they had narrowly escaped disaster once again, until the faint glow of headlights appeared in the distance. Mr. Marino reached for the door.

"What are you doing?" his wife asked, her voice trembling with fear.

"I'm going to wave down that car," he replied, determination etched into his features.

Unbeknownst to them, the downed power line slithered like a silent predator, inching closer to their vehicle. Mr. Marino opened the car door and lifted his leg to step out.

"Is it safe?" she asked, her hand instinctively reaching for his. Just as his foot made contact with the ground, his muscles tensed, and his body began to violently tremble. The electricity from the power line surged through the waterlogged ground, a deadly current snaking its way into his body. His wife's body jerked back, her movements eerily synchronized with his, as the deadly current found her too.

"Mom!" Mike Jr. screamed, reaching out in desperation for his mother.

"Mike, no!" Linda cried, yanking him back with all her strength. But it was too late—the electricity shot through Mrs. Marino, passing through Mike Jr., and then into Linda, exiting with explosive force, leaving a baseball-sized hole in her chest. The acrid stench of burned flesh and singed hair filled the air, a grim testament to the tragedy that had just unfolded.

In what the news would later hail as a miracle, the unnamed son, the lone survivor, sat frozen in the corner of the car, his chest pressed tightly against his knees. His wide, unblinking eyes darted from side to side, taking in the grotesque scene of charred muscles, skin melted away to reveal bone, and ribs grotesquely exposed.

He jolted awake, heart pounding, drenched in sweat. Could what happened to the Marinos be connected to the house? The digital clock glowed ominously—3:00 AM. The witching hour. He sighed, knowing there was nothing more he could do tonight. Tomorrow would bring more clarity, he hoped.

But sleep was now a distant memory. After futile attempts to calm his racing mind, he resorted to the one ritual that had always anchored him in times of turmoil. He slid out of bed and sank to his knees, the coolness of the floor grounding him as he tried to block out the physical world and connect with the spiritual. His lips moved in a fervent, silent prayer, words pouring out of him like a torrent as he pleaded for answers, his body trembling with the raw intensity of his desperation.

Then, like a beacon cutting through a storm, his mind stilled, and his thoughts sharpened with sudden clarity. The answer he sought had been just within reach all along... *Jillian*.

Chapter 40

WHEN JOSEPHINE KNOCKED on Jillian's door that afternoon to ask if she and her husband could come by later to talk, Jillian agreed without hesitation. They seemed like decent people—quiet, family-oriented, and genuinely concerned about the well-being of their loved ones. Nothing about them raised any red flags. If she had any concerns, she wouldn't have allowed her son to spend time with their nephew. Besides, Jillian mostly kept to herself and didn't have any neighbors she considered close friends. This might be a good opportunity to get to know them better, she thought.

A knock at the door pulled her from her thoughts. Jillian glanced at her watch.

5:30 PM. Right on time.

"Well, hello, neighbors," she greeted, opening the door with a warm smile. She pushed the screen door open. "Please, come on in."

"Thanks so much for having us," Josephine said, stepping inside.

"It's my pleasure—have a seat wherever you'd like," Jillian said, gesturing to the living room.

"Thank you," Emmanuel replied as they settled into the plush cushions of the couch.

"So, is there anything in particular you'd like to talk about?" Jillian asked. "Not that I mind the company. I just hope JR isn't causing you any trouble."

An awkward silence settled over the room.

"We found a Ouija board in David's room," Emmanuel said.

"Oh my," Jillian said, her brows shooting up in surprise.

"You didn't know?" Emmanuel asked. "About the Ouija board?"

"How could I have possibly known?" she replied defensively. "I hope you don't think I allow that sort of thing under my roof."

"No, of course not. I'm sorry," Emmanuel said quickly. "I didn't mean to be presumptuous. That's not what we're here to discuss."

She hadn't a clue where the conversation was going, but she suddenly felt uneasy. When they met before, Emmanuel had introduced himself as a pastor, and she left it at that, not seeing a need to ask for details. Now, she was questioning whether she had allowed herself to get sucked into a meeting she wanted no part in. Are these the kind of people who go around knocking on doors, leaving religious brochures? she wondered. She crossed her arms, leaned back in her seat, and said, "Listen, before you continue, I must assure you I am very happy with my religion and have no interest in changing it."

Emmanuel and Josephine exchanged wide-eyed glances. "We are so sorry—that's not what we're here to discuss," Josephine said quickly.

Jillian exhaled an audible sigh of relief. "Oh, thank goodness," she said with a laugh.

Smiles washed over their faces, breaking the tension in the room.

Emmanuel's gaze settled on a family photo hanging on the wall. "Will your husband be joining us?"

"Oh, no—I'm a widow."

"I'm so sorry."

She shrugged. "It's been five years... John was a truck driver. He fell asleep behind the wheel during an all-nighter."

"That's terrible," Josephine said, shaking her head with her mouth downturned. "I can't even imagine."

"I never liked him being a truck driver," Jillian admitted. She thought back to the countless disagreements they had about his line of work. He was on the road a lot with little sleep—always driving, rushing, at all hours of the night to meet impossible deadlines. The work was hard on his body too—he developed arthritis before he turned thirty from all that squatting and lifting, loading and unloading heavy cargo. If she had her way, he would have quit long before the accident that took him. But he was stubborn, and the pay was good, so she grinned and bore it. "It was hard... Still is. JR and I sometimes stay up late, watching old home movies—it makes us feel like he's still with us. But we're OK. I know I'll see him soon enough."

Emmanuel smiled gently. "You sound like a woman of firm beliefs."

"I certainly am."

"In that case, I hope you don't mind me asking... Are you familiar with the concept of spiritual gifts?"

"Yes," she responded quickly, without hesitating.

"You see, all of God's children have them."

"I'm aware," she said in a tone that made it clear she was uninterested in the topic. It wasn't the first time a keen observer had broached this subject after noticing her heightened level of awareness—her ability to sense things and see things that others could not. The conversations always followed a pattern. Someone always wanted something from her—asked her to use her gift—something she had promised herself long ago she would never do.

"Well, this is turning out to be a much easier conversation than I thought," Emmanuel said, forcing an awkward laugh.

Jillian stared at him with a tight, thin-lipped mouth and arms folded.

He cleared his throat. "Have you ever talked to anyone about your gift?"

"I know why you're here," she said, standing from her seat. "I'm sorry, but I can't help you."

"You can't or you won't?" Josephine asked.

"Does it matter?"

"Yes."

"Why?"

"Because I can walk out of here right now, no problem, if you *can't* help us. But no amount of church will hold me back if you *won't* help us."

"Josephine!" Emmanuel exclaimed.

"Are you threatening me?" Jillian asked, her voice tight with anger.

"Not a threat," Josephine said. "That's a promise."

"JOSEPHINE!" Emmanuel shouted. "That is no way to behave." He turned to Jillian. "I am so sorry. Please forgive her."

"Yes, forgive me... For what I'm *about* to do," Josephine said, rolling up her sleeves, her eyes glinting with anger. She stood up, hands clenched in fists by her side. "What kind of person are you, anyway?"

Jillian stood up too. "Excuse me?" she said incredulously. "You don't know anything about me."

Josephine's gaze flicked to the wooden crucifix hanging by the front door, then to the crucifix on the wall behind Jillian, and finally to the gold crucifix pendant around her neck. "I noticed all these crucifixes hanging on your walls and neck."

"So?"

"So what kind of good, God-loving person just looks away when someone comes to them in need?" She stepped toward Jillian with a fiery gaze.

Emmanuel gripped Josephine's arm and pulled her back. "What has gotten into you?" he said, scowling.

"I am just so fed up... So tired. And the fact that I am a pastor's wife does not exempt me from what I'm feeling... From what we are going through!"

Jillian's ears perked up at the sound of Josephine's voice, charged with emotion, and her words, loaded with desperation. She didn't know her very well, but she sensed that Josephine wasn't one to go around picking fights. Jillian cleared her throat. "If you don't mind me asking... What exactly are you going through, and what makes you think I can help?"

"Oh, like you don't know," Josephine said, her brows furrowing.

Jillian shook her head. "I'm sorry, I really don't."

"We sacrificed our beautiful, safe home so that we could move into that nightmare of a house next door, so we could pay the church's bills and keep the doors open. Now Candy is dead, and we're being terrorized by demons in our own home!"

Jillian gasped. "David's little sister passed away?" She sank into her seat as she absorbed the news. David had been over that day, and the day before that. He didn't say much, but that was nothing unusual. But now that she thought about it, he had been quieter than usual.

"You really didn't know?" Josephine asked.

Jillian shook her head.

"Honey, that's not how her gift works... She's not psychic," Emmanuel explained. He turned to Jillian. "Candy had an accident in the backyard just over a week ago, and there are clear signs of demonic activity in the house—activity powerful enough to be responsible for Candy's death."

Jillian placed her hand over her heart. "I assure you I didn't know," she said. "I mean, I'd be lying if I said I have never had a weird feeling, an instinct, that something bad was going to happen." She straightened her posture, her eyes locking with Josephine's. "But God as my witness, if I knew that little girl was in harm's way, I would have done something."

"I don't understand," Josephine said, turning to Emmanuel. "If she's telling the truth, how is she supposed to help us?"

"She can see things we can't... Like a metal detector for evil. If she comes to the house, she should be able to help us identify the source of the evil so that we can destroy it." He turned to Jillian. "So what do you say, neighbor... Can we borrow your metal detector?"

Chapter 41

DANIEL DROPPED EVERYTHING the moment he got the call from Emmanuel. His heart raced as he absorbed the news—Jillian, the neighbor, had agreed to come to the house. With her involvement, along with Emmanuel and himself, they finally had the resources and resolve needed to confront the demonic activity festering within the home. This would be Daniel's first time assisting with the exorcism of a place, and although the task was daunting, he was eager and ready.

Emmanuel had reassured him that the process was much the same as dealing with the possession of a person, but Daniel knew that nothing could fully prepare him for what lay ahead. The air around the house seemed to thrum with a dark energy, as if the malevolent presence inside was aware of their intentions. Yet, despite the creeping dread that clung to the edges of his thoughts, Daniel's determination burned bright. He was about to step into uncharted territory, but he was resolved to see it through.

While Emmanuel had spent years delving deep into the complexities of spiritual warfare, Daniel had a simpler, more straightforward approach. He had developed what he called *The Three P's* for understanding demonic possessions:

The Person: The young are particularly vulnerable because they haven't yet had time to develop strong moral values. Demons prey on this weakness, manipulating behavior and corrupting innocence. If no child is present, demons will target the next most vulnerable individual, much like a lion going after the weakest gazelle in a herd—those least likely to resist.

The Place: Though less common, demons can form attachments to specific places or objects. They seek out whatever they can gain authority over, exploiting any rights granted to them by the people in power. The extent of permission given to them determines their level of influence and activity.

The Pig: Drawing from the Biblical account, when Jesus encountered a man possessed by a legion of demons, they begged Him not to send them back to hell. Instead, they pleaded to be cast into a herd of pigs. This illustrates that demons would rather inhabit an earthly creature—be it an animal or insect—than be forced back to hell.

Daniel was confident that with *The Three P's* in mind, he could help Emmanuel and Jillian navigate the impending confrontation. Nearly everything Daniel knew about combating demonic activity, he had learned from Emmanuel. Under Emmanuel's guidance, he had come to view the battle against demons much like any athletic sport—whether it was basketball, football, tennis, or boxing. In every case, victory hinged on preparation, studying the opponent, and anticipating their next move. This situation was no different. Stepping into Emmanuel's home, Daniel felt like he was gearing up for a big fight.

"Hey Cap, I brought the supplies—everything you asked for," Daniel said, carrying a large paper bag.

"Thank you. Close the door behind you," Emmanuel instructed, his tone focused and calm.

Daniel shut the door firmly behind him. "Where should I begin?"

"Cover the electrical outlets and windows. I'll handle the back door and bathroom," Emmanuel replied. "And move fast."

Daniel nodded, already in motion. He knew that in a situation like this, speed and precision were crucial. The stakes were high, but he was ready to face whatever came next, trusting in the preparation and lessons Emmanuel had instilled in him.

He nodded, "Aye, aye." Daniel sprang into action, rushing through the house as if preparing for a hurricane. He unplugged anything that could fall under demonic control or be used to distract them—televisions, lamps, stereos, appliances, alarm clocks. The howling wind outside seemed to echo the urgency of his movements, a dark omen in the air. The floors groaned beneath him as he pushed furniture against the windows, transforming the home into a fortress ready to withstand the onslaught of sheer evil.

He hurried to the bathroom, breathless. "Do you need anything in here?" he asked, his voice edged with urgency.

"No, I've got this room covered," Emmanuel replied, spraying the surfaces and walls with flame retardant. "Cover the windows." He handed Daniel a roll of masking tape. "And hurry—I want to do this tonight before Jillian changes her mind."

"You think she'll change her mind?" Daniel asked, pausing only for a moment.

"I don't know, but for our sake, I hope not. Whatever we're dealing with—it's watching us. It must know she's coming, and I'm sure it's pissed."

"Aye, aye," Daniel said, grabbing the tape. He raced from room to room, his footsteps echoing like a drumbeat as he covered each window with tape to prevent shattering. He had seen demons blow out church windows more than once and knew the same could easily happen in a house.

As he finished, Daniel stepped back to survey his work, his eyes scanning the windows for any vulnerabilities. Suddenly, his breath caught in his throat, and he stumbled back, falling to the floor, startled by what he saw through the window. *Holy shit! What the hell was that!?* His heart pounded as he took a deep breath, forcing himself to approach the window again.

Outside, a mangy black dog stood, surrounded by a cloud of buzzing flies so loud that Daniel could hear them through the glass. The dog's single good eye gleamed with sinister intent, locking onto Daniel with an unnerving focus. Thick strands of saliva dripped from its snarling mouth, and its emaciated frame trembled with barely contained anticipation.

"Ugh," Daniel shuddered, tearing his gaze away. "You are one ugly dog. I would not want to be in the same room as you."

Chapter 42

JILLIAN NEVER TOLD A SOUL what she had really seen that day at the grocery store when she was young, nor had she revealed anything she'd seen since. Concealing that part of herself hadn't been easy, especially as her visions grew more frequent over time. Any inadvertent slips were quickly masked as women's intuition or lucky guesses. It was a defense mechanism she'd perfected, one that kept her safe. So when Emmanuel asked for her help, she instinctively gave him the answer her parents would have demanded, just as she had done her entire life. That would have been the end of the conversation—if she hadn't learned that Candy had died right next door. It could just as easily have been JR, she thought. So she agreed to help. And this time, her parents weren't there to force her to look the other way.

As the sun began its descent into the horizon, casting hues of blood-orange and crimson across the sky, the cemetery was bathed in an eerie glow. But as the last rays of sunlight faded, Jillian felt an unsettling chill settle over the once serene atmosphere. She turned to Emmanuel, unease evident in her voice. "Are you sure you wouldn't rather do this in the morning?" she asked, rubbing her neck as the tension crept in.

He shook his head. "Now is as good a time as any," he replied. There was rumbling as a car pulled into the driveway. Emmanuel glanced at his watch. "Right on time," he said.

"Is someone else joining us?" Jillian asked.

"Yes. Daniel," he replied. "He's a good friend and spiritually strong. He was here earlier helping me prepare the house. He will be assisting me."

Jillian's heart skipped a beat as her gaze fell on Daniel, who was driving the vehicle with a poised and confident posture. He turned off the ignition with a practiced ease that exuded self-assuredness—a quality she found unexpectedly intriguing. She hadn't dated since her husband passed, and she had no interest in doing so, but something about Daniel drew her in. Quickly, she pried her eyes away and turned around, careful not to be caught staring.

Daniel stepped out of the car, the door shutting with a decisive click. Butterflies fluttered in Jillian's stomach, and she felt her face flush like a schoolgirl with a crush as his footsteps grew louder, approaching her.

Josephine, noticing her reaction, placed her hands over Emma's ears, leaned in toward Jillian, and whispered with a knowing smile, "Handsome, isn't he?"

Jillian tried to shrug it off, but her lips curled into a small smile.

"Just so you know, he's available," Josephine added, her voice teasing.

"Is he?" Jillian responded, her eyes sparkling with a hint of surprise. Judging by the few strands of gray beginning to weave through his full head of thick, lustrous hair, he appeared to be just around her age—perhaps in his early to mid-thirties.

"Divorced," Josephine said.

"Oh," she replied with a tone tinged with disappointment. *With a face like that, he must be a womanizer*, she thought.

Emmanuel leaned in and whispered, "His ex-wife didn't support his work in the ministry—left him for a guy in a rock band."

"You don't say," she replied, smiling inwardly.

"Thanks for coming," Emmanuel said as Daniel approached.

"I'm Daniel. It's nice to meet you," he said, extending his hand to Jillian.

"It's a pleasure," she replied, shaking his hand.

"Are we ready to get started?" Daniel asked.

"Get started with what?" Emma asked.

Emmanuel crouched down to her level. "We're going to get rid of the things you've been seeing, mija."

Her eyes widened. "You are? You mean, you believe me?"

He nodded. "I'm sorry we didn't hear you before. I promise, from now on, we'll be listening."

Emma's face lit up in pure delight.

Josephine reached for Emma's hand. "Let's go angel. David is going to watch you at Jillian's house for a little while."

"Momma, wait," Emma said. She turned to her father. "Daddy, I have something to say."

"Yes, mija?"

"Look in David's room."

He nodded. "I will. I promise."

She smiled softly as she walked away with her mother.

"Let's get inside," Emmanuel said, turning to Jillian. "Josephine will catch up."

She nodded, but as Emmanuel and Daniel stepped toward the front door, Jillian found herself rooted to the spot, unable to move.

Daniel noticed and turned back to her. "Is something wrong?"

Suddenly, Jillian felt a wave of disorientation, as if her connection to reality was slipping away. Her heart pounded erratically in her chest, and her breath came in short, shallow gasps. *I'm having a heart attack,* she thought, panic surging through her.

"Jillian? Are you OK?" Daniel asked, concern etched on his face as he stepped closer.

Instinctively, she reached out, placing a trembling hand on Daniel's shoulder to steady herself, while her other hand pressed against her throat as it tightened. Her eyes widened in terror, and she gasped for air, the sensation of choking overwhelming her. "I'm choking," she managed to say, her voice strained and filled with fear.

"Let's lay her down on the ground," Emmanuel said urgently, his voice tight with concern. "She's being attacked." His words struck Jillian like a lightning bolt, igniting a fresh wave of panic that surged through her. Her mind spiraled into terror, conjuring the terrifying image of a demonic entity looming over her, its malevolent eyes piercing into the depths of her soul. She squeezed her eyes shut, but the vision only intensified, becoming disturbingly vivid. She saw it clearly: three twisted, enormous horns jutted from the creature's shrunken, shriveled head, which sat atop a long, sinewy body covered in blistered, crackling skin. Its cold, leathery hands wrapped tighter around her throat, each icy touch sending shivers of dread through her. The creature's breath, hot and foul, assaulted her senses, carrying with it the stench of decay and brimstone. Paralyzed by fear, Jillian thrashed her head from side to side, desperately trying to escape the invisible grip that was tightening around her, choking the life out of her.

"You're OK, Jillian. Just breathe. You are not being physically attacked. The demon is oppressing your thoughts. But you're stronger than it thinks. Do you understand?" Emmanuel's voice was firm, trying to anchor her to reality.

Focusing on his words, Jillian began to take slow, deep breaths, gradually calming her racing heartbeat. The crushing pressure around her windpipe started to ease, the tight grip of terror loosening its hold. "Thank you. I'm OK," she finally whispered, her voice barely audible as the fear slowly receded.

"See? Feeling better already, aren't you?" Daniel said, his tone gentle and reassuring.

Jillian pushed herself up into a seated position on the ground, her hands pressing against her abdomen as she tried to quell the nausea churning in the pit of her stomach. She longed to join them inside, to help uncover the source of the evil she had sensed lurking since childhood. But her body, still reeling from the ordeal, seemed unwilling to cooperate. Her face glistened with sweat, and her brow furrowed in frustration as she whispered, "I'm so sorry. I don't think I can do this."

Chapter 43

D ANIEL KNEW THEY COULDN'T identify the source of the demonic activity in the house without Jillian. In cases like this, where a place, rather than a person, was at the heart of the disturbance, they were at a disadvantage. There were no witnesses to question, no testimonies to gather about how the disturbances began or escalated. The usual trail of clues—who had been in the house, what they had done, and why—was frustratingly absent. They needed divine intervention, and Jillian was the key. She had the gift to see what they couldn't, to uncover the hidden origins of the evil plaguing the home.

But Daniel also sensed that Jillian needed them as much as they needed her. He recognized the symptoms she was experiencing—the shortness of breath, the racing heart, the sick feeling in her stomach. They were all too familiar to him. He had been there before, standing on the precipice of something terrifying and unknown, when his faith and his fear were in a fierce tug-of-war. He could see it in Jillian's eyes—the inner battle between wanting to run from what she sensed and the pull to confront it head-on.

Daniel stepped closer to her, his voice steady and reassuring. "We're in this together, Jillian. You don't have to face it alone. We need your gift, but more importantly, you have us to lean on. Whatever we uncover, we'll face it together."

Jillian's gaze softened as she met Daniel's eyes. "May I speak to you alone?" Daniel asked, extending his hand toward her.

She nodded, gripping his hand as he gently pulled her to her feet. Daniel turned to Emmanuel and Josephine. "We just need a minute," he said, leading Jillian a few steps away from the others. He turned to face her, his expression earnest. "Look, I know you don't know me from Adam, but I feel compelled to say something... I think I can relate to what you're going through."

"How could you possibly?" she asked, lowering her eyes on him.

"Your symptoms—do you feel waves of nausea? Like you could lose your footing at any moment? Maybe an impending sense of doom?"

She furrowed her brow as though confused by how much he knew. "You have the gift, too?"

"Of discerning spirits? No," he replied. "But I know a thing or two about anxiety, and you just had a panic attack. "

She nodded. "I figured that. I mean, not right away. At one point, I imagined I was being strangled by a demon."

He giggled.

She glared at him incredulously.

He cleared his throat. "Sorry."

"What if it happens again?"

"Nah," he replied, shaking his head. "You were caught off guard, that's all. We weren't even in the house yet. You'll be ready next time."

"So what caused it?" Jillian asked. "Your anxiety, I mean."

"The short answer—my ex-wife," he scoffed and shook his head, thinking back to the days when he tried so hard to make the marriage work. They met at church, which he hoped would make for the beginnings of a long, happy marriage. He went into the marriage in his thirties, ready to settle down, believing that divorce wasn't an option. *There wouldn't be a problem we couldn't work out together*, he thought. But she was much younger, sheltered, less mature. "In retrospect, we weren't a good match."

"So what's the long answer?" she asked.

"I'm not the person she wanted me to be," he replied. "I tried for a long time. I thought I could fake it till I made it... We went to couples' retreats, marriage counseling, therapy. In the end, I couldn't meet her demands without dimming my light–changing who I was–I mean, who I really was. Turns out, faking who you are takes a toll on you after a while. I developed so much anxiety, it made me physically ill. That's what happens when you dim your light, shrink yourself to fit someone else's expectations."

She nodded. "Your story reminds me of *Dirty Dancing*."

"What do you mean?" he asked, titling his head quizzically.

"You know–the movie? Except in the movie, Johnny believes in Baby's ability to shine and be herself, despite the expectations and limitations imposed by others."

"Sorry, it doesn't ring a bell," he said, shaking his head.

"Are you kidding?" she said with a disbelieving glare.

He shrugged. "Have you ever had to dim your light for someone?"

She nodded. "My parents... Especially my father. He was worried that if I exposed my 'light,' evil would come knocking."

He scoffed.

"Excuse me?" she said, leveling a glowering stare at him.

"I'm sorry, but that's just..." He hesitated as he searched for the right word. "Well, ignorant."

"Ignorant?"

"Light shines brighter in the dark; believe me, you shine your light, and evil will not come knocking—*it'll go running*."

She shrugged. "I get that. But my father lost his family when he was young; he was the baby. It was really tough on him. I guess that's why I gave in, gave him a break."

"I'm sorry to hear that," he replied.

"Can I show you something?" she asked. She reached into her purse, retrieved a piece of paper from her wallet, and hesitantly handed it to him before pulling back. "Promise you won't laugh?"

"I promise."

It was a newspaper clipping—dated August 9, 1976—that had been laminated with strips of scotch tape. "What's this about?" he asked, his eyes glued to the article.

"Read it."

He read to himself:

GIRL HAILED HERO AFTER LEADING POLICE TO MISSING
KIDS

Chicago police responded to a home on Jet Lane in Chicago Sunday afternoon after a local girl, eleven-year-old Jillian Marino, courageously tipped off an off-duty police officer at the Hyde Park Co-op Sunday morning regarding the welfare of a child.

Daniel's crystal blue eyes strayed to Jillian. "Jillian Marino? Is that you?"

She nodded. "Marino is my maiden name. I still go by my married name these days—Russo."

He repeated the name in his thoughts. *Marino, Marino... Why does the name sound familiar?* he wondered. He couldn't place it. "Are you divorced?" he asked.

"Widowed."

"I'm sorry." He turned his gaze back to the newspaper clipping and continued reading:

Jenna Harvey, age 10, who has been missing since the summer of 1973, was found with the suspect, forty-two-year-old William Shumer, inside the grocery store. The suspect then led authorities to his home, where they found two juvenile children, a boy, age 13, and a girl, age 15, locked inside a 12x12 foot room in a shed behind the primary residence. Investigators said the children had no way to exit the building, no running water, no bathroom, and were deprived of adequate hygienic care and food.

"You've carried this around with you all these years?" he asked.

She nodded.

"Why?"

"A trophy, I suppose? That's when I realized I had a gift. I still remember how I felt that day." A nostalgic smile tugged at the corners of her mouth. "I was just a little girl, but I felt like I was ten feet tall. Brave. Strong. Confident..."

"*Unstoppable*."

She locked eyes with him. "Yes—exactly... I haven't felt that way since."

Daniel reached for her hand and locked his gaze onto hers, searching for the hidden treasure he knew was in her soul. "You're still that hero, that unstoppable force of nature," he said, his voice trembling with the weight of his convictions. "We believe in you, but that isn't enough. You need to believe in yourself."

She straightened her posture and smiled gently. Her eyes glimmered with a subtle hint of newfound confidence.

"Now let's get out there and let that light of yours shine bright, because nobody puts Baby in a corner," he said, smiling.

She scoffed, "*Nobody puts Baby in a corner*, huh?"

Chapter 44

JILLIAN DIDN'T THINK ANYTHING could convince her to change her mind. The fear that had gripped her earlier felt insurmountable, paralyzing her with a force that went beyond the evil lurking in the house. It was the voice inside her—ingrained by her parents—that had conditioned her from a young age to shrink back, to retreat rather than confront. That inner voice whispered, *Jillian, you can't. It's not safe. Look the other way.*

She wrapped her arms around herself, pulling into a deep stretch as if trying to physically push away the self-limiting thoughts that had always held her back. She knew she was capable—more than capable—but that old programming was deeply rooted, difficult to shake. As she focused inward, a new resolve began to form, slowly but surely. *I can, and I will,* she thought, determination gradually replacing doubt.

"Everything OK?" Emmanuel asked from a distance, his voice tinged with concern.

"Just dandy," Jillian replied, her voice steady. She walked toward him at the door with long, purposeful strides, Daniel following closely behind. The fear was still there, but it no longer controlled her. She had made up her mind. "I'm ready," she said, a newfound confidence in her tone.

"Good. Remember, we're searching for the source of the demonic activity," he reminded her.

She nodded, her resolve firm.

He pushed the door open. "Let's go."

The family's pint-sized pet, brimming with excitement, darted toward the door.

"Come here, Blue!" Josephine called out, crouching down. The pup's ears perked up, and with a burst of energy, she leaped into Josephine's arms. "I forgot about her. Should I run her over to your house?"

"No, let her stay," Jillian replied. "She might help. Dogs have a way of sensing things."

They stepped further inside.

"This is the living room," Emmanuel said, gesturing grandly like a real estate agent showcasing a home.

"Yes, I can see that," Jillian said, her eyes scanning the room's simple layout—sofa chair, couch, coffee table, television set. Everything seemed ordinary, yet a sense of unease lingered in the air.

"Do you see anything? I mean, is anything being revealed to you here?" Josephine asked, her voice tinged with both hope and anxiety.

Jillian took a deep breath and closed her eyes, centering herself in the room. "I feel a sort of heaviness—the air is thicker here than it is outside." She stood still for a moment, attuning herself to the atmosphere, but nothing else stirred. Opening her eyes, she focused on the faint ticking and humming from the ceiling light. "It's much darker here than at my house," she said, rubbing her palms together as if warding off an invisible chill. Her gut told her they were right—something malevolent was lurking nearby, just out of sight, waiting.

"Shall we move on, then?" Emmanuel asked.

"Yes."

She followed Emmanuel through the living room into the kitchen. "Looks a lot like my house," she observed, running her fingertips lightly over the wall.

"I'll give you a minute," he offered, pulling out a chair from the kitchen table.

"That won't be necessary," she replied, sensing nothing out of the ordinary.

They continued through the kitchen and into the connecting hallway. Jillian pressed her palm against the first door down the hall, feeling for any unusual energy. "I assume this is the main bedroom?" she asked.

Emmanuel nodded.

Her gaze settled on the exquisite, though heavily tarnished, brass door-knob—crafted with the meticulous detail of a fine heirloom. "This is gorgeous," she remarked. "I've never seen anything like it."

"The gems are amethyst," Emmanuel said. "Daniel did some research and found out that the stone is associated with spirituality and protection."

That can't be a coincidence, Jillian thought. She turned the knob and pushed the door open just a crack. Instantly, she was overwhelmed by an energy unlike any she had felt in the rest of the house. It was as if the very air around her thickened with intensity. She breathed in deeply, then pulled the door shut, her mind racing.

"Aren't you going to go inside?" Josephine asked.

"No."

Josephine released a loud gasp, her face contorting into a look of dread. "Oh my God, it's been in our bedroom this whole time!?"

"No," Jillian replied.

"What is it, then? Why not step inside?" Emmanuel asked.

"Is that where you pray?" she asked.

"Yes," he replied. "My wife and I both do."

She nodded, "I sensed that."

"How?"

"The air was light... Felt peaceful."

She stepped to the next door.

"That's Emma's room," Emmanuel said.

Jillian turned the knob and pushed the door open. A smile tugged at the corner of her lips as she stepped into the room, which sparkled like no other in the house. Plush pink carpeting enveloped her feet like a gentle hug. Fresh pink wallpaper and velvet curtains adorned the walls, while a polka-dot-pink comforter draped the bed, its surface almost buried beneath a sea of fluffy stuffed animals and plush pink pillows. When her husband was alive, she had dreamed of having a daughter, and she had always imagined her room would look just like this. "You did a lot here," she said, her gaze sweeping the room. "Much more than in the other parts of the house."

"Yes," Josephine replied.

"Why?"

"Why what?"

"Why did you put so much work into this room in particular?"

"I wanted Emma to feel at home."

Jillian's gaze lingered on Josephine, whose eyes were filled with an emotion she recognized but couldn't quite place. Sensing there was more to the story, she pressed gently, "And?"

"And... I wanted her to feel safe."

I recognize it now, Jillian thought, as she saw the glint of despair in Josephine's eyes. After losing John, Josephine had questioned her ability to raise JR alone. Despite her best efforts, she often wondered—

Am I doing enough?

Providing enough?

Loving enough?

And most of all...

Am I good enough?

Moved by the familiar struggle, Jillian stepped closer, placing a reassuring hand on Josephine's arm. With a gentle squeeze, she said, "You're a wonderful mother." It wasn't a prophetic message, but a message of affirmation—one she had wished someone had given her during her own difficult times. The words carried a deeper meaning: "You're not alone. When I see you, I see a mother who would do anything for her child—even if it means taking on the world."

Josephine giggled, tears welling up in her eyes. "Thank you," she whispered, her voice thick with emotion. A tender smile of compassion played on Jillian's lips as her touch lingered on Josephine's arm, a silent promise of solidarity.

"Let's move on," Emmanuel said, gently breaking the moment as he turned to leave the room. They stepped to the next door. "This is David's room," he said, swinging the door open.

As the door creaked open, Blue released a high-pitched yelp, his tiny frame trembling, his fur standing on end. Jillian's heart skipped a beat, memories of her own childhood pup rushing back—how animals always seemed to sense things beyond human perception. "Oh boy, that's not good," she murmured, her voice laced with concern.

Chapter 45

BLUE'S WHIMPERING FILLED THE AIR as Jillian hesitated at the threshold of David's room, peering inside from the hallway. The pup, normally so fearless, cowered in David's arms, trembling. Whatever was in that room had rattled her so much that she refused to even approach the doorway.

"You can put her down," Jillian said softly, her voice low but reassuring.

Josephine set Blue on the floor, and they watched as the tiny dog bolted down the hallway, her little legs carrying her away like a blur, eager to escape whatever unseen presence had spooked her. The sound of her claws tapping frantically against the hardwood echoed in the silence that followed, leaving the two standing there, unnerved by what they couldn't see but felt deep in their bones.

Jillian turned her gaze back to David's room. There wasn't much to see—just some mattresses laid on the floor, a small dresser, and clothes scattered haphazardly, as one might expect in a teenage boy's room. The musty scent of sweat and dirty laundry wafted into the hall, making her wrinkle her nose. "I suppose I should go inside," she said nervously, clearing her throat.

"Go get 'em, tiger... We'll be right behind you," Daniel said, his voice carrying a mix of encouragement and warmth.

Although the phrase was clichéd, Jillian sensed the genuine authenticity in his words, and it bolstered her confidence. She smiled, straightened her posture, and stepped into the room. The floor squeaked beneath her feet with every step, a reminder of the tension in the air, as the others followed closely behind.

"Long and narrow. Odd shape for a room," Josephine said, her voice trailing off.

"Come again?" Jillian asked, turning back to Josephine.

There was no answer.

Her vision began to blur, and she instinctively rubbed her eyes. Then, as though the room had been swallowed by an impenetrable void–

Complete silence.

Complete darkness.

She gasped as the sound of girls' laughter slowly filled the room, then faded just as quickly. A distant flicker of light pierced the darkness, like the brief strike of a match. Shapes and shadows began to emerge, hazy and indistinct at first. The light grew steadily, revealing more of the space around her until the entire room came into focus.

Her gaze fell on the door, instantly recognizing the intricate brass doorknob that now shone like new. She shifted her eyes around the oddly shaped room—long and narrow—its perimeter lined with unlit black candles. In the center, three teenage girls sat on the floor in a circle, holding hands, their faces obscured by the dim light.

An icy chill swept through the room, and the air seemed to crackle with a palpable tension. Jillian heard Josephine's voice, distant and barely audible. "Is she OK? Should we do something?"

"I'm OK. Are you seeing this?" Jillian replied, her voice tinged with both awe and fear.

There was no answer.

The subtle scent of wax and smoke filled the room, and without warning, the candles along the walls ignited one by one, their flames leaping to life in a chain reaction. Startled, Jillian stepped back as the room seemed to take on an otherworldly life of its own. *Leave!* a voice commanded. *Leave now!* The voice was unmistakable, resonating deep within her. The ingrained obedience from years of conditioning urged her to comply, and she instinctively took a step toward the door. But something in her resisted. She stopped, then took a resolute step back.

"No," she said firmly, her voice steadying. "*I'm not going anywhere.*"

Their eyes remained fixed on Jillian as she lay perfectly still on the bed. Her eyes were wide open, her gaze locked on some unknown point as if under a spell, devoid of any awareness of anyone or anything in the room. Daniel, having seen nothing like this before, fought the urge to worry, but it seemed impossible. He turned to Emmanuel. "What should we do?" he asked, anxiety lacing his words.

"Stand by," Emmanuel replied, his tone measured but tense.

Daniel crossed his arms, resisting the impulse to jolt Jillian from her trance.

The faint sound of a muffled voice broke through the silence in the room. "She's trying to say something," Josephine said, leaning in closer.

"Dark. Cold," Jillian murmured, her lips barely moving, the words escaping like whispers from a distant place. They hovered around her, anxious to hear more.

She fell silent.

They exchanged uneasy glances. "What is happening?" Josephine muttered, her voice tinged with fear.

Jillian spoke again, her voice clearer but still monotone, like a transmission from another realm. "Candles flickering. Blowing. Wind."

"She's trying to communicate with us," Emmanuel said, leaning closer. They watched in awe as Jillian used her body as a conduit to send a message from another realm.

"Three girls. Teenagers. Ritual."

"Ritual?" Daniel echoed, turning to Emmanuel with wide eyes. "We were right."

Jillian's lips moved again, but this time her mouth opened and closed, opened and closed, like a fish gasping for air.

"She's trying to say something," Emmanuel urged, tension tightening his voice.

Anticipation hung heavy in the air as they strained to decipher her message. With a vacant gaze, Jillian's mouth moved again, and she muttered, "Mah-ma."

Chapter 46

JILLIAN STOOD COMPLETELY STILL, her breath caught in her throat, as she watched as one of the girls stepped toward her. The girl's skin was a stark, almost unnatural white, like powdered snow, her eyes a chilling icy blue. Her long, nearly white hair was braided neatly down her back, framing a face that was both childlike and haunting. Jillian felt a deep, unsettling recognition—this was the woman who had lived here, now appearing as a girl. The girl moved with a confident, almost regal air, as if she were fully aware of the power she wielded, despite her youth.

Jillian held her breath, fighting the urge to step aside, trusting that she remained invisible in this strange, spectral encounter. The girl passed through her, a cold shiver running down Jillian's spine as she moved toward the door. *It's her*, Jillian thought, confirming what her instincts had already told her. Even in her younger form, those eyes—those piercing, all-seeing eyes—were unmistakable.

The girl opened the door with a quiet grace. "Mama, we're ready for you," she called out. The sound of footsteps echoed ominously from the hallway, each step resonating with an almost supernatural force. The girl stood by the door, holding it open with the poise of someone who had done this many times before, like a doorkeeper ushering in something far more significant than a mere person.

An African American woman entered the room, her skin a rich mahogany that seemed to glow with an otherworldly light. Her dark brown eyes were deep, soulful, and filled with a power that commanded attention. Her hair, styled in a crown of thick curls, added to her regal presence. Clad in a flowing black robe, she exuded an aura of both authority and mystery. The woman's every movement was deliberate, as though she were carrying the weight of generations in her stride. "Madeline, is everything ready?" she asked, her voice smooth and commanding.

"Yes, Mama," the girl, Madeline, replied. She stepped over to an altar draped in a black cloth, its surface cluttered with black candles, herbs, roots, oils, crystals, and glass jars. With careful hands, Madeline picked up a jar containing a crimson substance and handed it to her mother.

"Let us begin," the woman said, moving to the center of the room. Her face remained in shadow as she lit the tip of a smudge stick, its flickering light casting eerie patterns on the walls. The scent of sage, heavy and oppressive, filled the room as smoke curled around her. Jillian watched in awe as the woman traced intricate symbols in the air, her eyes burning with fierce determination. The girls, now holding hands, seemed to surrender themselves to the ritual, their voices rising in a chant that Jillian strained to understand.

Dark, ominous shadows began to dance on the walls, whispering secrets only Jillian could hear. The room grew colder, the air thick with a malevolent energy that made Jillian's heart race. She leaned in, trying to decipher the chant. *Lu-vuv-iz-life?* The words were strange, ancient, their meaning elusive yet powerful. The shadows on the walls seemed to respond to the chant, growing darker, more animated, as if feeding on the energy in the room.

This wasn't just a memory—it was a manifestation of something far more sinister. The ritual had left a stain on the house, a darkness that had seeped into its very foundation. Jillian's fear shifted from what she was seeing to what might still linger in the house, waiting to be awakened.

Chapter 47

"SHE'S COMING BACK TO US," Emmanuel said, his voice calm yet focused, his eyes never leaving Jillian. Slowly, she opened her eyes, blinking as though emerging from a deep, dark place. They had all agreed not to bombard her with questions, choosing instead to let her speak when she was ready. So they waited, the air thick with anticipation.

Jillian rose to her feet, her movements deliberate and slow. The room was silent as they watched her, waiting for her to break the tension with even a single word.

Daniel instinctively leaned forward, ready to move to her side, but Emmanuel gently extended his arm, holding him back. "Wait," he whispered. Jillian, seemingly unaware of their exchange, moved toward the corner of the room. She pressed her palm against the wall, but instantly recoiled, her body jerking back as if she'd touched something scorching hot.

"What is it?" Emmanuel asked, urgency creeping into his voice as he stepped closer.

Jillian's eyes squeezed shut, a low hum of pain escaping her lips as she shook her hand, trying to dispel the searing sensation. "Let me see," Emmanuel urged, concern deepening in his tone. She hesitated, then slowly extended her hand.

Her palm was bright red, with blisters already forming, as though she had pressed it against a hot stove.

"There's something there," she whispered, her voice trembling. "The albino girl put it there."

"Albino girl?" Josephine asked, her voice laced with confusion. "What albino girl?"

"The one that lived here," Jillian responded, her voice barely above a whisper.

Emmanuel sensed the growing unease in the room. "We need to stay calm," he said, his tone steadying the group.

A heavy silence fell over them.

"Did you get her name? The albino girl?" Emmanuel asked gently.

"Madeline," Jillian replied.

"The girl from the diary," Josephine said, the realization dawning on her.

Emmanuel turned to Daniel. "Bring my toolbox—it's in the bathroom under the sink."

"Aye, aye," Daniel replied, hurrying out of the room.

Emmanuel moved to the wall, pressing the tip of his finger against it. The surface was cool to the touch. He scraped at the white, yellowing paint with his fingernail, revealing the sheetrock beneath, likely original to the house's construction. "I don't see anything unusual," he said, squinting at the wall.

"Search lower," Jillian directed.

He knelt down, running his fingers along the wall. A thin slit ran across it, nearly invisible at eye level. "It's been patched," he said, frowning as he examined it. "From the inside."

"From the inside? That's strange, isn't it?" Jillian asked.

He nodded. "To say the least."

"Maybe someone cut through it to access the wall heater on the other side for a repair," Josephine suggested.

Emmanuel, who had spent countless hours troubleshooting the troublesome wall heater, shook his head. "Unlikely. All the access points are more easily reached from the bathroom wall."

Daniel returned with the toolbox. "Here you go," he said, handing it over.

Emmanuel set the toolbox down and pulled out a hammer and a crowbar. He passed the hammer to Daniel. "You punch the holes in the wall," he instructed, pointing to a targeted section. "I'll peel back the sheetrock."

Daniel gripped the hammer tightly and swung it with force. The impact reverberated through the room as the hammer broke through the wall. He continued striking, each blow louder and more intense until the wall finally gave way. Emmanuel inserted the crowbar into one of the punctures and began prying back the sheetrock. A cloud of fine white dust billowed into the air as the plaster crumbled to the floor.

"Be careful not to hit the gas line," Josephine warned, her voice edged with concern.

Emmanuel worked meticulously, pulling back the sheetrock until the hole was wide enough to peer into. "Pass me the flashlight," he said. Daniel quickly retrieved it from the toolbox and handed it over. A bright beam cut through the dim light as Emmanuel switched it on. He crouched down, aiming the light into the dark, dusty cavity within the wall. The smell of dampness and decay wafted up, likely from water seeping in through the shower on the other side.

"See anything?" Daniel asked, leaning in closer.

"Not yet," Emmanuel muttered, his voice tense. Suddenly, his eyes widened, and he jerked back slightly in surprise. He leaned in closer, the flashlight trembling slightly in his hand.

"What is it? What do you see?" Daniel's voice was thick with anticipation.

Emmanuel swallowed hard, inhaling deeply before murmuring, "God help us," as he slowly pulled his arm from the depths of the wall. All eyes were on him as he emerged, holding a glass mason jar, covered in grime. Recognition flashed in Emmanuel's eyes—he had read about such things in his research, but never imagined he would come face to face with one.

"Is that what I think it is?" Josephine asked, her expression a mixture of confusion and disbelief. She leaned in closer. The clear glass jar was filled to the brim with an indistinct, red, gelatinous substance. "Is that strawberry jam?"

"It's a spell jar," Emmanuel said, his voice steady as he rose to his feet. "Used in the ritual."

Josephine pressed her fingertips to her forehead, struggling to piece together the information. "The ritual happened at the cemetery—that's what the articles said, not in the home. So what's it doing here?"

"In hoodoo practice, some spells involve a prescribed altar ritual that takes place in two parts," Emmanuel explained. "The first part occurs in the root doctor's home, in their ritual room. The second part is carried out in a cemetery."

"This was the ritual room," Jillian said, her voice steadying. "Madeline's mother was the root doctor."

"Let me see that," Daniel said, reaching for the jar. Emmanuel handed it to him. Daniel held the jar up to his face, scrutinizing its contents. "It appears to be a petition spell," he said, turning the jar slowly in his hands.

Josephine turned to Emmanuel, her eyes questioning, waiting for more explanation. "A petition spell requires the spell jar to be placed on an altar in the root doctor's home for a set number of days before completing the ritual at the cemetery," Emmanuel explained. "Black pepper, black candle wax, and black cloth are commonly used in curses, hexes, and revenge spells. The choice of this particular jar wasn't accidental either. Jars that once held sweet jams or jellies are often used in relationship spells."

"What about the menstrual blood? From the diary?" Josephine asked, her voice trembling with a mix of curiosity and fear.

"My guess is it was included as part of the root doctor's unique recipe," Emmanuel replied. "Ingredients vary depending on the root doctor's expertise and understanding of the power at their disposal."

"Check this out," Daniel said, pointing to a black substance inside the jar. It appeared as though black candle wax had dripped down the sides and accumulated at the bottom. "It must have been burning for a long time."

Emmanuel got back on his knees, shining the flashlight into the wall once more. "I found something else," he said, his voice tinged with unease. "There must be at least fifty of them." He reached into the wall and retrieved a small burlap pouch.

Josephine's eyes glimmered with recognition. "That looks exactly like the pouch I said I found in the chest," she said, her voice barely above a whisper.

Emmanuel opened the pouch carefully, pouring its contents into the palm of his hand. A black and white mixture, crumbly and powdery, spilled out. He brought his hand to his nose, inhaling deeply. The scent of burnt wood and something more earthy filled his nostrils. "It's charcoal and salt," he said, recognizing the familiar aroma. "Used in the Gullah culture to ward off evil spirits."

"I don't understand—didn't the people who lived in this house summon the spirits to begin with?" Josephine asked, her voice tinged with disbelief.

Emmanuel nodded solemnly. "Yes... And it looks like they got more than they bargained for."

Chapter 48

DANIEL EXAMINED THE SPELL JAR through the murky glass. Beyond the remnants of jam, the contents were enigmatic, and they needed to identify exactly what kind of spell they were confronting. He turned to Emmanuel and said, "I'm going to open it."

Emmanuel nodded, signaling his agreement.

Jillian and Josephine instinctively stepped back, the tension in the room thickening.

Daniel took a deep breath and held it, bracing himself for whatever pungent, otherworldly odor might be trapped inside. His heart raced with a mix of anticipation and dread as he twisted the lid of the tightly sealed jar.

A faint but distinct pop echoed in the silence.

"Get a whiff of this," Daniel said, peering into the jar's opening with one eye closed. "Smells... earthy." He handed the jar to Emmanuel. "What does that look like to you?" he asked, pointing at a densely packed brown area within the jar.

Emmanuel squinted, bringing the jar closer to his face. "Dirt. Must be goofer dirt."

Jillian and Josephine exchanged puzzled glances.

"Goofer dirt? Is that some kind of joke we're not in on?" Josephine asked, a note of skepticism in her voice.

"No joke," Emmanuel replied seriously. "In hoodoo practice, goofer dirt is taken from the grave of someone perceived as powerful, or from someone whose cause of death carries significance. It's used to invoke spiritual power and enhance the potency of a spell."

"Someone like Snorky," Daniel added.

"Snorky?" Jillian asked, confused. "Who's Snorky?"

"You know—Snorky, also known as Scarface, Big Al... Seeee," Daniel said, adopting a playful 1940s gangster tone. "Public Enemy Number One... Seeee. The American gangster and crime boss... Buried just across the street, seeee..."

Jillian scoffed, rolling her eyes. "You could have just said Al Capone."

"What's the fun in that?" Daniel replied with a grin. "Anyway, the dirt was probably dug up while it was still fresh. Must be a powerful spell."

"So powerful that it still burns after all these years," Emmanuel said, his voice grave. He turned his gaze to Josephine. "Now we know what's responsible for the wall heater turning on."

Daniel continued his examination of the jar, his fingers brushing over something scratchy attached to the bottom. It wasn't smooth like the rest of the glass. He held it up, squinting to get a better look, and noticed a piece of paper taped there, covered in handwriting. Furrowing his brow, he read aloud, "Michael David?"

Josephine's eyes sharpened as if pieces of a puzzle were falling into place. "Michael David—Madeline wrote about him in her diary," she said, her voice tinged with realization. "She had a crush on him—all three of the girls did. They were furious at him for loving another girl. They said she was the love of his life and that he would pay."

"Love of his life?" Jillian echoed, her face lighting up with sudden understanding. "During the ritual, I thought I heard the girls chanting 'Luvuv-iz-life.' They must have been chanting 'Love-of-his-life.'" She paused, her voice dropping as the gravity of the situation settled in. "The spell must have been intended for his girlfriend."

Emmanuel crossed his arms and exhaled deeply, clearly weighed down by something he was hesitant to share.

"What is it, Cap?" Daniel asked, picking up on the tension.

"I think the spell missed its target. Michael David—that's my nephew's name," Emmanuel said, his voice heavy with implication.

Josephine's eyes widened in shock. "Since when?" she asked, her voice barely a whisper.

"Since always," Emmanuel replied. "My sister named him Michael David when he was born. Michael, his father, left when David was just a month old. He's gone by his middle name ever since."

Josephine placed her hand over her mouth, the realization hitting her like a physical blow. She stumbled backward, collapsing onto David's bed. "Candy," she muttered, her voice thick with grief and dawning horror.

As the group absorbed the weight of this new revelation, Daniel's thoughts turned to the article he had read about the family killed in their car shortly after Al Capone's grave was disturbed. The connection seemed tenuous, but he couldn't shake the feeling that it was significant. He turned to Jillian, his expression serious. "Your father... You said he was the youngest and the only one to survive the car accident that killed his family, right?"

Jillian nodded, her curiosity piqued. "Yes," she said slowly. "Why?"

"Did your father by any chance have a brother named Michael?" Daniel asked, the question hanging in the air like a specter.

Chapter 49

JILLIAN'S EYES NARROWED AS SHE thought about her family, the implications of Daniel's question slowly dawning on her. She had visited the family plot with her father countless times over the years. Her grandparents and uncle were buried alongside her uncle's girlfriend, their names etched together on a single black granite gravestone. "My uncle's name was Michael David Marino," Jillian said, her voice heavy with realization. "He was named after my grandfather, who died in the car with him."

Josephine's eyes widened with realization. "Could it really have been *your uncle* that was the original target of the revenge spell?" she asked.

Having lived in Hillside all her life, Jillian knew what every Hillside Elementary student learned—Hillside began as a village in 1905, named after the Illinois Central Railroad stop. The name came from the uphill climb the westbound trains had to make in that area. She also knew that residential development started in the 1920s, and by 1940, the population was just over a thousand. "Hillside was so small back then; how many teenagers named Michael David could there have been?" Jillian said, a mix of sorrow and frustration in her voice.

"I'm sorry," Daniel said gently. "This must be difficult to hear."

Jillian's heart ached for her father, who had lost his entire family in such a tragic way. She couldn't even begin to fathom the depth of his pain, being left utterly alone in the aftermath. Her thoughts drifted to Candy, so young and innocent, caught in the crossfire of forces far beyond her comprehension. The weight of it all pressed down on Jillian, overwhelming her with emotion. With tears welling in her eyes, she stepped up to Emmanuel, her voice trembling with grief and disbelief. "How could this happen?" she whispered, the anguish evident in every word.

"The spell, the evil—it's very powerful," Emmanuel replied.

"That's not what I meant," she said, her gaze intense and fiery. "You're a pastor—how could God allow this to happen? And under your own roof?"

He straightened his posture and locked eyes with her. "Jillian, I know you're angry—I am too. But God did not allow this to happen. Satan did." She broke away from his intense gaze, crossing her arms as he continued. "You must understand, the war between good and evil, angels and demons—it's not conceptual, not a myth or legend. It's very real." He stepped closer, his voice steady and firm. "Do you understand that?"

Jillian had learned long ago in church that God gave His children free will and that evil could cloud judgment, leading to bad choices. People weren't robots; when they made decisions—like invoking evil spirits—terrible consequences were often inevitable. But Candy was just a child, innocently following her cousin, doing what children do. She didn't choose any of this. It didn't make sense to her... And if she was going to use her gift to fulfill a higher purpose, she needed to understand. "I guess I don't," she admitted, her voice tinged with frustration and confusion.

Daniel stepped up to her, his expression compassionate. "I think I can help explain."

She turned to him, searching for clarity. "I'm listening."

"Jillian, God didn't conjure up the evil responsible for what happened," he began, his tone gentle but firm. "The people who unleashed this, the ones who conjured the spell—they are responsible. Whether they knew it or not, whether they intended it or not, *they did this*. They toyed with dark forces and, in doing so, became soldiers for evil. Their actions unleashed something so malevolent that it not only took your uncle and his girlfriend but also your grandparents, and now Candy, even after all these years. And if we don't stop it, no one will."

Soldiers for evil. His words ignited her imagination: she envisioned armies locked in battle—one side driven by darkness, fueled by desires for revenge and chaos, spreading havoc across the world. The other side, a force for good, striving to contain and extinguish the darkness, to prevent it from consuming everything. And then there were the inevitable casualties—innocent lives, like Candy's, caught in the crossfire of this relentless struggle. The thought made her angry. So angry that it stirred something deep within her—a fierce determination to join the battle for good.

"I hope that helps," Daniel said. "It's what made me understand why sometimes bad things happen to the best of people—*good, innocent people*. And it's what makes me that much more committed to fighting the good fight."

She took a deep breath. "Yes, it helps." With an intense glare, she turned to Emmanuel and said, "Now, how are we going to fight this thing?"

Emmanuel appeared focused yet distant, his gaze locked onto hers, as though calculating something in his mind.

"It couldn't hurt," Daniel said, picking up on the intensity in her voice. "It's a powerful spell—we may need the help."

But Jillian knew it was Emmanuel who had the final say in the matter. Suspense hung heavy in the air as she awaited his response.

Emmanuel eyed Jillian up and down, as though silently weighing her resolve. "You are of strong spirit—"

"Yes," she interrupted confidently.

"That wasn't a question," he replied, his tone firm. "As I was saying, you are of strong spirit, so you may stay." Jillian's eyes lit up with excitement. "But let's be clear," Emmanuel continued. "We're not putting on a show here. I'm allowing you to stay because I want you to recognize how valuable your gift is and learn to wield it—not fear it."

She nodded, feeling the gravity of his words. "I understand. Thank you." This was her moment—a chance to shine her light and avenge the deaths of so many—her grandfather, grandmother, uncle, his girlfriend, and Candy. Not to mention, prevent the spell's future victims. She was prepared to go to war, ready to unleash her fury. She assumed everyone else felt the same resolve, so it shocked her when Josephine announced she was leaving. "Why are you leaving?" Jillian asked, unable to mask her surprise.

"It's not her role," Emmanuel interjected.

Jillian's disbelief quickly turned to anger. *He did not just say what I think he said*, she thought. "It's not her role?" she repeated, her voice sharp, shooting Emmanuel an incredulous glare. "What the hell is that supposed to mean?"

"It means I have nothing to contribute at the moment, and I'm fine with that," Josephine said, her tone matter-of-fact. "Thanks for looking out for me, though," she added with a small smile.

"Oh," Jillian replied, her defenses lowering. "I see."

"I'll be going now," Josephine said, stepping up to Emmanuel. He met her halfway. They exchanged quick kisses, murmured "I love you," and shared a brief hug. Jillian tilted her head, puzzled by what she was witnessing—a simple, almost mundane goodbye between the couple. No fear, no tears, no lingering embrace. Emmanuel was about to face demons, yet Josephine was saying goodbye as if he were heading off to just another day at the office. Jillian reminded herself that every marriage is unique and that how they interacted was none of her business. Still, she couldn't shake the feeling that something about it was... off.

Emmanuel walked Josephine to the door. "I'll come get you when we're done here," he said, closing the door behind her.

Josephine pushed the door back open, her expression suddenly animated. "Wait—I almost forgot..." She whistled and called out, "Come here, Blue!" The sound of tiny paws skittering across the floor filled the room as the pup eagerly rushed into her arms.

"Like I said before, dogs have a way of sensing things," Jillian said, eyeing the Chihuahua. "Don't you think she should stay?"

Josephine cradled the tiny dog, shaking her head with a smile. "Oh no—not for this," she said firmly. "Trust me, the last thing we need is a little Cujo on our hands." She chuckled, then added with a scoff, "Can you imagine? A *Cujo* remake starring our little girl Blue, the teacup Chihuahua."

Daniel raised his hand, a grin spreading across his face. "I'd pay to see that."

Chapter 50

EMMANUEL WAS SERIOUS WHEN HE told Jillian they weren't putting on a show. The act of casting out demons is no spectator sport. There's no room for passive observers; anyone in the room—anyone in the building, for that matter—becomes an active participant in the battle. Everyone has a role—a responsibility. Emmanuel would lead the exorcism, casting out the demon(s), and Daniel would be his right-hand man, ready to step in if needed. A crucial part of the process is learning the demon's name, which weakens its influence and control. The name is like a key that binds the demon, forcing it to yield to authoritative power. But without a physical body to interrogate, Emmanuel needed Jillian's help.

"Your job is to get the demon's name."

"And how am I supposed to do that, exactly?" she asked, her voice tinged with apprehension.

"The same way you'd get anyone else's name—ask. And if it won't tell you, gather as much information as you can so we can figure it out."

Her eyes darted around anxiously before she nodded. "OK, I can do that."

Emmanuel had no doubt that she could, but it was clear to him that she was nervous, just as he had been the first time he assisted with an exorcism. He felt it necessary to warn Jillian, just as he had been warned. "You need to be prepared for the demon to come after you," he said, his tone serious.

"Me? Why me? Because I'm a woman?" she asked, incredulity in her voice.

He shook his head. It wasn't about gender, although statistically, women are more frequently reported as being demonically possessed than men. Emmanuel didn't put much weight on that, suspecting the statistic was skewed by the fact that women are more likely to seek help, while men often resist it. In this case, it was about experience. Emmanuel and Daniel were seasoned in the rituals of exorcism. Gender and physical strength aside, between the three of them, Jillian was the least experienced. And as the least experienced, she was the weakest link—something the demon would almost certainly exploit.

"I don't doubt your spiritual strength, Jillian, but there's always a hierarchy. And judging by the panic attack you had outside earlier, the demon has likely already figured that out," he said, his voice firm but not unkind.

She took a deep breath. "Fair enough. Thanks for the warning."

"Now, do you have any questions before we begin?"

"Just one," she replied. "What was your wife's Cujo reference about?"

He nodded. "Demons can possess animals, even insects," he said. "When a demon gets exorcized, it seeks a new vessel. Of course, possessing a pet would never be a demon's first choice, but it beats the alternative."

"What's the alternative?"

"A demon would rather possess a person over anything else—someone they can use as a Trojan horse to control and manipulate into carrying out evil," he said. "Now, are you ready?"

She shifted her gaze to the floor and nodded.

She doesn't look ready, Emmanuel thought. *She needs more coaching*. "Just remember, demons—they are not stupid. They know they don't have a chance in hell against the power of Christ—"

"Chance in hell—get it?" Daniel scoffed.

His lips tight, Emmanuel glowered at him.

"Sorry," he said, shrinking in response.

"As I was saying… Demons know they don't have a chance, so they will fight dirty."

"Fight dirty? Meaning what?" Jillian asked.

"Hit below the belt, sucker punch—do anything with the little power they have to scare, trick, and manipulate you into putting your guard down, making you believe they have the upper hand so they can–" His fist collided forcefully with the palm of his hand. "STRIKE."

She gasped.

He continued, "And when they strike, they will attack you when you're down, like the cowards they are." He stepped closer, unblinking. If she took anything from his advice, he prayed it would be this: "Do not be afraid. Watch their every move, and whatever you do, keep your guard up."

Chapter 51

J ILLIAN LISTENED CLOSELY, absorbing every word Emmanuel said. To her, he was like a seasoned detective, and she was the rookie—competent enough to wear the badge, but not yet confident enough to draw her weapon. It stung to be seen as the weakest link, the most vulnerable, the one most likely to be targeted, but she knew he was right. *I'd be a fool not to heed his advice,* she thought, steeling herself. *And I'll be damned if I let that demon get in my head again.* She took a deep breath and nodded firmly. "Okay, I'm ready," she said, her voice steadying.

Emmanuel handed her the spell jar. "Open it up and see if you can get a flame going."

Jillian removed the lid and peered inside. "There's no wi—" she began, but her words were cut short as a bright flame suddenly ignited within the jar, burning brilliantly despite the absence of any wick. Her eyes widened in shock, and she instinctively pulled the jar away from herself. "Take it," she said, thrusting it toward Daniel.

"No," Emmanuel interjected, his tone firm. "You hold the jar."

Jillian opened her mouth to protest, but the words faltered.

"You didn't think you were just going to stand around and watch, did you?" Emmanuel added with a knowing smile.

Jillian hesitated, then tightened her grip on the jar, the flickering flame casting a determined glow in her eyes. "What am I supposed to do with it?" she asked.

"Daniel will walk you through it," Emmanuel replied. He picked up his Bible from the coffee table and pressed it against his chest like a shield. "Are you afraid?" he asked, his gaze steady.

She swallowed hard, but her voice came out firm. "No."

"Good." Emmanuel stepped to the front door, retrieving a small glass bottle from his pocket. He uncapped it and let the oil drip onto his fingertip. "We start with anointing," he said, tracing the sign of the cross over the doorframe with the oil. "Like a coward, you hid in the walls and preyed on the young and vulnerable... But there is no hiding now. You have been exposed, and it was only a matter of time before we smoked you out." He stepped back, leaving the door wide open.

Daniel leaned toward Jillian. "He's leaving the door open to give the demons space to escape quickly—to clear the energy," he whispered. A cold wind swept through the dim room, causing the flame in the spell jar to flicker. "Protect the flame," he added. "The demon allowed it to ignite like a party trick, trying to scare us off. But now it's trying to hide—demons thrive in the dark."

Jillian nodded, cupping her hand protectively around the jar's opening.

Emmanuel moved to the corner of the living room and applied more oil to his fingertip. "I renounce all agreements made with Satan and his demons, in the name of Jesus," he declared, anointing the corner wall opposite the door.

Jillian shut her eyes tightly and winced as the air erupted with a high-pitched screech, the sound drilling into her ears like nails on a chalkboard.

Daniel turned to her, his eyes wide. "What's wrong?"

"Don't you hear that?" she asked, pressing her fingers to her ears, trying to block out the unbearable noise.

Emmanuel continued, his voice unwavering. "I renounce and reject any satanic offerings that were made in this home, in the name of Jesus!" He moved to the opposite corner of the room.

The screeching intensified, slicing through Jillian's eardrums. She winced, resisting the urge to scream. "There it is again—sounds like nails scratching a chalkboard."

Daniel scanned the room, his brow furrowed. "I only hear Cap."

"Son of a—" Jillian bit her lip to stifle a curse. "It's so loud—high-pitched screeching, wailing—it hurts."

"It must be your gift," Daniel said, his expression serious. "Evil is being revealed to you."

"Some gift," she muttered under her breath.

Emmanuel's voice grew louder as he moved toward the kitchen. "I renounce lust, perversion, pornography, immorality, and every unclean spirit that anyone has made a pact with in this house, in the name of Jesus!"

They followed him. "He's going to anoint all four corners of the home," Daniel explained.

"Why?" Jillian asked, struggling to understand.

"To ensure there's nowhere for the darkness to hide. It's part of the exorcism."

Jillian's eyes widened. "An exorcism? I thought those were only performed on people."

"Yes," Daniel replied, never taking his eyes off Emmanuel. "But homes can be possessed too. What did you think we were doing?"

Casting out demons, Jillian thought, shaking her head. She hadn't realized that this was, in fact, an exorcism. "Shouldn't we be holding crucifixes?" she asked, suddenly unsure.

Daniel shot her a teasing look. "Oh no! The crucifixes! That's right!" He slapped his forehead in mock panic. "Whatever will we do without them?"

Jillian leveled a flat stare at him. "I get it—you're not Catholic."

Daniel smirked, a dimple forming in his left cheek. "The cross doesn't cast out demons—the Holy Ghost does. Trust me, there's more than one way to skin a cat."

Chapter 52

H E COULDN'T HEAR WHAT JILLIAN was hearing, but he didn't need to. The silence had lingered too long, and Emmanuel's experience told him it was a deliberate tactic. The demon was hiding, hoping that if it remained quiet enough, they might leave it undisturbed. But Emmanuel wasn't fooled. He could feel the malevolence seeping from the shadows, like the stench of a rotting carcass unearthed from a shallow grave.

He stepped into David's room, where the final two corners of the home awaited consecration. As he entered, he began to recite prayers of deliverance, his voice firm and unwavering. "I renounce and rebuke all witchcraft, occult practices, divination, and sorcery that was made in this room in Jesus' name!" Emmanuel exclaimed, anointing the room's corner with oil.

Suddenly, the air crackled with an intense energy, and the light bulbs throughout the house exploded in a violent symphony of shattered glass, as if the very walls were rebelling against his words. The house plunged into darkness, save for the small, flickering flame in Jillian's hands.

Daniel flinched, instinctively raising his arms to shield Jillian from the shower of glass shards raining down around them. As the echo of the explosions faded into silence, he turned to her with a wry smile. "Must have hit a sore spot," he said, his voice a mix of tension and grim humor.

"I destroy all demonic activity and every demonic thought that has ever been opened in this home. I shut it down in the name of Jesus Christ!" Emmanuel exclaimed. A surge of malevolent energy coursed through the room, pushing the dresser from one end of the room to the other, slamming it against the wall with a deafening bang.

Voices growled and croaked eerily through the darkness like a grizzly bear disturbed from its slumber. "I can hear them now," Daniel said. "We must be getting close."

Emmanuel continued, "I renounce any allegiances to the kingdom of darkness and Satan made in this home in Jesus' name!" The croaking grew louder, as though competing to drown out his commands, and the room grew colder as the demonic energy in the room depleted it of heat. "Satan, you have no power over us! You have no power over our kingdom!" he shouted. The dresser surged back and forth, scraping the floor and pounding against the wall, jolting the room. The mattress flailed and flopped like a fish out of water. The bedroom door swung open and slammed shut, again and again, in a violent tantrum. Emmanuel raised his voice, his breath forming a fog in the cold air, and declared, "I renounce and uproot every demonic word that has ever been spoken, giving Satan rights over this home! Be broken, in Jesus' name!" The pounding from the dresser grew louder, more forceful and deafening, as if it was being used to blast an opening through the wall of the windowless room, seeking escape.

Gripping the spell jar in one hand, Jillian inched closer to Daniel, plugging her ear. Emmanuel detected a glint of fear in her eyes. "Jillian, do not be afraid!" he exclaimed with a deep, resonant voice that carried the weight of his authority.

A gust of icy wind swept through the room. They watched as Jillian's ankles were seized by an unseen force, knocking her off balance. She gasped, her eyebrows shooting up, mouth agape. "JILLIAN!" Emmanuel shouted. The room shook with a reverberating thud as she landed on her back. Her eyes wide with terror, she kicked and screamed, resisting the demonic attack, as she was pulled out of the room, the door slamming shut behind her.

Daniel stood frozen, his mouth agape.

"Don't just stand there—go after her!" Emmanuel ordered.

Chapter 53

THE DOOR SLAMMED SHUT BEHIND JILLIAN as she kicked and screamed, refusing to succumb to the unseen force dragging her down the hallway like a rag doll. Her hands flailed, desperately trying to grip the walls, but her nails only scraped helplessly against the floor as she fought with every ounce of strength she had. "Daniel!" she cried out, her voice echoing with terror. "HELP!"

In the distance, she heard Daniel shouting her name, the sound of his fists pounding against the door in a frantic struggle to get it open. "Jillian! Jillian! You have to fight it!"

Suddenly, everything went silent.

Time and space ceased to exist.

It was dark, and she was lying on her back, alone. The spell jar was still clutched tightly in her hand, the flame within flickering in rhythm with her shallow, panicked breaths. Shadows danced and swirled around her, dark and menacing, taunting her as her eyes darted around, trying to keep up with their erratic movement. *You can do this, Jillian,* she told herself, forcing the fear down. *They can't hurt you.* She closed her eyes and focused on calming her frantic breathing. *I am not afraid. I am not afraid. I am not afraid,* she repeated, willing herself to believe it.

With a deep breath, she opened her eyes and pushed herself to her feet, shaking out her blistered hand. Her brow furrowed in confusion—there was no pain. She stared at her palm, expecting to see angry red welts, but there was nothing. No redness, no evidence of injury at all. *It must be a trick,* she thought, determined not to be deceived. She cupped her hands around her mouth and shouted into the darkness, "I'M NOT AFRAID OF YOU! DO YOU HEAR ME?!" She outstretched her arms, the spell jar clutched tightly, her stance daring whatever lurked in the shadows to come for her.

A subtle draft brushed against her knees. Startled, she glanced down. Her legs were bare. She wiggled her toes—no shoes. Panic began to creep in as she realized she was wearing a red fitted tube-top dress that barely reached her thighs. She patted herself down, her breath hitching as she discovered—no bra, no panties. A wave of shock and vulnerability surged through her. *How did this happen?* she thought, her mind racing. But she steadied herself, refusing to let the fear take hold. *I'm not falling for it. You son of a bitch.* She paced barefoot in the dark, empty space. "There is nothing you can do to scare me, let alone hurt me."

Silence.

"Boy, that must really kill you," she scoffed. "Knowing that you are no match for my God—and by extension—no match for me. It's no wonder you pick on the young, exploit vulnerabilities... YOU COWARD!"

More silence.

"Aren't you going to do anything?" she demanded, her eyes searching the void for any sign of movement.

A sudden, grating sound shattered the stillness as a chair came screeching toward her, seemingly pushed by an unseen hand. It forced her down, the seat catching her off guard as she collapsed onto it, her breath catching in her throat. "Is that all you've got?" she spat, her voice dripping with disdain. A small round table, draped in a black cloth, materialized beside her, a flickering black candle atop it casting eerie shadows that danced across the walls.

Then she heard it—a voice she knew all too well, a man's voice, one that hadn't graced her ears in years, except in the crackling playback of old home movies. "I saw the way you were eyeing him," the voice said, tinged with jealousy. "The way his gaze traced your figure."

Jillian's heart skipped a beat as she turned toward the source of the voice, her eyes widening in shock and disbelief. "John?" she whispered. Her dead husband stood before her, as solid and real as the day he died, yet there was something off—something she couldn't place. She had longed for this moment, dreamed of seeing him again. The years since his passing had been a slow, torturous ache, the void in her heart growing wider with each day.

He approached her slowly, his presence both a comfort and a terror.

Is it really him? Am I dreaming? Am I dead? she wondered, her mind spinning. *Or is this some cruel trick, a manipulation by dark forces?* Anticipation mingled with fear, her heart pounding like a caged animal desperate for release. She reached out, her hand trembling, yearning to touch him, to feel him, to know it was really him. He stepped closer, the candlelight softening his features, making him look so achingly familiar. She brushed her fingertips over his skin, gazing deep into his hazel eyes. "Is it really you?" she asked, her voice barely more than a breath.

"Did you ever look at me like that?" he asked, kneeling before her, his hand sliding up her knee, then higher. "Did I ever make you feel the way you felt when you saw him? What's his name? Daniel."

His touch sent a shiver down her spine, arousing sensations she had buried deep within. Her eyes roamed over his body, taking in every detail. She wanted so badly for it to be him. He looked like John, sounded like John. Bringing her forehead to his, she breathed him in—it even smelled like John.

"God damn it, God damn it! FUCK YOU!" he suddenly screamed, his eyes rolling back in his head. "YOU DID THIS!"

She gasped as a familiar sensation stirred deep within her—a need for release that she had denied for so long.

He locked eyes with her, his voice softening. "I'm sorry. I don't mean to be contentious. It's my fault. I left you all alone... unsatisfied," he murmured, his hand creeping further up her dress. "A woman has needs. We all do."

She clung to the belief that it was John, battling the instinct that something was terribly wrong. *It must be him,* she told herself. She knew him better than anyone—every freckle, dimple, and blemish. She studied his face closely—everything seemed to match. Desperation clawed at her as she reached for his hand, gently caressing each of his fingers, one by one. But as she did, a chilling realization gripped her—doubt clouding her thoughts. "They're all there," she said, forcing a tight, strained smile.

A gentle smile tugged at the corners of his lips. He brought his hands in front of his chest. "Ten fingers, ten toes," he said. "It's me."

Her eyes narrowed as she rose to her feet. "Is it really you?" she asked, her voice trembling.

He stood to meet her gaze. "In the flesh."

"In the flesh, you say?"

He nodded, his expression confident. "Absolutely. And I'm never leaving you again."

It was exactly what she needed to confirm her suspicions—he wasn't who he claimed to be. Glaring at him with fierce determination, she swung her arm back and shouted, "Bullshit!" His eyes widened in shock as her fist struck his throat, sending him crashing to the ground. Relief flooded through her, but she wasn't finished. With a swift motion, she drove her foot into his groin, a savage satisfaction coursing through her as he writhed in pain. "That's better." Red-faced and gasping, he curled up on the floor, whimpering. The nostalgia that had clouded her judgment evaporated, replaced by the cold clarity of her mission.

Planting her foot over his throat, she leaned in, her voice icy and commanding. "*Demon, tell me your name.*"

Chapter 54

J ILLIAN'S EYELIDS FLUTTERED OPEN to find Daniel's palm on her
face. "I'm OK," she said, bringing herself to a seated position.

"Did you get a name?" Daniel asked.

"No," she replied. "But—"

"Save it for Cap; there's no time," he interrupted. "We have to go. Now!"

"Where are we going?" Jillian asked, gripping his hand.

With a gentle tug, he pulled her to her feet. "He's about to anoint the last
corner of the house—let's hurry," he urged, his voice quick with the excitement
of someone who didn't want to miss the main event. Grasping her hand, he led
her swiftly back into David's room.

Emmanuel fixed his gaze on Jillian. "Did you get its name?" he asked.

"No—it wouldn't give it up. But I have intel—I watched its every move.
Hopefully, it's enough."

"What did it look like? What did it say?"

"It was disguised as my husband. It swore a lot, repeated, 'God damn it.'"

"Blasphemy."

"Then it apologized, said it wasn't trying to be contentious."

"Liar." His eyes widened, as if struck by a sudden revelation. "First hierarchy—Berith," he declared. With deliberate precision, he dipped his fingertip

in the oil and painted a cross at the final corner of the home. "BERITH BE BROKEN! IN JESUS' NAME!" Emmanuel shouted, his voice ringing with conviction.

The air thickened with an ominous presence, pressing down on them like an unseen weight. The walls trembled, fissures spreading like pulsating veins, as black wax began to seep and trickle through the cracks. "I rebuke you in the name of Jesus Christ and the Father!" Emmanuel cried out, gripping his Bible with unwavering resolve. He raised it high, like a knight brandishing his sword in the face of evil.

The atmosphere crackled with tension, the very air charged with the supernatural power of the Holy Ghost. "I REBUKE YOU, BERITH!" he roared, his voice deep and resonant, each word heavy with divine authority. The floor beneath them rattled violently, as if the ground itself was responding to the battle unfolding within the house.

"Oh my God," Jillian said in a quivering voice. "The walls!" she exclaimed, her breath catching as the foul stench of decay filled the air. Her mouth fell open as the walls seemed to close in, expelling two mummified corpses from the cracks. Their parchment-like skin was stretched taut, brittle and ravaged by time. One corpse stood upright, its limbs shriveled and eye sockets hollow, while the other lay twisted and contorted in a grotesque pose, as if frozen in eternal agony. "Who could have done this to them?" she whispered, her voice tinged with horror.

Jillian closed her eyes and plugged her ears, her senses overwhelmed by the high-pitched sounds and decayed bodies erupting from the walls. Suddenly struck with a vision, she stepped back. She turned her gaze to the albino woman not far away, on her knees and cutting a small section of the wall with a sheetrock knife.

Madeline.

Jillian watched as Madeline carefully set the cut-out section aside, a growing unease gnawing at her. *What is she doing?* Jillian wondered. Her breath caught as the aura of darkness she had been sensing suddenly materialized, coalescing into a thick black fog that swirled menacingly around Madeline. Without a word, Madeline stood up and left the room, returning moments later, dragging an elderly Black woman—her mother—by the arm.

"No, Maddy. No!" her mother cried out, her voice quivering and rasping with desperation. She dug her heels into the floor, resisting with every ounce of strength her frail body could muster. Her muscles strained, veins bulging as she fought against her daughter's grip. "Just let me be, child! Let me be!"

Madeline laid her mother on the floor and rolled her onto her side. "Stay still, Momma," she said, placing her palms on her mother's shoulder and forcefully pushed down.

Jillian flinched at the sickening sound of a grotesque snap. *Oh my God, she broke her mother's collarbone,* Jillian thought, covering her mouth in horror as the chilling scene unfolded before her. *She's torturing her.*

The room seemed to swallow the old woman's cries, muffling them into a haunting echo. Yet still, she persisted, her voice strained with pain and desperation. "Please, child! Stop!" she pleaded as Madeline cruelly forced her shoulders together, bending her frail body in half. "It hurts! It hurts so much!"

"Momma, it's better this way," Madeline whispered, her eyes darting around nervously in a fit of paranoia.

Jillian watched in horror as Madeline stuffed her mother's shriveled, frail body into the hole in the wall. The old woman's long, gnarled fingers, adorned with cracked yellow nails, extended from her wrinkled hands, gripping the edge of the wall as she tried to resist, but it was no use. The sound of bones cracking and tendons tearing filled the air. The old woman erupted with agonizing screams that echoed through the house, her pain so excruciating that it seemed to seep into the walls with her.

"Momma, you hush now, or it'll find us."

The vision faded. Jillian turned to Daniel. "I saw something—I know what happened. Madeline... She tortured her mother, stuffed her inside the wall. She must have gone in and closed the wall from the inside," she said. "She was hiding them from something."

"You mean they were still alive when she closed the wall?"

She nodded.

He shook his head, his eyes glinting with disgust. "At least it's almost over." He turned to Emmanuel, expecting him to deliver the final blow, but he was quiet, seemed transfixed.

"Mija, you're not supposed to be here," Emmanuel said. It appeared as though he was in a trance, staring at the corpses.

Daniel and Jillian gasped at the sound of a guttural shriek. "The demon, it's on the ceiling, over the corpses," Jillian said, looking up.

"I don't see anything," Daniel said, furrowing his brow. "What is it?"

"Looks like a bubbling black lava with twisted, deformed arms, hundreds of them, reaching through," she said. "It could be some kind of portal."

The repulsive scent of rotten eggs and the sound of a low, guttural growl filled the room. "You've got to be kidding me," Daniel said as his eyes landed on the mangy black dog, its fur on end, its single eye glowing red. It snarled angrily, lips curled, showing its teeth like it was out for blood. He took a deep breath. "Go to Cap, try to snap him out of it. I'll take over for him until he comes to."

"What about the dog?"

"I'll fight it off with my bare hands if I have to."

She nodded.

Daniel took the Bible from Emmanuel's grip and raised his hands in the air. "*In the name of the Father, the Son, and the Holy Ghost, be destroyed, Berith!*" he shouted.

Chapter 55

"EMMANUEL IT'S A TRICK!" Jillian shouted, her voice straining to cut through the cacophony of otherworldly sounds that swelled around them, attempting to drown out their cries. "That is not your daughter!" But her words seemed to fall on deaf ears as Emmanuel remained unresponsive, his gaze locked on something only he could see. Panic surged through her. "He's not coming out of it!" she yelled, turning to Daniel, her desperation clear.

"Keep trying!" Daniel urged, his voice steady despite the chaos. He cleared his throat and grounded his stance, raising his voice with renewed determination. *"In the name of the Father, the Son, and the Holy Ghost, be destroyed, Berith! Leave this home and go back tgo the fiery gates of hell where you belong. This home does not belong to you. The people in it do not belong to you! We belong to our heavenly Father, and you must bow down to Him! I command you! I command you! In the name of the Father, the Son, and the Holy Ghost, I command you!"*

The room responded violently. The walls erupted into flames, the fire roaring to life with an intensity that sent waves of heat crashing against them. Beads of sweat streamed down Jillian's face as the fiery glow cast eerie, flickering shadows that danced menacingly across the walls. Her breath hitched as she turned to Daniel, searching his eyes for any sign that he, too, could see the inferno closing in around them. But there was no time for questions or hesitation—only action.

She stepped closer to Emmanuel, her heart hammering in her chest as the fire raged on, their faces now mere inches apart. "It's a trick, Emmanuel!" she pleaded, her voice trembling with urgency and desperation. "If only you could see what I see."

Without another thought, she closed her eyes, feeling the searing heat intensify around them, and pressed her forehead against his. She poured every ounce of her will into the contact, hoping to bridge the gap between their realities, to share the terrifying vision that tormented her mind. *Please, God, let him understand.*

For a moment, everything seemed to pause.

Still holding the spell jar, she opened her eyes to find Emmanuel and a false-faced Emma in Emma's bedroom. *It can't be*, Jillian thought. Her gaze swept the room. The plush carpet, velvet curtains, pink polka dot wallpaper—it all matched up. She stepped up to Emmanuel, sitting on the bed alongside the imposter. "It's a trick. You need to snap out of it. Daniel needs your help."

He shook his head. "I won't leave her."

"Emmanuel, listen to me—this isn't your daughter."

"I know my own daughter," he said. "She's the only one I have."

"Please don't leave me, Daddy," the false-face implored him with wide, innocent eyes.

He shook his head. "No mija, of course not. I would never."

Jillian watched as he gazed at the false-face with loving eyes. It was the look of a father who would do anything to protect his daughter. *I would do the same for JR*, she thought. *No, NO! Snap out of it, Jillian!* she told herself. Suddenly, Emmanuel's warnings flooded her mind. The demon is attacking his vulnerability–the love for his child, she thought. She inhaled deeply, searching for a way to convince him that the doppelgänger before them wasn't his daughter. It resembled and sounded like her, but unlike John, she didn't know Emma well enough to identify anything that would prove otherwise. "You told me yourself—demons aren't stupid. They'll hit below the belt, sucker punch, do anything to manipulate you into putting your guard down, and making you believe you have the upper hand so they can strike!" she exclaimed, hopeful that using his own words would convince him.

"I said, I won't leave her." He stood from the bed and stepped up to her with a compassionate gaze. "You must understand, don't you?" He cocked his head to the side. "She's my baby."

She stood frozen, her eyes widening as the truth dawned on her:

It's not manipulating him—it's manipulating me.

She raised the spell jar closer to his face. His eyes began to darken, spreading through his eyes until it consumed them like the blob-like lava she saw on the ceiling, its form ever-changing and unpredictable like a swirling abyss. He wrapped his hands around her throat. The doppelgänger stepped up behind him, its eyes dark and nightmarish like her false-faced father's. "You're outnumbered," it said, tightening its grip around Jillian's neck as it lifted her off the ground.

Jillian's lips began curving into a smile as the imposter tightened its grip and exposed its clenched teeth. "That won't be a problem," Jillian said, cocking her head to the side and flashing a closed-lip smile. "Because you're overpowered. In the name of the Father, the Son, and the Holy Ghost, I rebuke you!"

Chapter 56

EMMANUEL GASPED WILDLY as though he was coming up for air after being forcefully held underwater. His grip on reality returned, his eyes clearing as he blinked, seeing through the illusion that had held him captive.

"Are you OK?" Daniel asked, still fighting back the demonic forces.

Emmanuel nodded. "I was in some sort of holding cell—it was dark, quiet."

Their gaze turned to the mangy black dog stepping closer. Jillian stepped back slowly. "It isn't here for us," Emmanuel said, speaking calmly. "Let it be." He stepped alongside Daniel and gripped the Bible. Together, they held it up and shouted in unison, *"In the name of the Father, the Son, and the Holy Ghost, be destroyed, Berith! Satan, you have been defeated!"*

Jillian blinked, her eyes wide as she scanned the room, her breath catching in her throat. "The fire—it's gone," she whispered, her voice trembling with a mix of amazement and disbelief, as if her mind was struggling to grasp the sudden transformation.

Daniel looked at her, his brow furrowed in confusion. "What fire?"

The room grew suffocatingly still, the tension thickening like a dense fog as an ominous presence took command of the space. All eyes were drawn to the growling canine, its low, guttural snarl reverberating through the floorboards, sending a shiver up their spines. The creature crouched low, its powerful muscles coiled like springs, ready to unleash its fury. Its single red eye, glowing like a smoldering ember, burned with a malevolent intensity, casting an eerie, flickering light across the room.

"It's a Plat-eye," Emmanuel murmured, his voice heavy with dread, the weight of his words sinking into the pit of their stomachs. "An evil spirit, born from the souls of those who were wronged in life." The revelation hung in the air like a dark cloud, making the creature's presence all the more terrifying.

"What does it want?" Jillian asked, her voice barely more than a whisper, the fear palpable.

Emmanuel's gaze remained locked on the creature, his expression grim. "Revenge," he answered, the single word carrying the weight of generations of anger and pain.

The Plat-eye's low growl reverberated through the room, sending shivers down their spines. Time seemed to slow, each heartbeat echoing in their ears as they watched it lunge into the air, its form twisting and doubling mid-flight. The ground trembled beneath their feet as two identical beasts landed with a thunderous crash, each one poised menacingly in front of the lifeless corpses. Their jaws, impossibly wide, unhinged to reveal rows of jagged, yellow fangs, dripping with venomous intent. With a sickening crunch, they sank their teeth into the cold flesh, tearing it apart with a ravenous fury that defied nature. The grotesque symphony of bones snapping and sinew ripping filled the air, drowning out all other sounds, until nothing but silence remained—a silence as eerie as the grave itself.

"I've seen that thing stalking the cemetery for decades. It was hunting them all along," Jillian whispered, her voice trembling with a mixture of disbelief and horror.

"Legend says they roam the countryside, seeking vengeance on those responsible for their suffering, haunting the very cemeteries where their bones lie," Emmanuel murmured, his words heavy with the knowledge he carried.

"That explains the steel door and the bars on the windows," Daniel muttered, a chill creeping up his spine. "They must have known it was after them."

The beasts turned toward them, their lips curling into what could only be described as a sinister, satisfied grin. For a moment, their glowing red eyes locked onto the group, as if savoring the fear that hung thick in the air. Then, without warning, the creatures began to fade, their forms dissolving like smoke into the darkness. It had vanished completely, leaving nothing behind but the echo of their growls and the chilling memory of their presence.

Chapter 57

EMMANUEL RECALLED THE FIRST DAY he visited the house and the unsettling fall he had outside. Even then, he had sensed something was off, a malevolent energy lurking beneath the surface. When he approached the front door, it wasn't just the physical stumble that unnerved him—it was the feeling of an unnatural force tugging at his ankle, pulling him down as if to warn him away. The pull was almost tangible, a dark whisper urging him to leave before it was too late. But Emmanuel was not one to back down, especially when he believed the fight was worth waging.

Now, standing in the dimly lit room, he uncorked a small bottle of anointing oil, his movements deliberate and calm. The scent of the oil filled the air, mingling with the heavy atmosphere. He held the bottle out to Jillian, meeting her gaze with a steady, purposeful look. "May I?" he asked, his voice filled with quiet determination.

Jillian nodded, her eyes wide with a mixture of trust and a flicker of hope.

Emmanuel dipped his fingertip into the oil and gently touched her forehead, tracing the sign of the cross before raising his hand in prayer. "I break off from Jillian all demonic residue, in Jesus' name," he intoned, his voice firm.

He turned to Daniel, repeating the gesture with the same solemnity. "I break off from Daniel all demonic residue, in Jesus' name. Amen."

As the prayer ended, Jillian's gaze fell upon the spell jar. Its once-vibrant flame had extinguished, leaving only a thin wisp of smoke curling into the air.

"Lights out, Satan!" Daniel exclaimed, a triumphant grin spreading across his face.

Jillian turned to Emmanuel, her mouth opening to speak, but the words caught in her throat. "What is it?" Emmanuel asked, concern lacing his voice.

"How did you figure out the demon's name?" she finally managed to ask, her voice barely above a whisper.

"The same way he knew about the Plat-eye," Daniel interjected, his tone admiring. "He used his gift."

Jillian's brow furrowed in thought, her mind racing as she searched for an explanation. "You have the gift of knowledge?" she asked, uncertainty coloring her words.

Emmanuel nodded. "Are you familiar with the three hierarchies of angels?" he asked, his voice patient.

"Somewhat," she replied hesitantly. "But not really."

"Allow me to explain," he said, his tone gentle yet authoritative. "The hierarchy of angels is a ranking system—nine choirs or categories, grouped into three hierarchies. Higher-ranking angels possess greater power and authority than those below them."

"You deduced the demon fell from the first hierarchy?" she asked, her curiosity piqued.

Emmanuel nodded again. "Yes, but it was your observation that confirmed its identity. You mentioned it was spewing blasphemy and sowing discord—traits characteristic of Berith."

"Incredible," she whispered, awe in her voice. She dropped her head. "Meanwhile, it fooled me twice."

"It *almost* fooled you twice," Emmanuel interjected, his voice gentle. "I couldn't have done it without you." He glanced over at Daniel, a smirk playing at the corners of his lips. "And you helped too... I suppose," he quipped.

Daniel waved him off with a grin. "Ah, shucks," he said, kicking the floor like a bashful child. "It was nothin'."

Emmanuel chuckled, the tension in the room easing for the first time in days. "Don't be modest. You had your moments."

Jillian smiled, the warmth of the exchange cutting through the lingering shadows of what they had faced. "Well, either way, I'm glad we're all on the same side."

Emmanuel inhaled deeply, the air lighter, as though the weight of the darkness had been lifted. The moonlight poured through the windows, casting a serene glow over the room—a stark contrast to the oppressive gloom that had gripped it moments before. "The house feels different now—peaceful," he said, his voice barely above a whisper.

Without warning, a sharp gasp shattered the calm. Daniel stumbled backward, his eyes wide with terror as a grotesque creature scuttled across the floor, its many legs skittering in a chaotic rhythm. Jillian didn't hesitate; she brought her knee up and stomped down hard. The sickening sound of a crunch, followed by a wet splat, echoed in the room.

"Nope," she said firmly, her voice steady. "Not taking any chances."

Chapter 58

JILLIAN SAT AT HER KITCHEN TABLE, her mind racing as she slowly came to terms with the chilling realization that she had been watched the entire time. The demon had observed Candy, knowing her desires, and manipulated her thoughts. It had sensed Emma's longing for her friend and attempted to lure her in with the promise of a new one. Worst of all, it had been surveilling Jillian, absorbing every detail of her life—her husband's appearance, the sound of his voice, even his scent—all gathered from photos, belongings, and the home movies she watched in the privacy of her own home.

"Are you sure the kids don't need you?" Jillian asked, inhaling the rich aroma of fresh coffee grounds as she poured herself a cup.

Josephine took a sip from her own steaming mug. "They're in bed, probably getting the best sleep of their lives. Emmanuel and Daniel are cleaning up and replacing the light bulbs in the house." She noticed Jillian's gaze drop to the floor, her cheeks flushing slightly at the mention of Daniel's name. A knowing smile spread across Josephine's face. "You like him, don't you?"

Jillian shrugged, trying to play it off, but the blush in her cheeks deepened. "Maybe just a little," she admitted, her voice tinged with shyness.

Josephine leaned in, her eyes sparkling with mischief. "I'll get the wheels moving on that—but first, tell me what happened in the house. Emmanuel mentioned you got dragged down the hallway and saw your 'husband.'"

Jillian nodded, her expression growing more serious.

"How did you know it wasn't really him?" Josephine asked, her curiosity piqued.

Jillian took a deep breath, recalling the surreal encounter. "He was exactly as I remembered him—it was bizarre. Even the freckles on his face and neck were in the right places."

"So... what gave it away?" Josephine pressed, eager for the answer. "Was it just a gut feeling?"

"No."

"Was it your gift? Did you have a revelation?"

"It wasn't just my gift. I tried to ignore the revelation. I was stubborn—I wanted so badly to believe it was him."

Josephine, bursting with anxious energy, stood from her seat, her hands gripping the back of the chair. "How'd you know it wasn't him then?"

Jillian exhaled deeply, steeling herself to recount the painful memory. "Remember I told you I didn't like John being a truck driver?"

"Yes."

"He had been injured before... It was a freak accident, really. The plastic insulation had worn off the wire attached to his truck's air horn valve. He was stepping off the truck, and he grabbed the wire instead of the truck handle to brace himself. His weight pulled his finger down on the wire. The wire sliced right through a good third of his finger."

Josephine flinched, her hand flying to her mouth. "Oh my God, that's horrible! Were the doctors able to reattach it?"

Jillian shook her head, the memory still raw. "They tried—his buddy even put it on ice and rushed it over to the hospital with him—but there was nothing they could do."

Josephine's eyes widened, her face pale with shock.

Jillian continued, her voice softer now, tinged with bittersweet nostalgia. "That was my reaction, too, when I first saw it. At least it was just the tip, I thought. But John was mortified—worried about his golf swing, how he would hold a baseball bat. In time, he got used to it, and eventually, we could laugh about it." She smiled faintly, remembering the lighthearted teasing. "I used to ask him for a high-four or tell him he couldn't flip me the bird if he wanted to. He always reminded me he still had one good middle finger on his other hand."

Josephine chuckled softly, the tension easing slightly.

"I knew it wasn't John the moment I realized all of its fingers were intact," Jillian said, shaking her head. "In the flesh, my ass."

Josephine burst out laughing. "Ha! That's one way to put it." She pushed her coffee cup away and stood up. "What a night. I should probably let you get some rest."

"Before you go, can I ask you something?" Jillian asked, her tone suddenly serious.

"Sure," Josephine replied, taking her seat again.

"Emmanuel told me Daniel's wife left him because she didn't support him being in the ministry. Is that true? Is there more to it?"

Josephine's expression grew thoughtful, her brow furrowing as she considered how to answer. "To be clear—she didn't support him being in the deliverance ministry," she explained. "The work we do is not for the faint of heart, and many people can't handle the idea of their loved ones being involved in something so... intense."

Jillian nodded slowly, understanding the gravity of what Josephine was saying. "Not for the faint of heart, indeed."

"And she didn't like him using his gift," Josephine added.

"His gift?" Jillian's interest was piqued. She leaned in closer. "What's his gift?"

Josephine smiled, as if the answer were obvious. "Why, the gift of service, of course."

Jillian nodded, the pieces falling into place. "He does seem like someone who's always ready to help."

Josephine's smile softened, and she added, "And that's a rare and precious gift."

Jillian leaned back in her chair, contemplating the complexities of the life Emmanuel and Daniel had chosen—the constant battle against darkness, the toll it took on their personal lives. "So, how do you do it?" she asked after a moment, her voice tinged with admiration.

"Do what?" Josephine asked, curious.

"I was watching the way you said goodbye to Emmanuel, like you weren't worried about him at all."

Josephine shrugged, a modest smile playing on her lips. "Must be my gift."

"And what would that be?" Jillian asked, her eyes gleaming with curiosity.

Josephine's smile deepened, her voice gentle yet unwavering as she answered, "Faith."

KEEP READING...

AN EXCERPT FROM THE AUTHOR'S NEXT NOVEL

THE IMPACT OF THE WHITE PORCELAIN vase shattering against the wall coincided precisely with the deafening clap of thunder that reverberated through the building. Dr. Everhart, dressed casually in khaki pants and a gray cardigan, leaned back in his chair, crossing his legs as the relentless sound of pouring rain broke the unsettling silence in the room. Outwardly, he appeared completely unfazed by what had just occurred—the vintage, trophy-style vase with its elegant gold-leaf pedestal, a cherished family heirloom passed down from his great-grandmother, had levitated from his desk and hurled itself across the room, shattering into countless pieces. He didn't so much as flinch. Inwardly, it was anybody's guess what thoughts were running through his mind. Clearing his throat, he asked, "Is that some kind of, I don't know, party trick?" His tone was light, but his eyes were sharp as they focused on his subject, Brianna Brown, a first-time patient. "I must say... I'm impressed."

All eyes in the room turned to Brianna in unison.

"It wasn't me," she replied coolly, tucking a strand of her dark, curly hair behind her ear. Despite being barely sixteen, she remained fully composed, her posture and demeanor strong and unyielding. She crossed her arms and legs, her gaze sharp and intense as she locked onto an object across the room—a puppet perched atop the desk. Her father had placed it there in a seated position, its black marble eyes facing the group as though it were an active participant in the session. "It was Oscar," she said sternly, her tone dripping with disdain.

The puppet remained still, its bright red, wispy hair swaying gently in the draft that swept through the room. Its black, beady eyes seemed to stare everywhere and nowhere all at once, a sinister presence that seemed to shift the very air around them.

"Enough!" Brianna's father suddenly exclaimed, his voice cutting through the tension like a knife. He slammed his fist on the desk with commanding authority. It was a tone he used sparingly, one that, when coupled with his piercing gaze, left no room for negotiation.

Brianna bit her lip and dropped her head, her defiance crumbling in the face of her father's stern command. Until now, the only sign of vulnerability she had shown was the slight bouncing of her knee, a subtle tell of her underlying anxiety. She had maintained an aura of perfection—poised and composed, not just on the surface but seemingly in every aspect of her life. But in this moment, her prim appearance, her years of steadfast obedience, her status as a model student, and her regular attendance at Sunday school—all these things seemed to vanish, replaced by the uncertainty and fear that now clouded her expression.

Brianna's mother, her face etched with worry, directed her tearful gaze toward Dr. Everhart and Reverend Rogers, who were seated side by side. "Haven't you seen enough?" she asked, her voice trembling as she sniffled and wiped her tears with a tissue.

The two men exchanged glances, their responses coming simultaneously:

"Yes."

"No."

They exchanged glances again, a silent tension brewing between them.

"Dr. Everhart, with all due respect, I believe it's clear what we are dealing with here," Reverend Rogers said, his voice firm, his attire—black slacks, a striped tie, and a white-collar shirt—exuding the solemnity of his office.

"Is it? If that's the case, why come to me?" Dr. Everhart retorted, standing from his seat and walking across his office to the water cooler. His casual demeanor clashed with the gravity of the situation, a stark contrast to the reverend's urgency.

The reverend scoffed, a trace of frustration in his voice as he shrugged. "A formality, I suppose."

Dr. Everhart scoffed in return and rolled his eyes skyward. "I don't sign off on formalities," he said, pouring a cup of water. He turned to Brianna and handed her the cup. "Here you go," he said, his eyes void of judgment.

"Surely you don't believe the puppet is behind this," the reverend said.

Dr. Everhart returned to his seat, leaned back, and fixed his gaze on the puppet. There was no denying that the thing was unsettling, enough to send a shiver down his spine. Of course, that in itself wasn't a point of argument. There's a reason, after all, that pupaphobia—fear of puppets—is so common, just below the fear of clowns. Perhaps it's the eerie suggestion of life where there should be none, a hollow vessel animated by unseen forces, that makes even the toughest of characters uneasy. He stared at it for a moment, contemplating the bizarre nature of the situation, before shifting his gaze to Brianna. Her posture was upright, her eye contact steady—certainly not the body language of someone exhibiting signs of fear or trepidation.

"I don't know yet," he finally said, his tone measured and noncommittal.

The reverend released an exasperated sigh, frustration etched into every line of his face. They had been in the same room for just over an hour—hardly enough time for Dr. Everhart to reach a formal conclusion—but the reverend's patience was clearly wearing thin. "What about my observations?" the reverend asked, his voice tinged with impatience. "Are you taking them into consideration?"

Dr. Everhart flipped through the pages of Brianna's file, his fingers tracing the words scrawled by Reverend Rogers in hurried, anxious handwriting. The reverend had noted several concerning observations:

Depression, dark thoughts—likely brought on by demonic oppression.

-Physical resistance, fighting when stepping foot in a place of worship.

-When physically restrained and forced to sit in the church:

-Wailing, panicked breathing.

-Convulsions, jerking, and stiffening.

-Drooling.

-Unresponsiveness.

"Into consideration—yes," Dr. Everhart replied, his eyes still on the file, his voice cool and detached. "Into account? Not even close."

He didn't bother to look up to acknowledge the reverend, the sharpness of his words hanging in the air like a challenge. The reverend's face flushed with indignation, but he held his tongue, recognizing the futility of pushing further just yet. The tension in the room was palpable, the divide between the rational and the spiritual widening with every passing second.

MORE FROM THIS AUTHOR...

Twenty-nine-year-old Emma is an intelligent, strong-willed, and ambitious PR exec, has always relied solely on herself. But when her recurring nightmares start taking a toll on her health, she turns to renowned University of Chicago psychiatrist and oneirologist, Dr. Edward Clark for help.

Dr. Clark learns that Emma's nightmares all revolve around her past love interests, a theme not uncommon among his patients. But, as they delve deeper, they discover a disturbing truth—Emma is losing touch with reality. The traumas from her nightmares are bleeding into her waking life, leaving her trapped in a waking nightmare.

In a race against time, Emma and Dr. Clark uncover the dark secrets buried deep within her psyche. As they unearth violence, control, and manipulation from her past, they realize that her diagnosis is more horrifying than they ever imagined. They must fight for Emma's life or risk succumbing to the relentless grip of unspeakable evil.

During his research on Near-Death Experiences, Dr. Prasad Vedurmudi, a genius neurologist at the prestigious University of Chicago, made a mind-bending discovery. A specific region of the brain acts as a gateway, transporting the departed to the next dimension. But there's more—a tantalizing possibility nobody has ever explored...Until now. Prasad believes that if he repairs that crucial part of the brain before death, he could unlock a profound secret—the key to controlling the afterlife experience itself. The implications are staggering.

With the help of his colleague, renowned psychiatrist Dr. Edward Clark, Prasad is determined to provide a service to humanity that surpasses all that came before. Endowed with unparalleled expertise and passion, they venture into uncharted territory, driven by an insatiable thirst for irrefutable evidence. But their pursuit comes with a price. As they delve deeper into the mysteries surrounding life and death, they encounter forces eager to silence their breakthrough.

In this gripping tale of courage and scientific brinkmanship, The Eternal Secret takes you on a roller-coaster ride through a twilight realm where the line between life and the afterlife blurs. Mary Romasanta weaves a suspenseful narrative that will leave you questioning the very fabric of existence. Prepare to be astounded, captivated, and haunted by the mesmerizing secrets concealed within the human mind.

Acknowledgements

I want to take a moment to acknowledge my husband, whose unwavering support has been the cornerstone of bringing each of my books to life. *Infestation* marks the first time I've been able to fully immerse myself in my passion for writing, and it's all thanks to him. His steadfastness and belief in me have not only provided the foundation I needed but also encouraged me to pursue my dreams with confidence. He is my best friend, my greatest champion, and—though it goes without saying—I'll say it anyway, my soulmate. Thank you for not only standing by me but for propelling and even pushing me to become the person I was meant to be. Although you often call me the brave one, you are the true hero in our story.

To my children, my biggest cheerleaders: every sentence I write is a testament to your unwavering support and a tribute to God's love that fuels our family.

To my parents, who introduced me to the spiritual world from the very beginning—never sugar-coating the truth, but always guiding me with love and conviction.

Thank you to the editor of this book, as with the previous two, Alejandra Gonzalez—a woman with the uncanny ability to speak her mind with both conviction and consideration. Her contribution to this work has been invaluable.